Love Bites More

A stand-alone, m/m/m, follow-up to
the Darkness and Light Duology

By TL Clark

Love & light

T
 xx

Published in the United Kingdom by:
Steamy Kettle Publishing

First published in electronic format and in print in 2023.

ISBN: 978-0-9956117-8-8

In loving memory of Pusskin,
my beloved familiar and writing buddy.
She was my "mews" for the Darkness & Light Duology.
And I continue that legacy here, with a follow-up to
my 'cat people'.
The green eyes on the cover of Love Bites were also
inspired by her. She even had a matching collar.

I miss you every day, despite it being two years since you
crossed The Rainbow Bridge, Pookie.

Acknowledgements

Cover design by Robin Ludwig Design Inc.
http://www.gobookcoverdesign.com

Thank you ever so muchly to my sensitivity, beta
and proofreaders. And my editor.
I truly do appreciate your hard work and support.

Thanks as ever, must go to my supportive husband.
I couldn't be any luckier.
You are my own soul-matched mate.
I couldn't do this without you.
Thank you. I love you.

And of course, thank you, dear reader, for legally
obtaining this book. I sincerely hope you enjoy it.

Table of Contents

Table of Contents Contd.

Recap – A Re-Introduction

You don't *have* to know all of this, but it gives context…

Maybe you read the Darkness & Light Duology (Love Bites and Love Bites Harder) a while ago, and your memory is a little hazy.

Or perhaps you've only bought this book without reading the others - you're absolutely welcome to do that. It is honestly a stand-alone novel. You're equally welcome to go and read books 1 and 2; Love Bites won an award so, y'know, might be worth your time. No pressure, though.

Either way, here's a little reminder of or introduction to the story so far…

❦❦❦❦❦❦

Shakira was always a bit of an outsider and had never felt like she had fit in. An itch which couldn't be ignored any longer took hold, so she took the brave decision to move away from everything she'd ever known in Surrey.

Driven by instinct, she found herself in a quiet Welsh village.

Shakira had been getting bad back pain, and uncharacteristically felt rough. It turned out that this was the forerunner of her transition. She'd had no idea that she wasn't human until that moment – oops!

Thankfully, there was a friendly, local witch named Cerys on hand to assist her.

Cerys helped her transform into her elinefae body (an extremely perilous time). She then explained what on Earth was going on.

Elinefae are a different species from humans. They have feline DNA running through them, along with magick. Some strange humans took the tales of these blood-drinking people and ran with it, creating the horror stories of vampires. Not that they like to be reminded of that; sore point!

They're not like those stories at all really. They're more like hippies living in a commune, attuned to nature if one must draw comparisons. Yes, they hunt at night, have fangs, drink blood, are a bit pale, have fantastic reflexes and supreme hunting skills but that's as far as it goes. Alright?

The problem is, Shakira isn't even pure elinefae. She is also part sorceress thanks to an unsavoury episode. This caused huge problems; elinefae do not allow any muddying of their gene pool waters. In fact, her own elinefae parents (the real ones, not the adopted human ones who brought her up) had been executed for giving birth to her.

That clan thought Shakira had been killed too. But Lily, another lovely witch, had rescued her as an infant and handed her over to the humans, thinking that's where she belonged. Shakira seemed human, and the witch hoped the baby would be safe in that world. Lily had taken her all the way from Scotland to Surrey via a portal, so she should have been safe enough.

But Shakira's instincts had brought her to her soul-matched mate, Pryderi (pronounced "pruh-DAIR-ee"). By the way, you'll find a handy glossary of names and words at the back of this book.

It was love at first sight, and they instantly bonded. He gave Shakira her new name Kiera (which is far easier for elinefae to pronounce).

But then Kiera's other genetic father (she technically has two), a sorcerer named Threaris discovered where she was. He needed her, or at least her blood, to break his curse. He had bred her for this purpose. So he captured her.

Threaris had been a bad man. His true love (a witch named Azalea) had been killed in the Time of Battles, by elinefae. Threaris took this way too personally and set about killing the clans involved. That didn't reduce his grief, so he sought to kill more and more of them.

The elinefae obviously didn't take too kindly to this and called in the help of a sorceress. Althea trapped Threaris in his own home and tasked him to seek amends via a spell.

But we're talking about an embittered male here, so he didn't take the hint. He spent years trying and failing to break his curse.

Frustrated, he managed to escape his prison for short periods, which was just long enough to meddle in elinefae life. Threaris set two clans against each other. One clan was where Kiera's mother had come from, the other was her elinefae father's clan.

Kiera was reunited with Frydah, who was the faery enlisted to protect her in her youth. The faery had also been captured by the psychotic sorcerer but helped teach Kiera how to use her magickal powers. And yes, natural/real magick is spelled with a 'k'.

There was also a nereid at Threaris' home; Zondra. She'd been enslaved by the sorcerer and was Kiera's allotted maid. Understandably upset by her imprisonment, and growing fond of Kiera, Zondra also helped the girl.

With their assistance, Kiera updated Threaris' curse, to try to get him to see the error of his ways. He was firmly stuck in place and unable to harm anyone at all, thanks to the bracelet the three females had magickally created and Kiera's spell.

Kiera then travelled to the warring clans as soon as Cerys alerted her of their plight. Lives were lost, but she managed to stop any further damage, and Kiera brokered peace between her maternal and paternal clans. They were ever so grateful and she was welcomed by the Irish clan Leader, Ailene.

Bolstered by her success, Kiera went to Rhion, Pryderi's clan Leader in Wales. The pair sought permission to live together in their 'happily ever after'.

But Rhion was not as impressed by Kiera's intervention. He blamed her for it starting in the first place and feared the terrible power she could wield. Sorcerers were nothing but trouble as far as his experience had shown him.

He offered Pryderi an ultimatum; choose the clan he was sworn by blood oath to protect, or his mate and be forever exiled. But that was no choice at all – one cannot break a blood oath. So, book 1 ended with the pair being torn apart by the idiot Leader.

(*takes a deep breath*)

But in book 2, we learned that Threaris had, in fact, been controlled by a daoi-sith; a dark elf named Donnagan – the last of his kind. When Kiera had banished everyone from Threaris' home who intended harm, that inadvertently included the pesky elf.

Kiera helped her father come to terms with all that had happened whilst he was a puppet to Donnagan. And then he sought vengeance, like any decent sorcerer would.

After a fight which nearly cost him his life, Threaris had to admit he needed help – ouch!

But Donnagan was now after Kiera, so Frydah took her to the fae realm, safe from his evil clutches. She learned some important stuff, had fun, made some friends (including a gruff unicorn named Roger)…and then her mate link was stretched too far for too long.

At last, the whole team formed a plan and cornered Donnagan, who was promptly executed, mainly by dragon fire courtesy of Shui, the familiar to a Chinese witch named Chen.

Turns out, Kiera's former boss and landlady was none other than the goddess Rhiannon, who had kept up-to-date with the assistance of her birds. She helped dispel the remnants of dark energy.

But that was not all! Kiera still had to face-off with Rhion, Pryderi's Leader. She's a feisty heroine, though. And with the help of her friends, Rhion was brought to see the error of his ways (as he too had been influenced by the dark elf).

The witches nominated Kiera Peacekeeper. And she was hand-fasted at long last to Pryderi. They now live amongst his Welsh clan.

Oh, and a dragon lord gifted her an egg which hatched into Terrah, a green dragon.

So, that's what happened.

In a nutshell; girl raised by humans, moves to Wales, and transitions into an elinefae. Then there's kidnapping, evil-doings, spells broken and cast, fae realm, fights, victory. Huzzah!

Magickal beings involved: witches, elinefae, a daoi-sith, faeries, elves, a unicorn, a nereid, a goddess and dragons.

Elan and Arwyn appeared a fair bit in the Darkness & Light Duology. They are best friends with Pryderi and helped him through the many tough times. In fact, it was Arwyn who challenged Rhion when he looked like he may still deny Kiera's status and home.

A quick note on language:
This book is written from multiple points of view. Each of those characters is an elinefae, so they technically speak in Eline. However, their language involves lots of cat-like noises and is incredibly difficult to write and would be incomprehensible to most readers.

So, for readability, I have written their thoughts and conversations in British English, given that the main clan lives in Wales. Sorry, Welsh isn't widely spoken, so, yes, it's in English. Although, some Welsh words have been included. And, if you listen carefully, you'll hear the Welsh accent. There are also hints of Arabic.

Again, there is a glossary at the back of the book to help with unusual/foreign names/words/phrases.

When people speak telepathically, I have indicated this in the dialogue tag, and have written those passages in *italics*. But there isn't much of that. Don't worry. It makes sense.

Oh, and there is swearing. Don't like it? Bite me – LOL, see what I did there? But seriously, if you don't like curse words, this is probably not going to be a book you enjoy. An f-bomb lands on page one, to give you an indication. But there was a warning in the book description.

Whilst I'm on the subject of warnings, I would like to remind you this is a m/m/m book. There are moments of violence, elinefaenapping and explicit sex scenes.

OK, you're all caught up. Let's dive into Love Bites More. Are you as excited as me right now? We're going back into the woods!

Chapter 1 – Stirrings
– Elan

Whimpering at the loss of the male as he withdraws from me, I steady myself against the bench. My buttocks sting as a playful smack strikes them.

"Aww, did you want a kiss and cuddle, Princess? You came to the wrong place," my hook-up mocks.

"Fuck you!" I fire back. Even though I know he's only teasing, the remark rankles.

"Again? Already? Now you're just being greedy," he replies, laughter ringing in his voice.

Dropping my chin down towards my chest, I utter with a sigh, "Yeah, yeah."

His breath hitches and his tone turns serious. "Do I hear a complaint?"

"No. Of course not. Just…oh, never mind. Ignore me."

I'm spun around and today's partner swipes his thumb across my cheek. "You are satisfied, Elan, are you not?"

We may have casual interactions in the Den of Sin, but ensuring joint pleasure is still a priority. My gut twists at the realisation that I've caused him concern.

"I am satisfied," I confirm with my best fake smile.

He believes me enough to wipe himself down, dress and stalk out of the room, without another word.

The noises and emotions coming from the only other pair in here does nothing to assuage my fraught nerves. But then again, neither has the perfectly adequate session I've just experienced.

Honestly, there was nothing to complain about. People come here to work off excess sexual energy with whoever is available and of the same mind. My giver was not selfish. At any other time, I would have been more than happy. But today? No, longer than that… recently, it's different.

This has been building for a while, and I don't know why. I just feel *wrong*. Incomplete. Restless. A feeling I cannot fully place. My inner cat is prowling.

Rolling my shoulders, I try to release the niggling doubt. I had hoped a quickie before my shift would ease my…stress?

Washing my hands over my face, I take a deep breath and blow it out. Picking up a towel, I quickly wipe away the mess on my body and the bench. The cleaning duty crew will wash down the room properly soon. I don't want to be too meticulous and interrupt the pair who are still going.

My session in The Den of Sin, which Kiera has been trying and failing to rename the Den of Fun by the way, was a desperate attempt. I do not *do* desperate. This is not me!

"Gargh," I cry, slamming the door on my way out.

An overly emphasised, "Ooh," sounds from inside the room, followed by laughter.

"RARRRGH!" I roar, furiously stomping down the tunnel.

Someone coming in the opposite direction looks my way with curiosity. My lip curls, revealing elongated teeth. The other clan member squeaks and hurries past as a growl rumbles from me.

I jump as a hand lands on my shoulder, pulling me to a halt. I pivot to face my foe, all too ready for a fight.

"Whoah, Elan! What has you snarling this early, Brother?" Arwyn asks, his face a mixture of concern and cheekiness.

My lip curls again. I am unable to control the bitterness spewing out. "If I knew, I would not be in this state." Turning on my heel, I walk ahead, my shoulders hunched, eyes fixed on the ground.

"Oh, no! You're not in love too, are you? Pryderi got all cranky when he met Kiera. Who is it? You can tell me."

I hiss. At my best friend. What is wrong with me? "And with whom would I be in love *with*, Arwyn?"

Goddess bless him, he just shrugs. "I don't know. Maybe Kiera has a sister or brother I have not heard of?" Grinning widely, he shoves my arm, wiggling his eyebrows.

His playfulness stops me in my tracks. Turning to look deep into his pale blue gaze, my shoulders relax as a sigh escapes me. Finally, a smile creeps across my 'anyone-would-do-many-bad-things-just-for-one-kiss-from', dark pink lips. Others have told me this about my mouth – it was *not* the flattery they intended.

Anyway, Arwyn is staring back with widened eyes. A rumble purrs out of my friend, which has me chuckling and shaking my head as my residual tension eases.

"I do not know how you do it, Brother." Bowing my head close to his, I offer myself to his consolation.

He does not disappoint. Ever. His forehead meets mine and we breathe deeply.

"We do not have to know, my friend. Just watch the magick unfold," he says, sweeping his hand out wide in front of us.

I shove his shoulder with mine. And together, we walk out into the bright light of day.

"Come, Brother, food will help," Arwyn suggests as we approach the dining area.

Kiera is already there, pouring our coffees, goddess bless her. Pryderi is sauntering over with their plates of food. With a nod of thanks, I walk to the servery whilst Arwyn takes a seat with our friends.

Without needing to ask, I pile bacon, scrambled eggs and bread onto a plate for Arwyn. The same as me. Only, I splurge some honey onto my bread. Licking my lips, I take our morning meal across and join the group. Arwyn's grateful, toothy grin is enough to melt my heart – I love providing for him, even if it is only in this small way. If only it could be more. I give a rueful smile back.

"Careful, Pryderi. Elan might bite this morning," Arwyn warns.

Pryderi raises a brow. "Is that so? Your bed not warm, Elan?"

"You lot will never know," I grumble towards my food.

"Ha, don't say I didn't warn you," Arwyn teases Pryderi whilst ruffling my hair. I shirk him off.

"Truly, is there something we should know? Or that we can help with?" Pryderi asks.

I hold my breath in. Is there? Not if I am to keep the oath sworn as a youngling. Puffing out, I shake my head. "Alas, nothing."

Glancing up, I observe three frowns directed towards me. Arwyn, sitting next to me, rubs my arm. Goddess, how I long for his touch. I thought it would get easier with time, but it only gets worse.

The thing is, Arwyn, Pryderi and I grew up together. We quickly showed signs of becoming Watchers. We are bonded as brothers-at-arms. We swore to one another never to get intimately involved with one another, not wishing to complicate our sacred relationship.

That was all well and good when we were young, but as hormones kicked in, I developed feelings towards Arwyn. In fairness, who wouldn't? Just look at him; tall, broad-shouldered, slim-waisted, sculpted, a dusting of stubble on those hollow cheeks, piercing pale blue eyes that shimmer with mirth, and a smile that could melt my leather trousers off. Seriously, that strawberry-coloured Cupid's bow would test anyone's resolve. Add in shaggy dark hair I want to run my fingers through, and his fiercely loyal yet teasing personality - how is a male to refuse?

I fully admit that it was stupid to make that vow. Elinefae are promiscuous when not mated. It wouldn't have had to mean anything. I hook up with others all the time. But I sigh, unable to lie to myself. It would mean something. Everything. And I won't be like *him*.

The frowns looking at me are only getting more furrowed. I shrug my shoulders, attempting a smile. They do not appear convinced.

Peering at Pryderi and his mate, Kiera, my smile turns genuine. I cannot be anything but happy for those two. They fought so hard to get her halfling-self accepted into our clan. There were literal fights. That sorceress side of hers was not to be argued with, though. Besides, any fool can see they belong with one another. He kisses her nose – the gesture turning my insides to goo.

Diverting our conversation to clan updates, I avoid the awkward topic of love once more. How many times have I done this? It is almost habit by this point. But I have honour – I will not break an oath, no matter how misguided it was.

This is the best and worst part of my day, sitting beside my best friend. Being so close that our thighs brush. It would be so easy to stroke his cheek, lean my head against his shoulder or stroke his shaggy mane. But I resist. Again.

Scoffing down my meal as quickly as possible, I get up to start my Watcher shift. There is a parameter to monitor. Duty first!

Chapter 2 – Longing
~ Arwyn

My heart plummets, watching my best friend walk away. Again. His trouser-clad arse is all too visible as he strides off. What I wouldn't give to chase after and claim him. But he would not thank me for it. Aside from our youngling oath, I think those feelings are mine alone. He has never given me the least sign of hope.

"Poor guy, he really does seem down," Kiera sympathises.

Pryderi shrugs by her side. "But what is there to be done? I asked him and he was not forthcoming."

"I'm not sure he even knows himself. Maybe I should speak with Cerys?"

I growl. "It is not for you or me to interfere if he does not wish it."

Pryderi growls back. "Watch your tone, Brother. That is my mate."

Said mate rolls her eyes at both of us. "Boys, please! You can both simmer down, thank you very much. Really, I don't know what's got into all of you. You'll be hissing next, and then I'll have to zap both your noses."

We both laugh. Oh, we know she would, but we also know at this stage she is teasing.

"We would not want a red nose all day," I reply, chuckling.

"Again," she reminds us, smirking.

Shaking my head, I laugh harder. Yes, that is how we know she would be true to her word. The last time she broke up our fight, my nose resembled a tomato the entire day. Stung like a bee, too. The mere memory has me wincing and rubbing it.

She truly is an impressive woman. Her soft brown hair and green eyes hide her fire. Feisty yet fair. One-third sorceress, two-thirds elinefae, she has the temper that rivals a nereid, and the power to be deadly. But she is as soft as a kitten with my friend. They truly are well-mated. That ache in my chest returns, my hand stroking it before I'm aware of my action.

Kiera raises a brow in silent question.

"Ate too quickly," I deflect.

Her side pout suggests her doubt, but to her credit, she doesn't force me to confess.

"I should be about my duty," I announce, standing.

"Yes. Come, my mate, we should too," she tells Pryderi.

They walk off in the opposite direction to me. Depositing all our dirty dishes, I slope off. My track takes me close to Elan's route, but not close enough.

I cannot help but worry for Elan. My heart bleeds to see him in such sorrow. Does he not know I would give anything to make him happy? Just say the word, and I will be there. Perhaps I should seek him out after our shift. Maybe get him alone and hold him in a safe embrace. True, it would be inviting temptation. But it is worth it if I can help bring him some peace. I am strong. I can keep it in my trousers. Probably.

Dragging my hand through my hair, I scan the area around me. All seems quiet enough. Chuckling, I think of the alert that went out when Kiera first accidentally crossed our barrier. She was more like a human then, utterly unaware of her true self. Oblivious to what she had done. Pryderi had been the one to investigate. They truly were fated.

How does one know? Pryderi did not seem to fully appreciate they were a soul-matched pair until he kissed her. And what an alarming event that was – it triggered her change, poor love. But he was drawn to her before that.

Coming to an abrupt halt, my ears prick up. There was a snapping twig. I reach out my senses. A scuffling. But whatever it was has run off by the time I investigate more closely. Probably a squirrel. We really should eat more of those pesky vermin; nothing but trouble. They have no respect, ignoring our magickal barriers and all.

Shrugging, I move on. Hands in my pockets, I could almost be out for a casual stroll. It is a fine day – the sun is shining through the canopy of trees and birds are signing. Another thing that sets our team of three apart; we all enjoy the warmth of the day. Most other elinefae grumble and take turns at day shifts, preferring the night. Not us, though. As long as the light is not directly in our eyes, the warmth is blissful.

Even on rainy days, which let's face it, is most of them, the petrichor fills my nose with wonder. My home. That fresh pine scent of these woods is clan to me. Well, that along with the pleasing aroma of apple and vanilla.

Picking a fern, my fingers fondle its fronds absent-mindedly as I saunter along my route. I cannot take this peace for granted. What happened last year to the Irish clan lives on in my nightmares. Pryderi showed me the horror of the battle which ensued. Fair, the daoi-sith who orchestrated it is now dead and gone, at the hands of Kiera and her helpers. Witches, fae, dragons and even a unicorn got on board with that execution.

But it was an important reminder of how fragile peace can be. Feeling the tranquillity here now, I would give my life to protect it. Not just because I am blood oath-sworn to do so, but because it is worth fighting for. This precious gift we have must be protected.

I snort at myself, realising I'm now holding the fern to my chest, stroking its fronds like some sort of nature doll. Ridiculous! I am a grown male. Who appreciates nature. I am just glad nobody saw my soppy display. Grr! Rough, tough Watcher, serving to protect. I chuckle. Who am I fooling?

My lips pull to one side as I ponder. I am a walking conundrum. Soft and squishy like one of Kiera's marshmallows – and thank the goddess she introduced us to those. But sure, I would fight tooth and claw if I had to – it is what I am built for. All we Watchers are.

I am the tallest, but not by much – Pryderi is fractionally shorter. Elan is the shortest. But we all tower over most of our clan. Tall and broad – we are clan security. We keep watch. Vibrant violet eyes spring to mind. Closing my own, I try to shut out the image of Elan's stare, but it only gets stronger.

So, focusing my gaze intently towards the ground in front of me, and gritting my teeth, I attempt to summon a different picture. Anything. Long, black, shiny hair waving as Elan runs. Grunting, I try again. Broad shoulders, rolling as he runs. No!

Pausing, I scent around. Aha! Sprinting off, I am upon the rabbit before he can even twitch his nose. My teeth gnaw down, crunching through bone, making it a quick and all too easy kill. Waste not, want not – I snack on the entire thing as I continue my rounds. Mmm, delicious!

Invigorated by the bunny, I pick up the pace of my patrol. Passing the irrigation system, I make a pitstop at the latrine. I'm a good boy – I don't befoul the woods unless desperate.

Back out on the path, I cannot shake the feeling of being watched. But every time I stop to check, there is nobody there. I must be getting paranoid. To keep myself from reverting into a frightened youngling who jumps at every sound, I hum a merry tune as I walk.

The rest of the clan are not allowed, but as we're such a close team, Kiera lets Elan and I listen to her treasured iPod in their den. Cerys is mean not to share this wonder with clan. The music which comes from the tiny machine is fantastic.

The words of a singer called Adele come out of my mouth, singing about all the things I would do to make a certain someone feel my love.

"Goddess dammit, Elan. That is you, is it not?" I yell, hearing a squeaked gasp as I finished singing my soppy little heart out.

I was supposed to be alone, enjoying privacy. The little sneak!

But my friend is not answering me.

"Hey, Elan. You might as well show yourself. I know it's you. You think I cannot feel and smell you?" I shout, walking towards where I'm sure he is.

"Haha!" I cry, jumping around the tree where I saw the edge of his arm.

"Fuck off," he all but screams in my face.

Wait. He was hastily doing up his trousers. His cheeks are flushed. That delicious scent of his is stronger.

"Hey, were you knocking one out on shift?" I ask, my voice husky all of a sudden. I do my best to look accusingly, but there is a different emotion tugging at my loins.

He flusters. "Maybe. But it's not as though it's forbidden to wank on duty. Who cares?"

"Enough! This is not you."

"Maybe it is, and you just didn't know it." He glares, challenging me to argue.

"But I *do* know. Please. There is something very wrong. Let me help." I pray to the goddess that my look does not turn into a leer as my thoughts stray to helping him with my hand…maybe my mouth.

"Leave me be, Arwyn. This is my problem and mine alone."

"Oh, no. No, no, no-no-no! There is no such thing as a problem which cannot be shared. And the fact you think there is tells me this is more serious than you are saying. After all the recent issues, you are going straight to Cerys after shift. You can complete this duty, can you not?"

Not waiting for an answer, I pull him into a cwtch – the most comforting hug imaginable. My heart aches for my friend. He has never been this way. We tell one another everything.

"It's OK. We'll solve this. Together," I murmur, rubbing his back.

I had expected him to pull away, but he's melting into my embrace, and it takes every ounce of self-control I possess not to allow my hands to wander. When he finally backs off, he looks up into my eyes. We both draw in a sharp breath. I look away before I do something we'll both regret. The last thing he needs right now is for me to complicate his life any further.

I keep Elan with me for the rest of our shift. He is mostly silent, which again concerns me. However, my mind is whirring, and the peace is maybe selfishly welcomed. Why is my friend causing such heightened lust now? I have always found him attractive. But denying my impulses has never been difficult.

I've been finding it nigh impossible to keep my hands off him lately. It is not normal. Maybe if we were a soul-matched mated pair this would explain things. But that cannot be. Raking my hands through my hair, I try and fail to explain these feelings away.

As I sigh, Elan casts a querying glance at me but I shake my head. I cannot speak with him, not about this. It pains me to admit that. But I don't want to cause him any more distress.

It's an agonising shift, but it finally ends. Without stopping for evening meal, I lead us straight to Cerys' den once we reach the encampment. Typically, she is not there. But Kiera takes one look at Elan and offers to take him to Cerys' cottage herself – she can transport them with her magick.

Me? I'm left behind to find some food. Not that I feel much like eating. But Pryderi is there, and I update him. Although, I think Kiera already mind-linked to let him know the situation.

"It's so unlike him. He is usually our joker," Pryderi muses.

"I do not like it. It is wrong." I may be pouting slightly.

"Is he ill?"

"He doesn't smell sick."

Pryderi runs a hand through his black hair, his bright blue eyes etched with concern. "I cannot explain it."

I sigh. "Hopefully, Cerys will reveal his truth. If anyone can, it will be her."

Pryderi nods in agreement.

Chapter 3 – Delving

~ Elan

Without even being sure what I'm doing here, I've allowed myself to get dragged along to Cerys' cottage. Kiera pulled me through, literally.

Numb. Everything is numb. Cerys is looking into my eyes.

"I'll bring him back when we're done," I hear Cerys tell Kiera.

She gives a nod. With a final look of concern creasing her eyes, Kiera disappears. I still cannot get used to her vanishing that way. The witches use portals, and even then, before Kiera was here, they had to have a witch at each end to operate them.

"Ow!" I yelp and flinch away from the fingers flicking my forehead.

"Oh, you are at home there somewhere then," Cerys mutters with one of her wry smiles.

I scowl. "Yes."

"Well, you could have fooled me, young Elan. You mind telling me why you didn't answer my first three greetings?"

What? "I did not hear."

With one hand on my shoulder, she turns me in the opposite direction. "Hello," she says.

"Greetings," I reply, my hands on my hips.

"So, you haven't gone deaf."

"It would appear not."

"Alright, back this way," she coaxes.

I'm frowning as I obey. She peers into my eyes, so close that her image blurs. My stomach rumbles. One of her eyebrows rises.

"Are you eating properly?" she quizzes.

"Of course. But I did not eat after my duty."

"Hmmm…" She rubs her chin with her hand.

Wandering to a shelf, she rummages around, mumbling. Pulling out a crystal bowl, she fills it with water at her sink. She turns a knob and water pours from the metal tube. No dipping of bowls or pumping of handles needed. I do not know where the water comes from, but it does not taste like rain.

Placing the bowl of water on the table next to where I am still standing, she picks up her tingsha cymbals. My head pulls into my raised shoulders, shrinking away from the high-pitched noise.

Ting ting, she repeats the strikes, going around my whole body. I am forced to cover my ears with my hands. My eyes are scrunched closed. I want to ask her to stop but know she is trying to help, so hold my tongue.

She pulls on one of my arms. I open my eyes and lower my hands, seeing she has finished.

"Spit," Cerys commands.

Wincing, I summon the requested phlegm and spit into the crystal bowl of water she's holding up. The water swishes and swirls as Cerys jostles the bowl.

"Hmph! Well, at least there don't appear to be any dark energies or hexes," she mutters.

The news is almost disappointing. "At least that would have explained this," I tell her, gesturing down my body.

"Are you tired?"

I nod. It is near my bedtime, and my agitation has left me more fatigued than normal.

"Sit yourself down then whilst I cook something up for you. I had sausages on the go. They good enough, are they?"

That brings a smile out of me. Eagerly nodding, I tell her, "Better than good. My gratitude."

"Ha, well, I am glad to see you can still smile. Won't be a tick. Tomato sauce alright with you, is it?"

"You know me so well. Thank you." Grinning, I settle my back against her soft sofa.

She reappears with a cloth. "Here, place this over your eyes whilst you wait."

"Am I to play a guessing game?" I tease.

Ruffling my hair, she replies, "Get away with you, youngling male. It is to soothe those red, puffy eyes that used to be violet."

"Oh. Err, my thanks." Casting my gaze down, I am sure a blush is now turning my cheeks red also.

Without another word, she walks away again. Tilting my head back, I place the cold, damp cloth over my eyes. A satisfied groan rumbles out of my lips. Mmm…it is indeed soothing. Twitching my nose, I smell…lavender. Our clan witch really is the best.

Stretching my legs and arms, I sink back further into the luxury of the cottage. Cerys' home is so cosy and plush. Taking a deep breath in, I savour the aroma of cooking sausages wafting through the room. My stomach rumbles again.

"Aren't you the picture of contentment?" Cerys asks as she carries the food to me.

"You make me feel like a spoiled youngling," I tell her, accepting the plate with both hands.

"Well, you are worth spoiling sometimes. You Watchers work so hard. Maybe too hard?" she asks, raising a brow as I take my first bite.

It is rude to speak with your mouth full, so I shrug. No way am I rushing this sandwich. Ahh…it tastes so good!

"Was that a purr?"

I finish my mouthful. "Might have been," I reply, grinning before taking another bite.

Cerys smiles. "You don't know how relieved I am to hear that noise. Listening to Kiera, I thought you were going to curl up in a corner and yowl all night."

I chortle around my sausage sandwich. Munching it down, I manage to say, "I am not that bad." Holding up the remainder of my food, I tell her, "And this helps."

She chuckles. "I am glad to be of assistance."

I'm allowed to eat the rest of my tasty morsel in silence. I gulp down the orange, vanilla and cinnamon tea after. "Ahh…delicious. I thank you."

"You are most welcome. Do you feel able to talk about what is troubling you now?"

I shake my head. "Alas, it is not so simple, Cerys. I do not know. I do not say this to be difficult. It is most frustrating. I just…ache, feel empty," I say, rubbing my chest.

"You feel heart sick?"

Scrunching my face, I inform her, "I do not think that describes it. It is more…you know when you put your foot down on solid ground, but it sinks into what is really a bog?"

She frowns. "Like something isn't there when it should be?"

"Yes. That is more the feeling. A wrongness. Missing…I do not know what."

"Ah, I see." That wry smile is back.

"Would you care to tell me, please? I do not understand, Cerys. Please."

Snickering, she shakes her head. "Tell me, Elan, has anything happened of late? Something significant?"

She is not going to tell me? My mouth hangs open a moment. "Apart from the clan battle, Kiera's arrival and mating with Pryderi?" A hint of sarcasm colours my answer.

She looks at me pointedly.

"What? I am happy my friend is happy. It does not make me sad."

"Uh-huh. You keep on telling yourself that, Elan."

I shake my head. "Truly. It brings me joy to see Pryderi and Kiera finally united."

"I do not say any different. But search your heart further. As well as that joy, did nothing change?"

"I still see him. More now than when they disappeared for their what she calls a honeymoon. It is not as if he left."

Sighing, she shakes her head. "Oh, elinefae are so literal sometimes. Not everything is black and white, Elan. Do you seriously mean to tell me that the balance in your friendship has not altered at all?"

Folding my arms, I grimace whilst considering what she has said. "Maybe?"

Patting my knee, she informs me in a quiet tone, "There is no maybe about it. You three have been a trio your whole lives. But you no longer spend all of your free time together. Yes, you still see Pryderi, but it is not the same."

"But I am not jealous. Truly, I am happy for him. He is my brother and friend, not my mate."

"No. No, he is not..." She pauses. I think she was about to say something but changes it. "Still, it is a change. I think you should acknowledge that. It is a happy one, granted, but that does not mean you do not need to adjust to it, all the same."

I nod with a tight-lipped smile. "Yes. I see the sense in this."

She pats my cheek then rubs it with her thumb. "Good."

Leaning towards her, I rub my cheek to hers. "Gratitude."

Moving so her forehead is against mine, she replies, "Welcome."

We smile at one another.

"Now. Did you want to stay the night?"

"I am not sick."

"No. But maybe one night away would do you some good?"

"It is kind. But no, thank you. I shall return to clan where I belong."

"Very well."

Running my hand down my face, I sigh. "Ah, but I made a fool of myself today. More pussy and less cat. How do I face them after that?"

Rubbing my upper arm, she tells me, "They will only be happy to see you more yourself."

I bow my head. "I hope that is true."

"Is it not what you would feel in their place?"

"Yes."

"Right we are then. My old witchy ways of travel still alright, are they?" she asks, tilting her head, smirking.

"You know I prefer yours. Kiera magick jumps so quickly it makes me dizzy."

"I'm glad I'm not the only one. Come on," she replies, leading me to her garden.

Once outside, she opens the portal her end. It takes a moment, but I see my home through it.

I rub cheeks again. "Honestly. Thank you greatly for your kindness, Cerys."

"Pah, off with you now."

Walking through the portal, I chortle, knowing the witch's gruff exterior hides a soft, squishy heart.

Breathing in deep, I smell all the woodsy scents of home as I meander back towards my den. I feel comforted and content once more. Could it really be so simple?

Chapter 4 ~ Comfort

~ Arwyn

As soon as Kiera returns from dropping off Elan at Cerys' house, I pounce. I waited with Pryderi in their den, eager to receive news. But she is back too soon. Still, I would ask.

"Arwyn, I can see from your expression that you want to enquire about your friend. It's good you are so loyal, but there's nothing for me to tell. Besides, it's private. I would not betray a confidence even if he had told me anything."

"This I know," I tell her, looking at the ground. I do know it, but that does not stop me hoping.

Placing a hand on my shoulder, she adds, "I am sorry, Arwyn. We are all concerned." She looks pointedly at Pryderi.

I put my arm around his shoulder too, and we share a group hug.

"I refuse to be useless. You are away tomorrow, yes?"

"Yeees," she replies, clearly unsure of what I will ask.

"Might I, err…be permitted to borrow…?" I gesture with my thumb, not wishing to speak the iPod's name out loud.

Her look of horror is pretend. I think.

"I promise to take care and not break it. Nobody else shall know, I swear," I vow, thumping a fist to my chest.

"I believe you. But why?"

I grin. "I have an idea. I do not lay blame, you must understand this. But there has been…disturbance with your arrival."

She smirks. "Utter chaos more like."

"I did not like to say. But yes, chaos. I would remind Elan we are unchanged. We are still here for him."

Turning my attention to Pryderi, I ask, "Brother, what say you to a night just for us three, like it used to be?"

He smiles broadly. "I say that sounds like a brilliant idea."

"I am allowed to have them occasionally," I say, cocking my head.

"For what it's worth, I think you could all use a boys' night in. I'm sorry if it's seemed like you couldn't," Kiera apologises.

"No, no. You are still newly mated. It is to be expected," I reply with a wink.

Pryderi slaps my arm. "Hey."

"Ha, tell me I am wrong."

"That I cannot do."

"See! Anyway. Kiera, can you contact Cerys, please? Once Elan is back. I want it to be a surprise. But would she bring snacks?"

She laughs. "Illicit contraband? And I thought you were such a good boy."

"Oh, I can be very very bad," I tell her, wiggling my eyebrows.

That earns me a thump from my friend. "Do *not* flirt with my mate."

I laugh at his overprotectiveness. "Brother, you know I would not. Forgive me, Kiera."

She's laughing at us both. "For the love of goddess, you lot get so *snippy*." The last word is in her English language.

I frown. "*Snippy*?"

She laughs more. "Sorry. I do not know the Eline. Um...short-tempered?"

"Oh, this is no joke. Do not laugh. Our mate is our world. You feel the same in return for Pryderi, I think."

"Ah, maybe I do. And yet I do not threaten a fight every time wrong words are used."

"No, you just zap people instead."

We all laugh at that.

"But you will ask Cerys, will you not?" I check.

"Of course. Anything for you boys. I'll ask her to secrete them in our den here."

"No!" I yelp but then moderate my tone. "I mean, please can you ask Cerys to take them to my den, please?"

She scowls but agrees.

I was chased away from waiting at Pryderi's den. "Three is a crowd," according to Kiera. I think they were going to have sexy time – I did not wish to be there for that.

I have been pacing my den, hoping my best friend will seek me out. But it becomes clear he will not. His den is a few doors away from mine – I sense his presence when he is once more nearby. I ache to go to him but force myself to remain here, knowing he will come to me if he wishes it.

My heart sinks when he keeps to himself. I wish to know why, after all these years, he now feels unable to tell me what troubles him. Argh, he is too stubborn. I carry on pacing a while, trying to calm myself.

This is no good. I must try to rest. We have duty tomorrow. And hopefully a good night after. I want to be at my best to help Elan through whatever this is.

Physically jumping back from the knocking on my door, I go to answer, my heart hammering in my chest. I can feel it's not Elan, though. Desperately trying to calm my anxiety, I plaster a smile on my face.

"Megan," I greet warmly, opening the door.

"Brother," she exclaims, rushing into my outstretched arms.

I hold her close, inhaling her sweet and woodsy pear with patchouli signature scent, calming me with her presence.

"It is good to see you," I whisper, meaning it with all my heart.

She closes the door behind her. "Apologies, I know it is late for you."

I wave it off. "Not needed."

"I am on clean-up duty in the Den of Sin…"

I grimace.

She giggles and then also pulls a face of disgust, her amber eyes squinting. "Admittedly, it is not my favourite. I came here as soon as I could. We always seem on opposite ends of the day."

I open my mouth, but she holds up a hand, stopping what I was about to say. "I lay no blame."

"Still, I wish we had more time with you."

Smiling broadly, she reassures me, "You are always there when most needed, Arwyn. You may rest easy, knowing you are a good brother. Besides, you work hard, so it is only fair you play hard too. Which you do, by all accounts."

My mouth opens again, but words are not forthcoming. This conversation has taken an inappropriate turn.

"It is not only your preferences I am aware of but your enthusiasm too." Her brow arches, and I know she sees me for my true self. "If I were not practically your sister, I may be a little jealous." She pushes her dark blonde hair back with a swish, the ginger highlights glinting as she does so.

Like all unmated elinefae, my sexual partners may be of any gender. However, I have a distinct lean towards males. Not that clan would hold judgement. But it is not something I boast of either; we are encouraged to seek a mate and further our species.

She continues, "I merely wished to convey it can be challenging to talk with you. And I needed to do so without Elan present. Is he alright? I have sensed great sadness in him. He is deeply unsettled, I think."

Sighing in relief at the change of topic and her concern, I reply, "Aye, he is. But he will not or cannot say why."

"This is saddening. You will let me know if there is anything I can do? I may have been born into another clan, but you are my own. You truly have been like brothers, all three of you, and there is nothing I would not do for you, Elan or Pryderi."

Kissing our foreheads together, I tell her, "The same can be said of us, Sister. That terrible day, when you lost your clan, was yet a blessing as it brought you to us. My mother, your mother's sister, was honoured to offer you sanctuary. We would not be without you. And you may ease your mind. I plan to surprise Elan tomorrow. The three of us are to relax as of days of old. It is my hope that it shall bring him comfort."

She smiles. "It sounds lovely. Let me know if it helps. I cannot linger. Duty awaits. But reach out any time."

We rub cheeks as I confirm, "Of course."

As swiftly as she appeared, she leaves me alone once more. I meant what I said, she has become like a sister to us. Our family dens were all close, and so we would play together as younglings. All clan are family, but some are more so than others.

Her visit is another reminder of the fragility of peace. Her original clan was attacked by another after a long-standing feud escalated. Most were tragically killed. But Megan's mother had managed to get her to flee, promising she would follow. Sadly, she was unable to fulfil her pledge.

From that distraught little female, a mighty woman has grown. She is perhaps the sweetest, best-natured soul among us. And now I feel bad for not inviting her to our evening. But, as she said, we are mostly awake at differing hours these days. I must try harder to make more time with her, though. I miss her brightness.

With her blessing, I feel excited about tomorrow. I just hope it works.

After what feels like one of the longest Watch duties of my life, I head to evening meal. Not that I would admit it, but my path was close to Elan's all day. It was impossible to be far away from him after yesterday.

Stubborn as always, Elan had insisted he was up to his task. Pryderi and I had shared uncertain glances but would not disrespect our Brother by accusing him of lying. He wandered off as if nothing at all had happened yesterday.

All day, my gut has been twisting. Maybe I had been expecting a repeat of yesterday's negative emotions. But, to his credit, Elan has, if not been calm, at least less disturbed.

Baby dragons are not especially small. Already, that is in the space of a few months, Terrah has grown from a tiny, green hatchling which could sit in Kiera's hands to the approximate size of a large domestic cat. She is now sitting in Pryderi's lap, her head on his shoulder, hugging him as he tries to eat his evening meal. A task made all the more challenging by her repeated attempts to help herself to his food.

Tapping her nose, again he tells her, "No, Terrah! Not for you. You had yours on our last walk. Remember the squirrels?"

I swear she understands every word. She's licking her lips as if in remembrance of her snacks.

"My turn now," he adds, stretching his hand with a spoonful of venison stew towards him.

Quick as a flash of lightning, Terrah's tongue extends like a whip and snatches the food before it reaches Pryderi's mouth.

"Bloody dragon! No, Terrah. Enough!" he says a lot more firmly, plonking the dragon on the ground.

She looks up at him with big golden eyes.

"It's no use you looking sorry now. Stay!"

Everyone else around us is laughing. I'm trying my best not to, knowing how much Terrah dislikes being laughed at. Even now, her wings have flattened along her back and her head is on the ground as she crouches down, trying to hide behind our legs.

Taking obvious pity on her, Pryderi reaches down and strokes her head. She nuzzles up into his palm.

"Alright. Just stay there whilst I finish eating. Good girl."

Having finished most of his stew, Elan places the bowl on the floor so Terrah can finish it off.

Pryderi splats his own forehead. "Nooo, now you're just reinforcing her bad behaviour, Elan. She's never going to learn."

He shrugs. "Meh, she was sitting there patiently like a good dragon. I was just rewarding her good behaviour. Wasn't I, sweetheart?" The last is said in a babyish tone towards Terrah.

She, of course, ignores him totally, too engrossed in licking the bowl clean.

"Spoiling her is what you're doing," I jeer.

"Oh, take his side, why don't you?"

Without warning, Terrah leaps onto Elan's lap. His arms wrap around her and he gets a meat-scented, slobbery lick on the cheek.

Wiping the drool away, he tells her, "You are welcome, youngling. I think."

Her chortling burbles are enough to melt anyone's heart.

"See, she appreciates me," Elan gloats as he gets another licky kiss.

"Well, someone has to," I tease.

"Hey, I could do a lot worse than this one."

I smack him upside the head. "*Twp!*"

"What was that for? Look at those big, beautiful eyes. Anyone would be lucky to have you, wouldn't they, Terrah?" He makes kissy faces at her, but she just nestles into his shoulder.

I laugh. "You think Pryderi had trouble getting Kiera accepted? Just imagine the fury over a dragon union."

We all laugh at that. It's an amusing image, for sure. Hopefully, they both know I wasn't serious.

Finishing my own meal, I give Pryderi a knowing nod. He is to keep Elan distracted as I make preparations, and I'm presuming that explains Terrah's unusual presence at dinner.

With every ounce of effort, I walk slowly away from the dining area. Only once out of sight, do I break into a jog to my den.

Gathering the blanket from my bed along with a spare and the pillows, I start to build a nest against the far wall. Goddess bless them, Cerys and Kiera have deposited their promised goods. These get stacked alongside the comfort area, the snacks piled high on my small table. There are even extra cushions provided. I do not think even an expectant mother could be happier with the arrangement.

Ensuring the precious iPod is tucked under a cushion, out of sight, I run back to my friends.

"Pryderi, for the hundredth time, I am well. I beg you to permit me to go to my rest," Elan moans, trying to pull away from his grasp.

Poor Pryderi rolls his eyes and huffs, exasperated at our friend's defiance. But he grins at my arrival.

"Ho, what is this ruckus, Elan? If you wish to fight, you know you can call on me," I tell him, lowering into a challenging stance but wiggling my eyebrows.

It is mildly surprising when he mirrors my action and rolls his fists at me. "You think you can take me?"

"Oh, I think we both know the answer to that," I tell him, smirking.

He lunges forwards, ploughing into my waist. I allow him to knock me onto my arse. Hey, he needs a win.

Elan's weight is on me in a second. I make a show of bearing my teeth but make no move to force him off. Not yet. One moment of close contact like this, under the guise of fighting will be enough to last me a while, I lie to myself. Only when my hips are dangerously close to grinding against his in an all-too-friendly manner, do I shove my hand against his shoulder, twisting him off of me.

I pause too long, trying to adjust to playfighting and not giving in to my lust. Elan tackles me, and this time it is not of my doing when I land with a thud on the ground. Playful snarls erupt between us as we tousle, but our fangs are not elongated.

It's amazing I have remained sane. How often have we done this? How badly do I wish he would pin me and turn this into a different type of fun? Every time! But he never does.

"Alright, enough," Pryderi interjects, breaking us apart before we play too rough.

Terrah is hopping around, snorting.

Elan and I help each other up. Nobody else pays us much attention; such things are commonplace amongst clan. Only if the snarls turn real, would anyone step in.

Looking ever so slightly down, I stare into Elan's violet gaze. "Do you trust me?"

His answering look is so earnest that I could melt on the spot. "With my life."

Our faces are a whisper's breath away from one another. It would ruin everything if my lips inched forwards to touch his temptingly pink and perky ones, so I resist. Just.

"Then come with us," I command, my voice breathy.

Grabbing his hand, I tug him to follow. Of course, he does. This is our level of trust – we would follow one another anywhere without question. Argh, but it heats my loins. Down, boy!

"I'm just taking Terrah home," Pryderi confirms before running off with her.

Elan and I walk on alone, together.

He cocks his head as we reach my door. "This is your big secret?"

I laugh. "So, it is not entirely out of the ordinary," I admit, raising my hands in a shrug.

His outward puff blows his long black hair up from his face a little. "I must admit to being a little relieved, Brother. I thought you were going to take me back to Cerys and force me to stay."

I laugh. "I would never force you to do anything."

Sadness passes across his eyes in a flash. "I know."

Forcing myself to look away, I open my den door, sweeping my arm out wide. "Welcome to boys' night."

His cheeky grin is all the reward I need. My friend is restored to me. "This looks cosy."

Pushing him in through the entrance, I inform him, "I have contraband galore. Pryderi will be with us in a mo."

Having placed a towel over the outside handle to ensure we are not disturbed, and ignoring my hopeful, twitching cock, I close the door. Not that I tend to bring anyone to my room for sexy times – I try to keep that in the Den of Sin. However, hope springs eternal.

Snatching the iPod from its hiding place, I ensure nobody squishes it. Kiera may actually kill me should any harm befall her treasured machine. She has kindly connected a small speaker to it, and when I press the button, I see she has selected a "boys' night" playlist. That makes me chuckle. Pryderi is lucky to have such a thoughtful mate.

Elan heads straight to the snack table to inspect the offerings.

"You just ate," I remind him.

"Ah, but there is always room for treats."

I smile at him before going back to inspecting the songs on the playlist, seeing if I recognise any of them. There is rustling behind me as Elan paws over the treats, but he oddly doesn't snatch any of them up yet. He must be full despite his protestations.

My head whips up at the sound of knocking. But I sigh and roll my eyes as I sense who's on the other side.

"Pryderi, you don't need to knock, come in," I call.

"But there was a towel…" he says, entering my den.

"Ah, no, that was so nobody else would interrupt boys' night." Did he really think Elan and I would be up to anything?

Trying to distract my thoughts, I press play on the iPod. We all laugh as the first song sings about predicting a riot. The little screen says it is sung by the Kaiser Chiefs. Given what just happened in the dining area, I have to admit that Kiera does know us well.

As lively music continues to pour into our ears, we jump around, dancing like nobody is watching. Pryderi has the longest hair – his black strands are flying wildly. I am sure that even my shorter, dark brown hair is messy. Some of it is clinging to my face by the time we pause for breath.

"Ahh…but it is good to immerse in such music," I declare, panting.

"My mate spoils us. I cannot believe we never knew of this. And most of clan still do not. If only Cerys would permit it," Pryderi says.

"I understand why not, though," Elan adds, "There are too many questions that come with such things. And in turn, our way of life would be compromised."

Pryderi rolls his electric blue eyes. "Yeah, yeah. I know. It is a pity, is all."

"I do feel a bit selfish," I admit, "But not so bad as to forego the pleasure."

Pryderi slaps the side of my head, so I give him a friendly shove. Elan knocks us both together. I end it by ruffling their hair, making them squirm like younglings. Laughter rings out through my den. And oh, but it warms my soul. I have missed this. Maybe tonight is as much for me as it is for Elan, after all.

"Mmm...salt and vinegar," I murmur, breathing in the divine scent as I open a bag of crisps.

Licking his lips, Elan reaches his hand into the bag. I do not think of that tongue lapping my cock. At least, I try not to.

"Here," I say, shoving the bag into his hands and turning to look at the drinks.

Some rearrangement of my trousers may also be happening on the sly. Our leather waistcoats got discarded as soon as we started dancing. Naked, sweaty torsos are distracting – one in particular. How are my hands not running up and down his body? My thumbs hooked into his trousers, tugging them down. My tongue lapping the tip...no, none of that.

"Ooh, cola," I cry, holding up the rare sugary drink.

Collecting his own can, Elan salutes, "Cheers!"

Pryderi echoes us a beat afterwards. Light brown bubbles spew out as I crack mine open, soaking my hand in sweet nectar. I lick and suck it off, so I'm not left sticky.

Elan groans as he sits on the blankets to enjoy our forbidden...well, not fruits. The opposite of fruit. Cerys calls it *junk food.* It's jolly delicious to me, so I will not call it junk or anything which infers waste. Feast. Whatever you want to call it, Pryderi and I sit either side of Elan on the blankets, our snack packets open and ready for sharing.

"Alright, that's spooky," I say, as calmer music plays through the speaker.

Wafting his hand, Pryderi tells me, "Pah, she probably used sorcery on the thing."

Cocking an eyebrow, I glare at him. "Have you heard yourself? You tell me your mate used magick on her, quite frankly, already magickal device, as if you were saying she went for a stroll in the forest."

Shaking his head, he chuckles. "I suppose I shouldn't be so used to it yet, now you mention it. But it's just her." He shrugs.

Elan shoves him shoulder-to-shoulder. "Only you could have a magickal mate."

Sliding my back down the wall a little, I snuggle into the cushions. This is the life – my friends, music, snacks and banter. I should not really ask for or expect more. This right here is gift enough.

We talk utter bollocks as we munch our way through our supplies. The night wears on and having danced off the sugar, our energies dip. Collapsing onto the blankets once more, we sigh deeply.

"Many thanks," Elan says to us both.

A tear does not well up in my eye. I am a fierce Watcher. "My pleasure," I murmur as Pryderi replies with something similar.

The music becomes soporific as we sit in silence. Oh, sweet goddess, Elan's head falls onto my shoulder, and I realise I was wrong before. *This* is as good as it gets.

Letting my eyes close in bliss, I know only peace and joy.

Chapter 5 – Kiera Meets...
– Hassan

Kiera has arrived in our clan. From her numerous winces during the greeting, I gather she does not approve of us. Whispers go around our clan as quick as wildfire. It's obvious our ways are not what she is used to.

It's frustrating, being kept away from our visitor. She sounds intriguing; an elinefae sorceress. Our witch has been chatting with her, as well as our Leader. But such conversation is not for the likes of me. She has surely only been permitted such freedom as she is accompanied by her clan's Leader. Females are usually kept far away from males. But rumours of her blunt manners seem to indicate that she is in no way shy.

Her plates have come back to the kitchen entirely empty. A glow spreads through my chest, realising she was happy with the food my team and I cooked for her. It is almost enough to displace the sadness which has taken up residence there. Fear fills my every waking moment and terrorises my sleeping ones.

I wish I could go back and erase that terrible experience and its outfall. Well, there are several times I would undo, but that one in particular. The most humiliating and dangerous one of my life. And it may yet end my existence.

Whilst I'm making wishes, convincing my *zib* that I'm not mated and have no place getting urges would be another. He's not listening to me. And having a preference for males puts me in danger; such things are against the law here in Saudi Arabia. As well I know.

Today, even with the threats hanging over my head, I need to work off my tension. Maybe it's the stress caused by our important visitors. But I'm as stiff as a board. There's no way this is going down without some action.

I've come out the back for a cigarette now that food service is over. Leaning my head back against the cool concrete wall, I blow out a cloud of smoke. I must be giving off a vibe as Omar is sidling over.

"Hassan, you're looking particularly delicious this evening," he croons.

I raise an eyebrow at him. "You mean you hope you do."

He grins. "If you say so. Would you like a nibble to find out?"

"What if you were to do the nibbling for a change?"

He snorts. "My way or no way."

Against my better judgement, I find myself stubbing out my cigarette on the ground and following him to a concealed area and getting down on my knees. I know what will happen, but it is better than nothing. At least, that is what I've told myself on numerous occasions before. And I'm desperate. It is as though Omar can sense it.

Glancing around again, he raises his thobe. The human clothing admittedly has the benefit of quick and easy access. Licking my lips, I lean forwards and tease his tip. My hand works his shaft as my mouth sinks down.

I know what he likes, and there is always an urgency, especially when visitors are amongst our clan. My head bobs as I suck harder, up and down whilst my grip works in tandem. I'm left to grip myself with my free hand; there is no hope he'll return the favour. He never does.

Within minutes, he's filling my mouth. I spit into the tea towel which had been left over my shoulder. Then use the same to catch my release as he walks off.

"STOP!" a female voice calls.

My heart freezes still along with the rest of my body. Oh shit! I can't move and have been caught doing the unthinkable. By none other than our guest, Kiera. I might be sick. Only, I can't lean over to wretch. Helplessly, I watch on.

Omar is apparently likewise rooted to the spot. Sauntering up to him, she sneers, "You are a very selfish male, aren't you? Shame on you."

He strangles out, "What?"

"You obviously didn't return the favour. Did nobody ever teach you mutual satisfaction is expected?"

She flicks her fingers and he manages to shake his head, but it may be more in disbelief. She swipes his nose. Oh, my goddess!

"Never again will you take without giving. Off you go now," she commands.

With another wriggle of her fingers, he stumbles forwards and away in a daze.

My stomach lurches as her white glowing gaze is turned on me. I gulp.

"Oh, there now. Don't be afraid. I'm not cross with you, Hassan."

"Urgh?" I garble.

"Oh, my apologies. I couldn't have you running off. We need to have friendly words. If I release you, promise not to scurry away?"

"Uh-huh."

I watch her fingers wriggle once more, and I stagger forwards a step as my limbs are released from her hold.

"What the—?" I start, but she holds a hand up.

"Like I said, I need to speak with you. Is here alright?"

I nod slowly.

"Fabulous."

"I apologise—"

But again, she stops me. "*You* have nothing to apologise for." She chuckles. "But I think your friend regrets being...well, let us say no more about it. I didn't come out here to spy. In my clan, such things happen in the Den of...oh, never mind, I'm getting distracted again."

I gawp at her. "You're not disgusted?"

"Oh, please. By a blowjob? I am only shocked by the non-reciprocation. But I honestly didn't mean to be a voyeur. There are more important matters at hand."

"But he...I..."

"Really, let's not get hung up on it. The male's a selfish git, and not worth our attention. Now, your Leader tells me your services are in high demand."

"I...err..."

"Now, don't be modest. You're clearly an excellent cook. And I have a plan I'd like you to be involved in."

Oh, my cooking. But this is too good to be true. By the time she finishes giving me all the details, I find myself agreeing to go to her clan. I'm not even sure how long for, but I practically bite her hand off at the chance to get away.

Chapter 6 – A Wake-Up Call
~ Elan

Inhaling deeply, I savour the faint orange and clove scent filling my nostrils. A smile spreads across my face…and then I open my eyes. It takes me a moment to realise where I am and who I'm with.

I must've slept in Arwyn's den all night. He's still asleep next to me, so I try not to make any sudden movements. Rubbing my neck, I try to alleviate the ache as I slowly come to a stand. With a yawn and a stretch, I take in my surroundings. There is no sign of Pryderi.

Looking down at my thoughtful friend's sleeping form, my eyes trace every line and curve. Raking my hands through my hair, I try to reason with myself. Kissing him good morning, no matter how tempting, is not an option. But, ahh, he looks so peaceful like this. What I wouldn't give to wake up to him every morning.

To avoid temptation, I slip out of his room like a thief in the night. I need to go and relieve my bladder anyway. There was no wake-up knock at the door – we have a day off. I'll let Arwyn sleep in.

The daylight's shadows tell me it's still morning. After a quick wash, I head towards the dining area. Morning meal is still being served. I grab cold meats and cheese – after last night's sugar overload, the honey is not appealing right now.

My cheeks spread into what must look like a daft grin as I sit and eat. Fun-filled memories of last night run through my head. With shoulders sinking down my back, I let out a contented sigh. The three of us felt right for the first time in months.

Cerys would be insufferable if I told her as much, but she was right. This *has* been an adjustment. I have been missing my friend. I cannot blame him; having a soul-matched mate is overwhelming, and I consider myself lucky to have seen him at all. But we have changed. However, last night shows that maybe I should have faith that we are still there for one another.

My shoulders snap tight as a hand claps my shoulder. "There you are," Arwyn greets, "You wandered off."

"I did not wish to disturb you."

"Aww, you were worried about me?" he mocks.

I slap his arm away before he can ruffle my hair. "Not so very much."

He chuckles. Does he know I'm lying through my teeth?

"So, what would you like to do today?" he asks.

I double-take, which has him laughing more.

"Elan, you did not think I would leave you in the lurch today?"

"I had not given it much thought," I lie. However, none of my intentions are remotely actionable.

"I thought you might want to come swimming with me," he suggests, his pale blue eyes shimmering.

"Now, there's an offer I can't refuse." Although I probably should; nudity will lead to even more forbidden thoughts.

For the millionth time, I question that stupid oath. We should just give in to our instincts; shag and get it out of the way. It's only sex. I'm sure that denying ourselves is what has brought us to this messy situation. It's unnatural. The desire keeps building as it has nowhere to go.

What I cannot tell anyone is that my desire and subsequent frustration are what lies behind most of what happened yesterday. Yes, Pryderi has unsettled our dynamic. And maybe that has made me focus more on Arwyn, or more accurately, what is not happening between us. When I heard his beautiful voice singing those words pledging deeds of love, it was as if he were singing to me. Something in my soul snapped and shattered. Because I would do anything for him. And yet I know that to him it was just a song.

And no matter what, I would never stand in the way of Arwyn and his mate. He hasn't met her yet, but it is surely only a matter of time. I feel he has one. I do not know how I know but I know. It is not something which is guaranteed to any of us. Fate has to unite mating pairs. But his must be close. Maybe that is why my body is screaming louder than ever to take the opportunity whilst we are both still single.

All of this remains unspoken as we head towards our favourite pool. We're the only ones here. A small, gentle waterfall cascades down the rocks – great for splashing around with. Just the thought of that has me all kinds of excited as I scramble out of my trousers and top.

The cool water is refreshing as we jump in. Elinefae don't feel the cold the same way humans do – that is why they do not come here. Well, that and the wards around our encampment. Still, my dick is dissuaded from becoming too excited with the cool temperature, thank the goddess.

Arwyn and I seem content to drift on our backs for a while, lapping up the rare, glorious day. It's utter bliss, wallowing this way. My eyes softly close as my body slowly glides around the pool. We're both silent. It is enough just to have my friend nearby; no words are necessary.

Coughing, I resurface after Arwyn pushes me under without warning. As soon as I catch my breath I lunge at him, but he evades my first attempt at retribution. I splash a wave at him with my arm instead. We're both laughing as he jumps on my back trying to pull me under. But I leap up and fall backwards, plunging him in first beneath me.

Spluttering, we separate, trying to gulp in air. It is harder to do when you're laughing, though. And he's still trying to splash me with his palm. Swimming to the side, I hook my elbows over a rock to give myself a moment to breathe properly. Within moments, a pair of pale blue eyes squint at me.

"You are alright?" he asks me, melting my heart.

"Of course. I am not so fragile. Just swallowed too much water."

I half expect him to dunk me again, but no. He waits and watches as I cough and breathe. Once composed, I lay my head on one side atop my folded arms, looking at Arwyn. His brown hair is clinging around his face like a drowned rat, and yet he's still as good-looking as ever.

Water cascades down the channels of his muscles. His broad shoulders are splayed out as he rests his arms on the side. Every sinew is taught. And I know all too well how his chest with a smattering of hair tapers into a slim waist. His perfectly pert buttocks leading down to his powerful legs.

With a wave of his hand, Arwyn flicks hair out of his eyes. My fingers were itching to do that for him, but it was too intimate. I will not cross that invisible friendship line which holds me captive.

"Tell me, how are you?" I ask him.

His brow furrows. "Me? I am well enough."

"But could be better?" He has been so good to me, and yet I wonder if there is no cost to himself – he has been more subdued of late.

"Pah! I have nothing to complain about. I have all I need." His slight wince does not go unnoticed.

"You would tell me if there were something I could do in return for you, would you not, Brother?"

He nods sharply. "Of course."

The passing sadness is well concealed, but I know this male as well as I know myself. My whole body urges me to swim up behind him, to hold Arwyn in my arms, shielding him from all harm. To my astonishment, I have started to paddle across to do just that. To evade such embarrassment, I attack his shoulders, pushing him back underwater.

"Elan! I was not ready," he grumbles as he reappears, squeezing water from his nose.

"Ha, that is the idea," I tease.

And then I find myself underwater once more. My face is level with his magnificent dick, but I close my eyes against the sight and force myself back to the surface. I will not wrap my arms around him. Grinding against Arwyn is absolutely not going to happen.

Pushing away from the side, I swim beyond temptation's reach. Infuriatingly, he follows. We swim around one another in circles without attacking. Somehow, it is more enticing this way. The promise of skin contact is within reach but yet a thousand miles away.

Eventually, we give in to our youngling selves and return to splashing antics, but no more dunking. Eventually, we tire. Pulling ourselves up onto the bank, we flop down on the earth and air-dry. I do not wait long, mindful to cover my nudity in front of my friend when I would not give it a second thought were I with anyone else.

Pulling my trousers on, I call across, "What next?"

He stares at me a moment. "It is for you to decide, Brother. This is your day."

"My day to do what?"

"Whatever pleases you most."

If only he knew! I merely offer a shrug.

"We should first find Pryderi. I need to double check he took the," he lowers his voice to a whisper, "iPod when he left. Kiera will kill me if it has gone missing."

My stomach lurches. "I had presumed...why did you not say before? We must find him at once."

Now I think of it, why did we not seek our friend out sooner? I think Kiera is still off on a mission. I was so swept up in excitement and denial that, to my shame, it did not occur to me to invite him to our swim session. But then, he is not as fond of the water as we are. I think it is something to do with his inner black panther.

It is hard to say how we are affected by our cats. We do not shift, but some traits seem to be inherent within us. For example, the Persian leopard which forms my signature is a water fan, and so am I – who influences whom? I cannot rightly say.

Arwyn's white tiger is the biggest water lover out of us. I wonder if we ever did shift and have somehow lost the ability. There are times I do not feel entirely alone in my body.

After our swim, I'm feeling bright-eyed and bushy-tailed. I wish I had an actual tail. A lot of people say we used to. See, it must be things like this which made our elders say that humans must not mix with us. I think we are missing a lot of what made us elinefae. I wonder if we can get any of it back? I push my stray thoughts aside.

Sighing deeply, I allow myself to feel happy. Deep down, happy. No more moping.

We approach Pryderi's den, having jogged here in silence. Arwyn is first to knock.

"Enter!" comes our friend's voice from inside.

We burst through his door together.

"Pryderi, tell me you have the iPod safe," Arwyn pleads.

Pryderi laughs. "Of course. But you are slow to check."

"Yes…we…err…got distracted."

Pryderi raises an eyebrow and smirks. "I bet you did."

I shove him. "Eww, no, we just went swimming."

"Ah, I see." There is a passing hint of…disappointment, I think, in his bright blue eyes.

"You would've hated it. I swear Arwyn was trying to drown me," I tell him, giving Arwyn a shove.

Shoving back, he defends himself, "Only after you tried to drown me."

"You started it."

"Did not."

"Alright, enough! By the goddess, let us not argue. You are both as bad as each other," Pryderi interjects.

"Sorry, Dad," we chorus, then look at each other and burst out laughing.

Pryderi rolls his eyes. "So, what are we doing now?"

"Arwyn says it's up to me. But I don't know. In truth, I am a little sleepy."

Arwyn ruffles my hair. "You can go and nap if you want. Is that your deepest desire?"

"Unless you want to join me in the Den of Sin?" I goad him, waggling my eyebrows, playing a dangerous game of dare.

He shakes his head. "Nah, you go sleep."

Ah, the obvious refusal. I had offered it as a taunt. But still, disappointment tastes bitter on my tongue.

"Alright. I'll see you later," I say, lowering my head and shuffling out of the room.

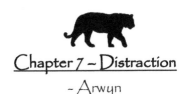

Chapter 7 ~ Distraction
~ Arwyn

"Well, I was going to say he seems his old self," Pryderi comments once Elan leaves the room.

I stare at my feet. "Yes, I had thought him improved. But the way he just stalked away..? You should have seen him playing in the water, my friend. We were so happy." I must look sappy as I think of the fun we shared.

Rubbing my upper arm, he replies, "Ah, Brother, I am sorry not to have seen it, but chin up. It sounds as if you enjoyed yourselves."

"Yeah, maybe too much."

He cocks his head at me. Shit! I said too much.

Rolling my eyes, I quickly add, "I think it tired him."

"You know you think too much? It is only natural to nap after play. Maybe you should go do the same?"

"Maybe. But first, tell me, is there any news of Kiera?" I have to ask.

After all they went through, it still makes me uneasy when they are not together. I cannot imagine what it must be like for him. I really should not have excluded him this morning. I hoped he was being distracted by Terrah. And I so badly wanted Elan to enjoy his water time. OK, maybe also I wanted to be alone with him too, but I hesitate to admit that to myself.

"She contacted me earlier. She is safe and it seems she will bring back our visitor, as planned."

"Are we calling him a visitor?"

"At least until he has had the chance to see our home, yes. It will be for him to decide whether he will feel comfortable among us. I do not know many details, but his clan seem very different from ours."

"Hopefully, ours is the better?" I ask, peering through my lowered lashes.

He smirks. "That, I am confident in. But I can only judge from my perspective."

I ruffle his hair. "Pryderi The Wise now, is it?"

We laugh. "Kiera's doing. We both know that is not a title I could claim on my own."

Nudging his shoulder, I tell him, "Pah, come now, Brother. You are no fool."

He seems uncharacteristically bashful as he looks away. "Maybe not."

I catch his chin in my hand. "Truly, you are not."

He shoves my hand away. "Fine. Have it your way. But that was not the point. Soon, we will have a new potential clan member who will need a lot of assistance if he is ever to settle here."

Placing my hand above my heart and bowing my head, I vow, "Every effort shall be made to welcome him."

"I know it."

I bid my friend farewell, but I'm too restless to sleep. Does Elan have any idea how close I was to accepting his joking offer to go to the Den of Sin? I know what's at stake. But nor can I seem to quell the deepening desire which threatens to consume me.

Elan and I can never share what I crave. Why does that bother me? We cannot be fated mates – that is not the way of males. All we could ever be is friends who fuck. That is somehow not enough. And I don't understand what's different. Pryderi, Elan and I have always been close friends, sworn not to complicate our close bond.

Combing my hands through my hair as I walk, I sigh long and hard. What was I thinking? I was there the day Elan heard of his father's death. Pryderi and I helped pick up his pieces and put our friend back together.

Elan had witnessed his father arguing with his best friend. Words were said. Things neither of them could ever take back. It was during that exchange that Elan learned the two males had been sexually involved in the past – nothing shocking for most elinefae. But even when one of the males was mated and Elan was born, they had apparently continued their liaisons. That was the shame that drove his father away. It shouldn't be possible. Soul-matched, fated mates are supposed to have eyes only for each other.

Turning my thoughts to Pryderi and Kiera, I know there is no way they would carry on with someone else. I'm not sure they'd even be up for a one-off threesome as fun. So, what happened to Elan's father?

The next morning after that argument, his father was gone. He had joined a battalion that had been passing, looking for recruits to join the ongoing clan wars. It was one of the final battles, as it turned out. But that didn't help his father as he lay dead on the combat field.

Things had never been the same again. His mother fell to pieces without her mate. Her spirit crumbled, unable to sustain life any longer. Pryderi's parents took him in. And his father's friend vanished, we think he went to find another clan. Nobody ever talks about him. And we're not permitted to ask.

And so, we made a vow to never let that be us. We will not be the cause of death to one another. Or even turmoil.

A purr erupts next to my ear, making me stop on the spot. "Arwyn, would you share your troubles?"

Looking round, I see it is one of the clan males I couple with the most. I blush, having been too lost in my own world to tell from his voice or scent, which I realise he's sending to me.

"Greetings, Gethin," I reply, gazing into his concerned, brown eyes.

"Greetings, my friend. But are you going to make me ask twice?" he asks, wrapping his arms around me.

"What? Err, no, sorry. Eurgh…" I let out a long sigh.

"Ha, that bad?"

"I don't even know where to begin."

"Does it threaten clan security?"

Shaking my head, I answer, "No. Nothing like that."

"Mmm…I was hoping you'd say that." His whisper tickles my ear, sending shivers to all the best places.

"I'll enjoy taking your mind off whatever it is." His head tilts as if he asked a question.

"How can I say no?" I say with a smirk.

His tongue flicks my ear in one quick lap. Augh, but that feels good.

Really, I can't deny the allure of the male. He never disappoints and is so eager right now, I allow him to take me by the hand and lead me to the Den of Sin. Still, I can't help but be saddened it is not Elan here with me.

My heart thumps hard as we enter the dark tunnel leading to our destination. My cock is already straining against my trousers – enthusiastic little fella. But I can't blame him, the male leading the way is definitely wiggling his arse more with each step, the tease.

Casting a look over his shoulder, it's clear Gethin is looking forward to this as much as me. His eyes are shining with naughty promise.

In the darkness of the Den of Sin, Gethin's eyes glow a deep, autumnal, burnt orange; darker than my own glowing pumpkin hue. The red light dims our night vision but enhances the glorious colour aimed my way. Those eyes beckon me with fiery desire.

We're both discarding our clothing as quickly as our fingers will allow. Mine are trembling as I struggle to untie my laces, but finally, I'm free. My cock juts out proudly. I can see well enough to notice his is mirroring my own, making me lick my lips.

"What are you waiting for, handsome?" he asks in a growled whisper.

Needing no encouragement, I fall to my knees as he leans back against a sloped bench. I barely notice the other people in the room. My focus is on him, as I lick my tongue down his length. It may not be the sweet apple scent I yearn for, but the dark, vetiver taste is a welcome distraction. Maybe this will slake my lust.

Gethin groans as I run another tantalising slow lick down his shaft. Then hisses as I tease his slit.

"You like that, Geth?" I taunt.

"Augh, you know what I want."

"Mmmm…but giving it to you all at once would spoil my fun."

His hand presses against the back of my head. "No waiting. Not today," he commands.

Fair game. I open my mouth wide and slide all the way down, sucking him in. His cry of pleasure spurs me on. Grabbing his arse with one hand and the base of his cock with my other, I work him in my mouth. He's throbbing in next to no time and his hips start to buck, ramming his cock harder into my mouth. His groans grow louder and I work more vigorously…faster. With a shudder, he squirts down my throat, roaring into the dark.

Getting to my feet, I stroke my way up his lithe body. He's not a Watcher and is shorter than my buddies. His muscles aren't quite so well defined, but they're still hard and rippled under my fingers.

Nuzzling his neck, I whisper, "My turn."

"No waiting for you either, greedy?" he retorts, but I see amusement in his eyes before he spins around and bends over.

Fucking this guy is amazing. We've done it often enough that we both know what we want and need, what gets us off the best. Running my finger around his hole, I discover he's all juicy for me already – praise be for his active gland. No coaxing required.

"And you call me greedy," I tease in a hoarse whisper.

"What? You want me to tell you how much you excite me?"

"Oh, those words are not necessary. Geth. I can feel your truth," I reply, running my fingers in another circle before sliding one in.

He whimpers, jutting his arse out further.

"So, so greedy today," I mutter.

Deciding to put the guy out of his misery, I line my cock up. Unable to resist tormenting him a little, my head halts at his entrance. But at his insistent wiggle, I plunge in. A satisfied moan shudders out of me.

"Augh, you feel so good."

"Mmmm…" is all I get in response.

Slowly, I start to pump backwards and forwards, revelling in the sensation of his tight warmth clamping around me.

"Ahhhh," I cry, unable to restrain myself.

My momentum builds as I thrust faster and harder.

"Yes, more," he cries back.

Pounding into him, heat fires through me, making my toes curl. Sweat beads down my face and back, heightening my tension. Sensation engulfs me. My balls tighten. Blood thunders in my ears. Banging into him with unleashed abandon, my cock erupts as I roar into my own release. I'm vaguely aware Gethin is clenching and crying out as I begin to still.

Once we both calm, I uncouple but give him a quick hug, and peck his neck. "Fab as ever."

"Likewise, handsome." He circles round in my arms. "You are fantastic."

I plant a peck on his nose. "Well, aren't we full of compliments today?"

"Just relieved."

I pull my head back and shoot him a raised brow. "Everything OK?"

He pulls me tight to him again. "Yeah, right now it is."

Scowling, I hold him as long as he needs, until he breaks away.

"Do you want to go somewhere to talk?" I check.

"No, we're good."

"You're sure?"

"I got the stress relief I needed. I'm fine."

"Uh-huh."

I have to take the male at his word. I offered a chat and he refused. It's not like we're mated, but clan looks out for one another. His worry is mine. I am not convinced he's as fine as he says. But he knows where I am, and there is always someone to talk to. Biting my lip, I bid him goodbye and make my way to my den.

As I lie down on my bed, I can't help the feeling that descends. I had thought Elan and I had merely been getting a weird dose of hormones. And Pryderi is understandably on edge without his mate here. But now Gethin is stressed. Something is going on with my clan, but my Leader, Rhion, is still away with Kiera; my concerns shall have to wait. It is not something I'm comfortable discussing with Ioan, his Second – he would take too much pleasure tormenting me if my fears prove unwarranted.

Right after morning meal, Rhion makes his return along with Kiera. As they make their way into the dining area with great authority, I get a glimpse of our new potential clan member.

He is wrapped up in the plain, white robe and head covering of his people, but his stunning green eyes are visible, along with a fine jaw which has a slim, dark beard running along its edge. Talking of slim, he is slender all over, from what I can tell. My jaw almost drops to the ground – he is perhaps the most gorgeous person I have ever seen.

Holding up his hands, Rhion commands the attention of us all. Even my own gaze is drawn away from the stunning male and back to my Leader.

"Greetings everyone. It is good to be back amongst you all. Ioan, my gratitude to you for looking after our clan in my absence."

My lip curls as the smug bastard bows to our Leader, soaking up all the glory.

"I thought it best to make introductions as a group. Please be mindful that our ways may be different to those our new clan member is used to. I urge you to respect his privacy."

"Yeah, don't all go bashing down his door at once," one of our clan catcalls.

Rhion rolls his eyes. "Yes, thank you. I know you will all make him feel welcome. Elan, where are you? Elan?"

He gives me a look of, 'I have no idea,' as he shrugs and makes his dutiful way through the crowd to Rhion. Pryderi is clenching and unclenching his fists – he must be itching to run to his mate, poor guy.

Bowing, his hand to his heart, Elan announces, "Here, at your service, Sir."

Rhion gives him a faint smile of acknowledgement and bows his red-haired head. "Very good."

Turning his yellow stare on us all, our Leader continues, "It is my pleasure to introduce you all to Hassan who joins us from a clan in Saudi Arabia. He is here to see if he can adapt to our way of life, not only for himself but potentially on behalf of others. So, let us all ensure he has the best opportunity to do just that."

Hassan makes a small bow to everyone before once more trying to shrink into Kiera's shadow. I guess he's shy. Or has something to hide.

Looking at my friend, and planting a hand on each of his shoulders, Rhion declares, "Elan, you are to show Hassan around on your shift today. It will be a good opportunity for him to see our land and familiarise himself with our home. I am trusting you with this. I know you will not fail me or clan."

Beating his fist to his heart, Elan confirms, "Sir, you can count on me."

Immediately, he moves towards Hassan who retreats a step. I chuckle, knowing that won't phase Elan in the slightest. And sure enough, he stops where he is and looks down, directly into Hassan's eyes.

I've edged closer as the crowd starts to disperse.

"Greetings," I hear him say softly, "I'm Elan. His Sun is it?" His smile shows me his mischief is surfacing.

Hassan shakes his head almost imperceptibly. "I beg your pardon, Sir. But my name is Hassan."

I have to stifle a laugh. Elan is playing but our new friend has not yet realised.

"Ah, a pity. Sun would suit you too. You're definitely radiant."

A smile creeps along Hassan's lips, but he tries to hide it as he inclines his head. "My gratitude, Sir."

Elan claps him on the shoulder. "How's about we just call me Elan, eh? I am not a Leader. I'm not even his Second."

Curiously, Hassan frowns as if confused by the response.

The hand which is still on Hassan's shoulder squeezes and rubs. "First difference, eh?"

Hassan nods.

"Well, that's one out of the way. Let's get you to your den, shall we? Then you can get changed before we head out."

Hassan's gawping mouth is horror-stricken. "Changed?"

"Well, you won't want heavy robes out on our tour. It's starting to rain."

Wrapping his arms around his middle, and sliding away from my friend's hand, he manages to say, "I think I will be fine as I am."

Kiera obviously thinks Elan's about to argue, so interrupts. "It's fine, Hassan. If you're more comfortable as you are, then by all means, remain so. We have a wax coat in your wardrobe, though, which you may wish to wear."

"I would just like to go, please."

Elan's mouth works without sound for a beat, but he ends up shrugging. "Fine. If that's what you want. Come on, then, green eyes."

Hassan paws at his face. "What? Green?"

"Yes, aren't they normally? What? What did I say?"

"Yes, no, errr… green is their natural colour. But our witch has a perma-spell so we all appear to have brown eyes."

Elan screws up his face but is stopped from saying whatever he opened his mouth for, as Kiera again intercedes, "There is no artifice in our clan, Hassan. Cerys and Chen, our witches, have a spell of their own here. Any glamours disappear on our territory. It keeps us honest. And it's a safety thing."

Hassan's brow furrows.

"Difference number two done. Shall we?" Elan asks, his head kicking away from the awkward group.

"Very well, Sir."

Elan rolls his eyes. "We'll start this way. It's the quickest path out to the forest," he says, leading the way.

Hassan, head down, follows like…ha, well, a bit like a sulky Terrah, quite honestly. Whilst Pryderi has finally managed to capture his mate in his arms and is kissing her from here to kingdom come. Terrah is winding around their feet, and it's a mystery how they remain standing.

I slope off. Fabulous! That's a great start, isn't it?

Chapter 8 – Newcomer
– Elan

Oh goddess, why me? It would've been nice to have been asked first. A little heads-up at least would've sufficed. Sure, it's a great honour to accompany our new clan member, and yes, he's drop-dead gorgeous, but wow, he's going to be hard work.

It's not that I don't have any sympathy. The poor guy looks like a fish out of water. I thought once we were out and about, away from the large crowd of people, he might open up a bit. But he's still not said a word. And the rain's coming down harder.

I've been trying to point out our boundary lines and places of interest but I'm not sure he's heard a word. A snuffling from behind a tree has his head whipping in that direction.

"Relax. It's only a pig."

"A pig? Here?"

"Aye. We let them roam free in the forest. It keeps the costs down for their feed. And it makes them happy."

"But aren't you worried they'll wander off? We…" he trails off.

Deciding not to press for the details he's clearly not ready to share, I inform him, "Well, they're happy and protected here. And also, the magick boundary keeps them within certain parameters."

"Huh."

"You'll probably see some chickens wandering as we get closer to the living area too. Part of the Watchers' job here is to look out for the animals, check none are sick or injured. We alert the animal medics if needs be."

"But predators..?"

"None. Foxes, badgers and any such like have not been seen around here in my lifetime."

"More magick?"

"Sadly not. I believe they were all killed the physical way."

"Oh."

"You're disappointed?"

"I sort of wanted to see a fox. I've read about them and seen pictures. My clan raise goats and horses. I do not get to see many other creatures."

"I'm sorry to disappoint. But foxes are indeed predators. Our food source is protected by necessity."

"I think I shall overcome my fanciful feelings then."

I'm not entirely sure if his last statement was sarcastic or serious. Either way, we fall back into silence as we walk along.

We're deeper into the forest now, where the canopy of branches offers some protection from the downpour. I come to a stop and beckon him to sit with me on a fallen tree. He's nothing if not compliant.

Shrugging off my wax coat, I lay it across his shoulders. My quick backward glances were to ensure he was still following, but I'm not blind. The rain has saturated his white tunic and is revealing some delectable muscles on his lithe body as the fabric clings to them. I'm not shy, but he seems to be, and I don't need the distraction as I obey my orders.

His face shoots across to look at me and not the ground. "Sir, I cannot."

"Funny, I don't remember asking a question. Unless you count the suggestion to call me Elan, of course," I tell him with a nudge and a wink.

His long dark lashes land on his cheeks as his beautiful green eyes close. "Of course…Elan. My apologies. I do not mean to cause offence."

I risk reaching my finger under his chin to make him look at me again. "Do I seem cross or offended to you?"

He takes a moment, his gaze wandering over my face and deep into my eyes. Finally, he shakes his head. "No, you do not."

Gently, I confirm, "That's because I'm not. I have not earned the title of Sir. It's strange for me to hear. But also, I want you to think of me as a friend and not some scary authoritarian. Does that sound good to you?"

His smile is so weak that it almost doesn't show, but I'm taking it as a win anyway.

"Good. That's sorted. So, Hassan, tell me, do you wish to go and change yet?"

His smile broadens as he holds up a dripping sleeve. "I think it's too late for that."

"Hmm…you'll catch a cold if you're not careful."

He cocks his head.

"Ha, this is something Kiera says. She is my friend, Pryderi's mate, so we talk a fair bit. You know she was not brought up here?"

His lashes lower again. "I…had heard she was raised…by humans."

I can't help but chuckle. "That she was. And it is no secret. I think it has given her a unique perspective. But it does also mean she says the funniest things sometimes. Apparently, a cold is a disease humans get when they get cold and wet for too long. They can be bed-ridden for a week with a leaking nose, hot head, and aching body."

He scrunches his face. "Sounds awful."

"Doesn't it, though? I'm glad we don't get such things. But her language is contagious. So, if I say something weird, don't be afraid of asking what on Earth I'm on about, OK?"

His smile is broader this time. "Thank you…Elan."

"It's no bother. We want you to be happy, don't we?"

His lips draw in a tight line and his eyes close as he takes a deep breath in.

"Oh shite, I said something wrong, didn't I? You mustn't mind me. Really, Rhion couldn't have paired you with a bigger oaf to show you around. It's beyond me why he—" but he cuts me off.

"No. You misunderstand…Elan. It's just that I…well…"

Seeing his distress and the water gathering in his eyes, I decide to finish his sentence for him. Taking his hand in mine, I guess, "You have not been happy?"

"No," he says with a sigh, gazing into the distance.

My heart lurches and my stomach drops. I do not want to imagine the horrors behind such sad looks as he's shared with me. The pain and anguish were there in his carefully unshed tears.

Barging him with my shoulder, I cajole, "Come on soppy chops, we can't sit around all day gasbagging."

His green eyes are turned on me again. "Gasbagging?"

"Ha, oh, that's a local one. Chattering." At his continued quizzical look, I try, "Gossiping?"

"Oh, gossiping, I understand."

"That's good then," I say with a chuckle, rising to my feet to get us back on our way.

We all speak Eline, but as each clan learns the local language in case of human interaction, some colloquialisms and inflexions infiltrate our dialect. Hassan, for example, hisses his h's most sexily at the back of his throat, so I've noticed. There is definitely something of the exotic in him. Yes, this male intrigues me.

Despite the continued rain, we make our way around the perimeter with more cheer. I swear with each footfall Hassan gains more confidence. He's still far too quiet, but I leave him to it. I don't want to make him uncomfortable by prying, but by the goddess, I would love to know more.

He's still wearing my wax coat, walking two steps behind. It's not cold so much as maddening. Every rain drop that hits my bare flesh sends tingles through me, and not the good kind. It's like my senses keep going on high alert for attack. If I had hackles, they'd be raised. And yet, there is a sense of satisfaction in knowing I'm protecting this male.

His frown deepens and contracts with alarming regularity. He's a thinker. Maybe too much of one? But then again, he must have a lot to process – it's a big, brave move for him on his own. The lengths we'll go to in order to find a true mate. The pull of the dong is strong!

I can't bear it anymore. I'm too concerned. His actions, words and looks hint at something troubling. I stop, and he almost bumps into my back.

"My apologies. Is something wrong, S…Elan?" he asks, looking up at me with doe eyes.

"Why are you apologising? You know what? Never mind. Hassan, we've only just met. And I know how important your stay is here. I wouldn't do anything…"

He looks so troubled at my rambling that I take his hands in mine and rub a thumb along the top of one. I'm biting my lip, trying to find the correct words as his frown deepens. I feel him try to pull away, but I grip on tighter to hold him in place.

"Please. It's nothing horrible. I just need to know so I can better help you."

His shoulders fall a fraction.

"Hassan, please, just tell me, are you here of your own choosing? You have not been forced?" My gut twists in a million knots waiting for his answer.

Squeezing his eyes shut and reopening them, he takes a deep breath. "Not in the way you fear, I think."

Pressing his hands more, I encourage, "You do not have to, but if it helps, would you like to tell me?"

Cocking his head, he regards me in that intense way of his. Releasing a hand, he rubs it along his furry jaw. "Yes, I think I would. But please, Elan, not today. Not yet. My friend?"

His look almost pleads with me to confirm his question. Before I know what I'm doing, I pull him into a cwtch and rub his back. "Of course. Of course, I am your friend."

I feel his shoulders shake before hearing his sniffle. Good goddess, what has brought this beautiful male to such a state? Anger broils in my stomach, demanding I do harm to those who have so clearly harmed him. But first I must be patient. My priority is to hold Hassan together as he sets some of his pain free.

He says nothing more, and he does not take long to recover. Backing away a step, he wipes his eyes. "Forgive me."

I can't help but chortle and shake my head whilst jabbing the ground with my foot. "Only you could apologise even now. You have much to learn, my friend, much to learn."

"You do not think it shameful to shed tears?"

I gawp. "Shameful? What the hell are you talking about now?" I slap his shoulder lightly. "Good for you, you had a feeling. Welcome to the elinefae race."

He half-laughs at my statement. "You are a very unusual male, Elan."

I chuckle in return. "You don't know the half of it. But, around here, I am not so utterly different."

"The rest of your clan…they are like you?"

Raising my chin, I reply smugly, "Well, they lack some of my charm, of course."

He actually laughs, and it is maybe the best sound I've heard in all my entire life - a raspy kind of staccato. Something tells me he doesn't use it much. But I pledge on the spot to make him repeat it often.

"Come, we are nearing the populated area. Do you feel up to saying hello? We can skirt around if you prefer."

His plump, peach lips form a closed-mouth smile. "I think I'm up to it, as long as you are by my side."

"No, I was going to shove you out alone," I mock, nudging his shoulder.

He shakes his head. "So strange."

Booping his nose, I observe, "It's good it's raining, though."

"Really?"

"Yeah, it hides your weepy eyes."

He actually nudges back. "You said it was not shameful."

"Oh, yeah. I guess it doesn't matter then," I confirm with a wink.

He shakes his head with a half-laugh. "Where do I begin to try to understand you?"

"Oh, you don't. It'll only hurt your head. Just go with the flow."

Chuckling, he says, "I will try, *Habibi*."

I open my mouth, ready to ask what that means, but decide I don't want to know. We're near the clan now, and don't have the time. In fact, a familiar woman is approaching already.

"Cerys. How lovely to see you, and not at all surprising that you are the first person we see," I tease.

"Get away with you," she says, shoving my shoulder.

"Hassan, this is our clan witch, Cerys."

He nods his head, and says, "*As-salamu alaikum*."

A wave of his delicious cinnamon and honey scent washes over me as he introduces himself – mmm…I have to try super hard not to groan out loud. And that flash of his black jaguar is all kinds of tempting; a velvety soft, dark delight.

"Err?" Cerys is muttering through my reverie.

"Pardon, my apologies. It means peace be upon you. An automatic phrase," Hassan explains.

"Please, don't apologise. It's rather lovely."

"But I am among my own kind. My greetings."

"Well, you have good manners, even if you do look like a drowned rat. Elan, you were supposed to be taking care of him."

"Please, Cerys, the fault is mine. I was too eager to explore and refused to listen to reason."

She eyes him with one brow raised, in her stern fashion. "I see. As stubborn as this one, eh?"

"He is stubborn?"

She laughs. "Oh, the worst."

"Excuse me, I'm right here," I butt in.

"Cerys, you were supposed to wait for me," Chen chides as he jogs up to us.

"Hassan, this is Chen. He's…" I begin.

Cerys supplies, "My lover, if we must use labels. Hassan, Chen is a witch from a Chinese clan, but now lives with me. It's all very complicated and boring, really. Just know that he has a red dragon familiar, so don't you be worried if you spot him marauding about."

"A fire dragon?" Hassan asks.

Chen smiles broadly. "No, don't let his colour fool you. He's actually a water dragon. But have you ever seen any?"

"No, only heard about them."

"Well, he is rather special. I'm sure it won't be long before he introduces himself. The nosey devil."

"Oh, like you aren't just as nosey, insisting we meet Hassan straight away, the minute he arrives back?" Cerys rebukes.

"I beg to point out, my love, that this may be the pot calling the kettle black."

At Hassan's worried look, I let him know, "It's OK. They bicker like cat and dog, but it's how they show each other their love."

Cerys stops short. "Oh, Hassan, dear. I do apologise." She shoves Chen's shoulder. "You've made a terrible first impression on the poor, young man."

"Me?"

"Well, we'll catch you later, then," I say, leading Hassan away.

"They are your witches?"

"Cerys is, yes. I suppose Chen is too now. It's a new-old thing. Huh, we have two. How greedy. Honestly, her bark is worse than her bite. She seems gruff but her heart is pure gold. If you ever need advice or medical attention, seek Cerys out and she'll see you right."

"This is good to know," he says with a nod.

"Not what you are used to?"

"Nothing here is the same, I think."

"Is that a bad thing?"

"I'll let you know? I hope it is good. I *think* it is."

A few more clan members timidly approach as we wind our way through the encampment. Rhion's warning of respecting his privacy seems to have struck the right note. And Hassan seems more comfortable with the one-at-a-time introductions.

"Right, this way," I instruct when he seems to have had enough.

Taking my hand, he lets me lead him to our homes. He stops at the doorway.

"You alright?" I check.

"You truly live underground? This is where this tunnel leads?"

"Yes."

"Oh."

"Hang on. You mean to tell me you don't? Pull the other one."

"I am not pulling anything. We do not live like this. We are a desert people. The sands shift continuously. To house ourselves underneath it is too dangerous."

"Huh, when you put it like that, I suppose it makes sense."

He smiles wryly. "To live in a house which does not threaten our lives? Yes, it makes sense."

"So, where do you live?" As I ask, I step into the corridor leading down.

I don't think it's a conscious thought, but he begins to follow as he tells me, "Our houses are on the surface and made of *concrete*."

"*Concrete*?"

"You do not have this?

"Never heard of it. Tell me more," I encourage, leading us further in.

"It is a human substance they make, grey and hard like stone. We used to live in tents. Our clan tries to appear as Bedouin. Most of them no longer live that way so neither do we. But I think they are more modern than we are. However, humans don't query our ways very much."

"Ah. So, you interact with the humans a lot, do you?"

"Out of necessity, *Habibi*."

"There's that word again. What is *Habibi*?"

It's dark, but my eyes have adjusted, and I can see his blush. "It literally means my love but as in a friend's love."

"Aww, how sweet. You love me," I chime.

"I begin to a little less when you say this."

Getting him in a headlock, I rub the top of his head through its covering. "Aww, you don't like the teasing?"

Straightening himself up, his smile is gone. "I am unused to such behaviour."

"I have truly offended?" My heart skips a beat as my blood runs cold.

He smirks. "I said I am unused to it, not that I don't like it. Maybe, just a little more gently, please?"

I plant a smacker on his cheek. "If you wish, I will try."

To my surprise, he kisses both my cheeks in return, stopping me in my tracks. "Thank you, *Habibi*."

"Now, with all this talk of love, it seems appropriate to let you know this is our Den of Sin."

Hassan cocks his head in question.

"Hmph, I'm not sure what you would call it. The room we singles go to when we have sexual needs to satisfy. Just go in and see if anyone else is in the waiting area before going into the darkened zone to have a quick shag."

His eyebrows almost shoot off the top of his head. "You what?"

"For the love of the goddess, tell me you have ways of satisfying your needs."

"Usually only on our own, unless called on specifically. Sometimes, we manage to partner but it is secretive. There is no dedicated room for such activities."

"Oh, we're going to discuss this a lot more later. But, for now, how's about I give you a demonstration?" I ask, wiggling my eyebrows.

He actually laughs again. "Kiera told me you were funny. I did not fully grasp her meaning." He walks past, making me scurry to catch up.

I don't know what's so funny, though. I sniff my pits – hm, clean. Nobody has ever told me I'm ugly. What gives? But, after what he just told me, I don't think he's overly comfortable talking about sex. I mean, is his clan even elinefae?

His face is doing that crumpling thing again as I lead him through the maze of corridors.

"OK, this is your den," I announce, "And mine is just down here." I walk him to where my den is, just so he's sure. Then take him back to his.

Opening his door, I chant, "Right this way, my friend."

He steps in, his mouth hanging open. "This is all mine?"

My hand swipes down my face. "So, you share in your clan?"

He nods. "Yes. Unless mated, all males sleep in one room, the females in another building."

"Each to their own," I mutter whilst secretly thinking his clan is very odd.

He glances all around the den.

"Right, since we are so very different, let me give you a tour. So, this is your bed," I say indicating the same.

"Not on a mat on the floor, understood."

I clench my fist, stopping another face palm. "And this is your washstand. There is soap here in this dish, and a fresh towel just here. When you're done, tip the wastewater into the bucket here on the floor. Once per day, take that to the barrel at the end of the corridor and empty it into that."

"It gets used for irrigation," I add at his look of dismay. "And anything you want washing gets put in this basket here. All our clothes have our names on the inside, so you know you get back stuff that fits."

"That, at least, is the same," he says with a sad smile.

Strolling to the cupboard, I open the doors. "And this is your wardrobe where said clean clothes will be placed. Have you got more of your own clothes? Or are you happy to dress like us?"

"Uhhh…"

"Never mind, just hang them in here if you have them. The choice is yours. No pressure. But here is the wet weather stuff. I urge you to wear it when it rains."

He smiles properly at that. "Yes, that lesson I have learned."

I go to ruffle his hair but stop, realising his head covering hampers my progress. So, I pat his cheek instead. "Clever lad."

He swats my hand away.

"Ooh, getting feisty. I like," I comment, chuckling.

His answering look could be defiance, a leer or an apology – it's hard to tell. Pah, I'll learn. To be honest, I hope it's defiance. He needs to learn to speak his mind. If he stays, that is. I must remember this is a trial period. Hassan may decide to return to his clan. Huh, my heart lurches at that. Weird!

"Alright then, so, I'll leave you to settle in? Are you able to find your way to the latrines and showers if you need? Look, just knock on my door if you need anything. Oh, our doors are kept closed. If you want, err, private time, hang your towel on the outside door handle."

His hand grabs my arm as I go to leave. "Please. Stay?"

"Alright, *Habibi*. If that's what you want." Hm, I don't think that word sounds right, coming from me. Oh well, I tried.

By the goddess, it takes all my willpower not to hug him close – I don't think he's overly fond of such contact. I go and sit on his bed, not quite sure where to put myself. He goes to take his robe off but hesitates.

"What? You're shy about your body, Hassan?"

He shakes his head. "Of course not. I just didn't want you to think I was being suggestive."

"Oh." Well, that's a relief. I think.

He takes off his wet clothes and…puts on the leather trousers and waistcoat similar to mine.

"There. How do I look?" he asks.

"Now, there's a leading question." Am I salivating?

He turns around, arms spread wide. There is almost a swagger to his movements. Mmm…appreciating this view!

I approach slowly and clear my throat. "There is one thing," I tell him, holding my hands to his head covering, waiting for his permission.

"My *gutrah*? It holds no religious significance. Nor do my clothes define me as a person. I am just used to wearing it."

"Do you mind trying without?"

His outward breath is almost a laugh. "I am here for a different experience. I suppose I should try."

"You don't have to. There is no pressure."

With a sharp nod, he widens his stance a little and commands, "Do it."

I pull off the loose covering, only to find a small cap underneath, which he takes off himself.

"Oh my!" I blurt.

"What? Too much?"

"No. No. Your hair…it's gorgeous. This shouldn't be covered up," I tell him, fingering through his lustrous, black mane which stops just beneath his ears, which are reassuringly elinefae-pointy.

Leaning into my touch, he purrs.

"Mmm…you like that, huh?"

"Another new thing, but don't stop, it feels wonderful."

Well, who am I to argue? I stand there, letting my hands rake through his soft, thick hair. He's so fluffy! If I'm not careful, his purrs will have me dragging him to the Den of Sin, and I know he's not up for that. So, why is this OK? I'm so confused. I stop before overthinking sets in.

Bringing our foreheads together, I whisper, "I am glad I could bring you joy on this difficult day, my friend."

"I am too. Thank you, Elan. I didn't expect it, but I am grateful for your friendship."

"Tidy. What would you like to do now? It's still a bit early for evening meal. Make your request. I'm all yours."

He chuckles. "Still strange. Umm…I do not know what to suggest. I am restless, but…you have seen how I am in crowds. Our clan is much smaller."

"I know! Come with me. But put your wet weather gear on, we're going back outside."

Chapter 9 – New Friends

– Hassan

This clan is strange. From the moment I arrived, I have been treated like an honoured guest. Having not been invited into any of the negotiations, I do not know exactly what has been said. I just hope they're not too disappointed when they learn the truth about me.

For now, I am surprised and relieved at the warm welcome offered by this male, Elan. He, at least, cannot know how far down the pecking order I am, otherwise, he would never have invited me into the place they have sex. It would have been dishonest to accept, and I fear losing his friendship if I tell him what I truly am. No, his loyalty must be won first. And, based on his looks as well as behaviour, I truly want to earn it.

When he went to leave me alone, I clung on like a lost youngling. It was not my place to do so. But he has been so kind, and I am not used to seclusion – I panicked. It is puzzling this clan did not command him to watch me at all times. I am a stranger here, so surely it is even more important they do so.

What must they think of me? I'm certain I've not shown enough gratitude for their kind hospitality. They have not put me to work yet, but when they do, I shall show them my full gratitude. They do know what I do, don't they? Kiera does, but I'm not certain she's told the others of her plans.

This time, I'm putting on the outer clothing suggested. But when I turn around, horror clenches my stomach.

"Please, Sir. Do not touch," I cry out, lurching to hold Elan's arm away from the leather roll on the table.

"Uh oh, I *am* in trouble. You called me Sir. OK, OK, no touching," he says, holding his hands up in surrender.

"My apologies, Elan. These are my only treasured possession. I mean no disrespect."

He ruffles my hair. "Hassan, if there is one thing I know about you, it is that you never mean disrespect. I apologise to you for my inquisitiveness. Cerys is always reminding me about the nosey cat."

I squint at him. He is always saying odd things which at first make no sense.

"Curiosity killed the cat? No? Never heard of that one, either, eh?"

"What a horrible thing to say."

"Huh, it isn't very nice, is it? Human phrase. It just means that you should stop being nosey. I call it being friendly, but you can't please everyone." He shrugs.

I chortle as I find a safe place to stow my bundle for now. Elan is the most forward person I have ever met. There is always a smile on those protruding, dark pink lips I want to nibble on. He says whatever pops into his head, and apparently, there is a lot going on up there. I've never heard anyone talk so much. Is he always this way?

His violet eyes always shine with mirth. I think there is a lot of mischief in this one. But so much warmth too. Without knowing the first thing about me, he has shown me kindness such as has never before been shown to me. Instead of ripping off my wet garments and having his way with me, he covered me with his coat. And he did not presume I would want sex – he actually asked. I think. Was he serious or just playing?

The apple and vanilla signature scent he introduced himself with made my mouth water. And that Persian Leopard is just asking to be fondled. If I had the honour of choice, I would wrap myself around him and never let go. He is intoxicating. I should have let him leave when I had the chance. There is so much trouble opening up to me.

And yet, here I am, following him outdoors once more. He could lead me anywhere and I would follow. After one look and word, I was hooked – entranced by this dazzling male.

Sticking his hand out as we get outside, he announces, "Huh, it stopped raining."

Smiling, I quip, "So, it doesn't always rain?"

"Cheeky!"

"Apologies."

"Will you please stop apologising? I was teasing back."

"If you say so."

"You are a timid thing, aren't you? Come on, come out to play, kitty," he coaxes.

His ensuing hug has tears reaching my eyes once more, but I blink them away. He leaves a kiss on my cheek before turning and walking off. I'm left bereft and chasing to catch up.

Elan says nothing – he seems in a hurry. We jog down a few winding paths through trees but eventually stop at a large pond.

"You are thirsty?" I ask.

He chuckles and shakes his head. "You don't want to drink this water."

Then he whistles. The semi-circles forming on top of the water tell me there is something swimming closer. I take a couple of steps back and am ready on sprung haunches to leap away further if needed.

"Calm, my friend," Elan urges.

I try, but my unease refuses to leave entirely. Bubbles burst on the surface. And then a red snout appears, closely followed by two large black eyes. I can't help but gasp. However, Elan is squatting down at the water's edge.

"Hello, Shui. I have a new friend to meet you."

A sort of burbling noise comes from the creature, which is now drawing itself onto dry land. I stagger back and fall on my backside – how humiliating!

"A…a…dragon!" I cry.

Elan grins. "Yes. You seemed intrigued that Chen's familiar is a dragon, so I thought I'd bring you to say hello."

I wave from my place on the ground. "Hello!"

Slowly, the red dragon approaches, still making the funny burbling sounds. His head hangs low as he reaches his snout to my hand and gives a good sniff.

"I am Hassan," I tell it, sending my scent and black jaguar image – seems the polite thing to do.

"Hassan, meet Shui," Elan introduces, which sounds like *shw-aay* with an upturn in tone at the end.

Trying to copy the way he says it, I speak to the dragon – who would have thought I'd ever say that? "Hello, Shui. I am pleased to meet you."

The bright red nose nuzzles my palm. In all honesty, he is smaller than I'd expect a dragon to be – about the size of a kid, as in baby goat, not a child. As his face slides through my hand, I follow the direction and stroke down his head and back.

"Huh, scaled but smooth," I observe.

"You get used to it. Also, just so you know, he grows and shrinks. He must like you to trust being this small. He grows to massive proportions so Chen can sit on him to fly. I've seen him carry three adults before."

"My, aren't you a strong one?" I comment towards the preening red being.

"Chen and Kiera can hear him talk. It's much like our telepathy, but mostly with images. I don't know why the rest of us can't. But we understand one another well enough, don't we?" His question is directed at Shui as he strokes down his other side.

Our fingertips meet. I quickly pull my hand back as a zing shoots through my hand, making Shui jump.

"My apologies, Shui," I say in a soothing tone.

He crouches and regards me warily. So, I placate him with slow strokes and shushing noises. "There now, my friend. All is well."

"You're good with him."

"Ha, if I was so good I would not have made him scared."

"Bah, he's forgiven you already."

We smile at one another across the dragon's back.

"You're obviously good friends with him. But should we not have Chen with us?"

"No, Shui is very independent. Aren't you, Shui? Oh, yes you are."

I can't help but laugh a little at his baby voice. "He understands you?"

"Of course. He's not stupid. You're very intelligent, aren't you, Shui? Yes."

I laugh as Shui stands more upright and gives a rather petulant nod in my direction.

"My apologies, Shui. Of course, you can understand us. It is we who are too stupid to hear you. But you make yourself understood, I think."

Another nod gets sent my way. I risk bringing my forehead to his. "It is a great honour to meet you, Sir."

Shui bobbles his head, and looks…smug, I think.

"Now you've done it. He loves being given the utmost respect."

"Don't we all?"

More sadness must've leaked into my question than I meant, given the way Elan's looking at me with sympathy. However, to his credit, he ventures no comment.

Shui waddles off a little, then takes a running jump into the air and flies around, above our heads.

"Show off!" Elan calls at him but laughs.

"That is very impressive."

"Honestly, wait until you see him grow."

Arching my brow, I can't resist commenting, "I'm pleased that size impresses you so much."

He playfully smacks my arm. "Monster!"

"Ah, so you took a good look, did you?"

He smacks me again. "Oh, my goddess. Who even are you? What did you do with my quiet friend, Hassan, huh?"

I shrug. "What can I say? You bring out the worst in me."

"Oh, no, baby, no. I think you mean best." His wink and tone set my groin on fire.

I'm suddenly aware of how snug and fortunately supportive these leather trousers are. Although, I am somewhat uncomfortable as my *zib* is fighting to get free. Elan and I both suck in an exaggerated breath. Biting my lip, I look away first. This is inappropriate behaviour.

As my apologies seem to rile him, I simply remain in awkward silence.

Clearing his throat, Elan announces, "Err, yes, well, we can probably go to evening meal now."

"Hungry, are we?"

With narrowing eyes, in a husky voice, he replies, "Like you wouldn't believe."

Pretending not to notice the mounting desire, I get up and call into the air, "We must leave, Sir. I look forward to seeing you again soon."

The dragon circles, comes to land and nudges my hand. I stroke his head once more and bid him farewell as a pouting Elan leads me away.

Arriving at the dining area with its covered seating, Elan guides me first to the servery.

"So, I don't know what you're used to, but grab a plate and help yourself," my friend instructs, as he picks up a plate and passes it to me, then takes one for himself.

As with everything, he is my guide and picks up a bread roll, already cut in half. Next, he places a dry-looking meat patty on the bottom half, followed by some limp lettuce and a slice of tomato.

Spooning many greasy onions on top, he comments, "Got to love burger night."

Wincing, I watch him squeeze on a great deal of tomato ketchup.

"If you say so," I reply before blowing out my cheeks.

This does not look or smell appetising at all. It does not bode well if this male is excited by such pitiful food. Taking a deep breath, I remind myself that this change is for the greater good, and there is nothing so awful that it cannot be made better. The burger on my plate looks at me as if in challenge to that.

"This meat, it is..?" I start to ask.

"Venison. We have many deer in this forest. We keep their numbers down, otherwise, the habitat would quickly get destroyed by them. The villagers know us as herders. It is not really a lie."

"I see."

Helping himself to a glass of blood, he cocks his head at me. "I don't suppose you have many deer where you're from."

Shaking my head, I tell him, "No. I do not think forest dwellers would like the desert."

My nose scrunches as I sniff my drink.

He squints. "Or vice versa?"

"That is not a fair question, as well you know."

He looks abashed as he lowers his head. "Sorry. I meant no offence."

I chuckle. "None truly taken. It is but my first day. I withhold judgement."

"Fair play. Look, if you don't like this just let me know and I'll take you to hunt for some rabbits after, OK?"

I smile. "Thank you for that kind offer." I may very well take him up on it.

"They don't taste as strong as deer."

"Good to know. Thank you."

Several people look our way as we walk between tables. However, it is with less scrutiny than before, perhaps. Or maybe that's wishful thinking. Then again, my change of clothes may have made me stand out less. Whatever the reality or reason, it is not so daunting.

"Oh, no, you go too far, Elan. I cannot sit here," I tell him as he approaches a table where Kiera sits.

"What? Why? These are my friends. Kiera you already know."

She smiles at me. "Hassan, please do not make yourself uneasy."

"Forgive me, but please show me where I should sit."

She frowns then points to an empty seat opposite herself. "Right there."

"You misunderstand me, I think. You cannot mean for me to sit with you?"

A growl emanates from the male next to her. "And why not?"

"Please, it is too much..."

Also, now I look around, females are all mixed in with males. I had heard tell of such things but have never seen the like. I had thought it a fanciful tale. Frantically looking around, panic surges through me. I don't know what to do. My breaths come out in short snorts.

A hand rests on my lower arm. "Breathe, my friend. It's OK."

Bile rises in my throat despite his calming gesture. Chucking my plate and glass on the table, I bolt. I can't stand it. It may be cowardly, but my feet are pounding the ground, speeding me away.

"Stop!" An already familiar voice calls from behind me, but one I cannot obey. "For fuck's sake, Hassan, stop."

Having reached a quiet area behind some bushes, I force myself to comply. But I cannot look Elan in the eye.

"What the ever living..?"

"You do not know what you ask, Elan," I all but scream at him.

"Then tell me. Explain," he demands through clenched teeth.

With effort, I slow my breathing down but am interrupted as I open my mouth to speak.

"Hassan, I am so sorry. I did not prepare you. The fault is mine. We have not had the chance for a proper conversation. I was hoping to talk more over dinner. I see now how stupid that was," Kiera says.

Two males stand on either side of us, the ones who were with her at the table. I hang my head.

"Would someone please tell me why my mate is apologising to him? And what the hell just happened?" One of the males asks.

"Pryderi, Hassan. Hassan, Pryderi," Elan informs.

I bow my head. "Greetings, Pryderi."

"Yeah, yeah. Hi. What the fuck is so offensive about my mate?" He challenges, elongated teeth bared, his face close to mine.

Elan steps between us, a hand on Pryderi's chest. "Back up, Pryderi."

"Not until he explains himself."

"NOW! I said, BACK UP." Elan's back is towards me, but there is no mistaking his readiness to fight. For me? No, it cannot be.

"My love, it is not what you think," Kiera tells Pryderi, pulling his hand to lead him off.

His teeth instantly retract, but his glowing eyes show his lingering fury. "If he thinks a half-breed is not good enough—"

"WHAT DID YOU JUST CALL ME?" she roars back.

"Not me. Him. It's what you think, isn't it?" he fires my way.

"A what? No." I stagger backwards, unable to find further words.

Kiera slaps his forehead. "You bloody idiot. Not everything is about my heritage, thank you very much."

"But—"

"Don't you but me, Pryderi. Argh!"

Bowing, I manage to mutter, "I did not mean to cause a fight. Please, I beg forgiveness."

Kiera walks over and meets my forehead to hers and strokes my cheek with a hand. "It is not your place to seek forgiveness, Hassan."

Pryderi looks like he wants to rip my head off. I'm frozen to the spot.

"Err…so, Hassan, hello by the way, you did not want to sit with us because..?" The other male who had silently watched on now enquires.

With another bow, I pluck up my courage. "My reasons are twofold. Firstly, the honour was too great. I should sit lower, somewhere near the back. But your tables, they are not set out that way. Also, males are not permitted to sit with females."

"Now I've heard everything," Pryderi comments, throwing his hands up in the air.

"Hey, be nice," Kiera warns. "I witnessed this myself in his clan, the divide of the sexes, that is. I should've thought. And that is why I was apologising, oh easily riled one."

Somewhat unwisely, I snigger but try to cover it with a cough.

Pryderi's head shoots my way even so. "What's so funny?"

"Pardon me. But I have never seen a female so feisty."

To my relief, Pryderi bursts out laughing. Without fully understanding why, I join in, as does everyone else. Doubling over, Pryderi slaps his thighs.

"Never a truer word," he says between gasps.

"Clearly, you don't remember our nereid friend, Zondra," Kiera retorts, kicking her head up.

"Ah, well, she does have scary levels of anger, true enough. But being honest, you, my love, are all sorts of defiant. It's one of the many things I love about you." He nuzzles nose-to-nose with her.

"Love you too."

Turning to me, she adds, "But why further back, Hassan?"

My head spins at the change of topic. "Err…I am of lower rank."

Three sets of eyes squint at me.

"Surely you know I am only a cook?"

Elan barks out a laugh. "Only a cook?"

I bow. "I never intended to deceive you."

"Kiera, what is he apologising for now? Honestly, all day he's been saying sorry like he's guilty for existing."

She shrugs. "I'm not sure I understand. Hassan, what do you mean only a cook?"

I look between them all, my brow wrinkling. "Just that. I am one of the lowliest of my clan. Especially with my…never mind."

The third male interjects, "Wait? Let me make sure I understand, a cook is less than the other clan members?"

"Yes, Sir."

"Ooh, I quite like that Sir. But I am a Watcher, like Pryderi and Elan."

I incline my head. "Yes, Sir."

"Errr..?"

Pryderi tries, "So, Watchers are high-ranking in your clan?"

I nod, thankful for some understanding. "Yes, Sir. The Leader, his Second and then Watchers. I could go on, but you all look confused as it is."

Kiera takes one of my hands in hers and squeezes. "Hassan. Thank you for explaining. I had no idea how different your clan was. Right, so here, our Leader is the alpha. There are female ones in other clans, incidentally. And yes, his Second commands some respect."

A couple of snorts sound behind her, and she rolls her eyes before continuing, "But that's it. Everyone else is equal."

"Equal?"

"Yes. Everyone."

"Huh."

A tummy grumbles. Elan, who returned to my side as soon as Pryderi calmed, asks cheerily, "Shall we all go back and eat now we got that cleared up?"

"*Twp*," the third male says, tapping the side of Elan's head, who tries to duck out of reach.

"What? A male's got to eat."

The male ruffles Elan's hair. "Yeah, I know. Some more than others."

That cannot be a twinge of jealousy twisting in my gut. It can't. It's been a very strange day. And set to get stranger as I follow the group back to the dining area. The plates are where we left them.

"It might be a bit cold. Would you like me to get you a fresh one?" Elan asks, ensuring I sit down this time.

"I doubt it will make much difference," I grumble.

If Kiera had not said she wished to speak with me, I would have asked Elan to show me those rabbits to hunt. I'm unused to so much attention. Inwardly, I cringe. Outwardly, I try to show the gratitude my new clan members are due.

"My apologies. Pryderi, isn't it?" I check.

He nods. "That's me. *Pruh-DAIR-ee*," he confirms, carefully pronouncing his name. I get a whiff of juniper, sandalwood and pine – a sort of petrichor smell, along with the image of a black panther.

I smile. "Not so very different," I tell him, sending him my black jaguar.

"Bit sweeter, though," he remarks, presumably referring to my honey and cinnamon scent; one I've always been appreciative of.

"I'm Arwyn, seeing as nobody else is going to tell you," male number three interrupts with a grin.

A rush of orange and clove hits my nostrils, making them flare. "Hmmm…hello. Oh, and your white tiger has the same blue eyes as you."

His grin broadens. "That's me."

I bite my lip to stop blurting out how much I like that. Silently, I send him my signature.

"So, Saudi Arabia, eh?" he asks.

Discreetly, I put down the burger with one bite out of it. It tastes worse than I feared. Fortunately, conversation is a good diversion.

"The deserts of, yes. It is not as if I have lived in Riyadh."

"As we don't live in Cardiff."

"Hm, I suppose so. Do any elinefae dwell there?"

"In Cardiff? No. Why? Are there any in Riyadh?"

I cast my eyes down. "Some."

Kiera bangs her knee on the table as she stands abruptly. "Ow! What?"

"You did not know?"

"No, I bloody well did not."

"Alright, calm yourself," Pryderi tells her, rubbing her lower back.

"Ahem. Yes, well." She sits back down, rubbing her knee. "I'm sorry. I mean, what?"

"You have to understand, our way of life is hard."

"Harder than here?"

I glance around. "Water falls from your sky in abundance. Animals multiply in such numbers as require culling. Forgive my bluntness, but yes, Sir."

"Sir? Oh, I'm not even going to start…" Taking a deep breath, she says, "Call me, Kiera. It'll make me not want to throttle you."

"Now who needs to be nice?" Pryderi teases.

"Well, really…!"

"Pardon, Kiera. I was not sure how to address one such as yourself. But, as I was saying, life is hard in the desert. We are no longer nomadic. Our site was hard fought for and won. But in these difficult times, we are being challenged more again."

"By humans?"

"Yes, humans mainly. It is very hard to keep one's true identity hidden at the best of times. During battle? Nigh impossible. Especially when outright victory would be suspicious."

"Hmm, I can see how that would be difficult," Arwyn comments.

"Always pretending," I say with a sigh.

Elan, sitting next to me, pats my shoulder. "Ah, mate."

My head whips towards him, my heart stuttering.

He chortles. "Kiera, that's your fault! Err, no. Mate as in friend."

I screw my face at him.

"Honestly. Friend. Like *Habibi*."

"Huh, OK."

The others look at us quizzically.

"You learned a new word, Elan?" Arwyn asks.

"Yes, I did," he replies, grinning.

"*Habibi*. My love, as in friend too," I explain.

"Uh-huh." Arwyn scowls.

"Well, it's nice you two are getting along so well," Kiera comments. "I was going to put you in the kitchen tomorrow. I thought it might be nice to do something familiar. But maybe you would like more time learning about our surroundings?"

I put up my hands. "Oh, no. The kitchen sounds perfect, please. Thank you."

"He's so polite," Arwyn observes.

Glowering at him, Kiera replies, "You could learn something from him, so pay attention."

"Yes, ma'am," he answers with a cheeky salute.

I hide my smile behind my hand, pretending to yawn.

"Ah, our new clan member. You're doing well, I trust?" Leader Rhion is actually addressing me!

These benches are a health hazard. I bang my knee as I rise to bow to the Leader. "Yes, thank you, Sir."

"Very good. I shan't keep you. Just wanted to check. Any problems, report them via any of this lot or directly to me. My den door is open."

My mouth drops open a moment. "Yes, thank you, Sir," I stutter.

"Behave," he says over his shoulder, I think to Elan.

"Come on, you must be tired," Elan says softly.

"It must be so much to take in. Sleep in tomorrow, as long as you need. Just help prepare the evening meals," Kiera kindly instructs.

I bow my head. "Thank you. And thank you all. I hope to make a better impression tomorrow."

"Oh, I don't know. It's a pretty good start already," Arwyn quips, which earns him a shoulder slap from Elan as we pass him.

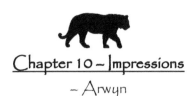

Chapter 10 – Impressions

– Arwyn

"So, what do we think of our newest clan member?" I ask Pryderi and Kiera once Hassan departs with Elan.

"Oh, don't be like that," Kiera fires back.

"Like what? I'm just asking."

"Arwyn, I thought it was Hassan who had green eyes. Don't pretend there wasn't jealousy in your tone."

"Was there? I didn't mean there to be. I'm just afraid he won't be able to adapt."

She raises a brow at me, making her resemble Cerys. "And what makes you say that? Granted, he was confused and had a moment of panic. I'm sure you would too if you found yourself in his clan. However, he *did* come and sit with us despite Pryderi's animosity."

"Don't look at me. What was I supposed to think?" Pryderi defends.

She kisses the tip of his nose. "I can't say I didn't like the way you rushed to my defence. But maybe keep more of an open mind?"

"Lesson learned already," he agrees with an eye-roll.

"Are you OK though, Arwyn?"

Running a hand through my hair, I tell her, "Yeah. I'll be fine."

Leaning over the table, she meets her forehead to mine. "Yes. You will be. Give things a chance. Maybe spend some time with our new friend. Get to know one another."

I nod, my lips pulling into a tight smile. The pair take their leave. As they reach the edge of the dining area, Kiera whistles, bringing a very happy Terrah to her. Making a fuss of her familiar, they all walk off together.

"I can't believe you even tried to let her eat with you lot," I hear Kiera tell Pryderi, her voice fading into the distance.

I can't help but chuckle. Kiera hasn't ever brought her dragon to eat with us. Yet again, she proves her wisdom. I don't think Pryderi will be trying it again any time soon.

Picking up their dishes as well as my own, I take them to the wash-up area, placing them in a pile with many others.

"It's good to see him looking happier."

I jump at the sudden intrusion. With my hand on my chest, I reply, "Megan, I didn't notice you there."

"Ha, too lost in your own world. Why do I feel sadness from *you* now?"

I ruffle her hair. "Always too nosey."

"And ever evasive."

"I'll be fine."

"Uh-huh. Have it your way. Just know I'm always here for you."

I rub cheek-to-cheek. "I know that. Thank you. It's nothing. Really. Just an odd day."

"But one which is pleasing to the eye?" she asks with a side glance.

My grin feels lopsided. "Aye. There may have been some good in it."

It seems we're not the only ones to appreciate the beauty of Hassan. Wandering past other clan members, I overhear many comments about our new addition. Some debate his outburst, but most are preoccupied with his looks.

I ignore them all. It wouldn't be fair to discuss him behind his back like this. Wait, wasn't that exactly what I just did with Pryderi and Kiera? Well, I suppose it's to be expected. I just don't want to discuss him anymore today.

Still, my gut twists. He and Elan seem close already. I'm proud of my friend – he can make anyone feel at ease. It's one of his many charms. Yet, yet...I sigh, not really knowing exactly what unsettles me so. I shouldn't begrudge him a new friend. But is it that I want Elan to myself? Or Hassan? Raking my fingers through my hair, I walk the long way to my den via a forest path. The trees lend me their strength as I wander past.

Feeling calmer, I stop at Elan's den door and knock.

"In!" he cries out.

"Hey, Brother. Thought I'd stop by and check how you are. Hassan all settled in, is he?"

Rolling his eyes, he confides, "I wouldn't say that exactly. But, yeah, he's in his den. There is a lot for him to think about. I can't believe how different his clan sounds."

"Are they even elinefae?"

He laughs. "My thoughts exactly. It seems they interact with humans far too much. Their behaviour is dictated by them. No wonder Cerys protects us so fiercely."

I half-smile. "Yeah, it makes me a whole lot more grateful for her."

"We should take her something nice tomorrow to let her know that."

I rub his cheek with the back of my hand. "That's so thoughtful. Yeah, flowers or rabbits?"

"Ha, I was thinking flowers."

"Fine, I'll pick some on my rounds tomorrow."

"Me too."

I grab him to me in a hug which he nestles into.

He breaks away first. "Not that I'm complaining, but what was that for?"

Blowing out a breath, I tell him, "Oh, I don't know. Just felt like it after a weird day."

Looking up into my eyes, he replies, "As strange as it was for us, it must have been a hundred times more so for Hassan."

His compassion is wondrous, yet it shoots an arrow through my heart. "Yeah, it must've been."

"Hey, it'll be OK. We'll make it work."

"You. You will make it work. It's what you do." I gently chuck his chin.

His intense gaze melts my insides. "You're not so bad yourself."

Rubbing cheeks, I wish him, "Goodnight, my friend."

"Good night, my friend," he echoes.

I reach my den, a few doors in the opposite direction from Hassan's. I think about checking on him, but he's probably had enough of other people today. Besides, Elan seemed to think he was alright on his own, mulling things over. But I want to reach out, let him know I'm here too. Maybe tomorrow.

Shucking off my clothes, I slump down on my bed. Bright green eyes appear behind my closed eyes. And a beautiful, full-lipped, bashful smile. Which is shared with…Elan. My stomach churns as my mind wanders over their shared glances. How he was ready to face off with Pryderi over this stranger.

All day, I had trailed behind those two, hiding my presence. Part of me needed to ensure things went smoothly for the good of the clan. But, if I'm honest with myself, there was an equal part that needed to be nearby. To protect Elan. Fine. And maybe to gawk at Hassan.

Argh, this male is going to be trouble. I just know it.

Weirdly, I am saddened by Hassan's absence at morning meal. Should I not find relief in normality? This is as things should be – my family. Elan, Pryderi and Kiera together again. So, why does it feel as if something's missing?

My plate awaits me on the table.

"Thanks, Elan," I tell him, taking my place at his side and a bite of my bacon and eggs.

"No bother."

"So, where's your new friend?"

"Kiera told him he could sleep in. From the snores coming from his room, I'd say he's taking her at her word."

"No! He doesn't snore?"

Elan laughs. "No, but I did poke my head around his door, and he was sound asleep."

"What are you like?"

"Charming," he answers, fluttering his black eyelashes.

"Yes. Yes, you are. Anyway, you two, what are your plans today?" I ask, turning to the mated pair.

"Well, I'm going to escort Hassan today," Kiera states, "Letting Elan get back to what he does best. Besides, I think he'll be headed straight into the kitchen."

"Huh, yeah, he did seem eager."

She lays a hand on my arm which is resting on the table. "Arwyn, go easy. I think it is his place of refuge."

"What?"

"So, you weren't listening that closely yesterday, then?" Elan asks.

"When?"

"Oh, only all day. What? You think I cannot sense you a mile away?"

"Someone had to look out for you," I mumble.

"They did, huh? If I can't manage one little cook on my own, I should probably not be a Watcher."

Holding my hands up in surrender, I admit, "Fine. You got me. You have a valid point."

He nods smugly.

Holding his chin in a pincer of finger and thumb, I hold his gaze. "But I cannot help it if I feel very protective of you."

A cough sounds from Pryderi.

"Ahem, as a Watcher myself, of course," I add, dropping my grip.

Kiera is doing her Cerys impression again.

"But you were saying, Brother, Hassan's refuge?" I ask Elan, bringing our conversation back to safer territory.

"Ah, yes, well, he didn't say too much in all fairness. But I did get the impression he's been mistreated."

"Yeah, I did gather that much. Poor guy. I don't think I even want to ask him for details. From the moment he appeared among us, it was as if he wanted to disappear into the shadows."

"And what is with all the hierarchy bullshit?" Pryderi chips in.

"Weird!"

Elan slaps the table. "Well, we'll just have to make him all the more appreciated here."

"Oh, I plan on making him feel very appreciated," I declare, wiggling my eyebrows.

Elan shoves me. "Oh, my goddess. You have a one-track mind."

"Tell me you don't."

He looks away with a nervous laugh. "You know I can't. But he turned me down."

My chin must be on the floor. "He what? Wait, you offered already? *Slut!*"

His chuckle is not filled with his usual mirth. "Well, we were passing the Den of Sin. It seemed like a wasted opportunity."

"And he said no? Kiera, send him back immediately. That elinefae is obviously broken beyond all repair."

We all laugh but end on a sigh.

"I hope not," Kiera says with downcast eyes.

"Hey, we'll make it work," Elan tells her.

Pryderi holds her close and kisses the top of her head.

"Yeah, it'll be alright," I tell her, contrary to the knot in my stomach.

What if our life is too much for him? What would happen then? My food threatens to revisit, but I force it to stay down. I really need to get a hold of myself.

Chapter 11 ~ Not So Familiar

~ Hassan

"Hey, you," Kiera says as soon as I step out of my den, making me freeze on the spot.

"Greetings. Am I in trouble?"

I am dressed back in my white thobe and gutrah today, fairly confident that there won't be any rain where I'm going. It is a familiar anchor in this strange new world.

"No, of course not. I thought you may like someone with you until you start cooking?" She peers at me kindly.

"No Elan?"

She huffs out a laugh. "No, he's back on duty already. Morning meal is finished, but I can take you to the kitchens. That way, you get a peek at your surroundings whilst grabbing whatever food you would like."

She's wily, this female. Inclining my head, I flash her a knowing smile. "My gratitude."

"You ready?"

"I...err..."

"Oh, of course. Sorry. I got over-excited about showing you the kitchen. Go do what you have to do. Is it alright if I wait in your den? Save me going all the way back to mine."

"Certainly."

With that, I make my escape and manage to find the latrines all on my own. I had fortunately used the water basin and soap in my room to clean my hands, body and face already. There are odd-looking contraptions raining water down on someone as I walk past. Is this the shower Elan eluded to? I don't mind giving that one a miss.

There is so much water here – it is everywhere. Shui even gets an entire pond to himself. Staggering! Sniggering, I shake my head. I may not have been present at the meetings, but the exchange did not go unnoticed as I was passed over, no better than one of the barrels of spices. Surely, Rhion and Kiera cannot fully appreciate how valuable water is to my people – they made an excellent trade. So very wily!

"Better?" she quizzes as I find her waiting patiently, hands crossed on her lap, sitting on a stool.

"All ready," I say, grabbing my leather roll.

"Ah, of course, mustn't forget those," she says, getting up and walking towards my door.

Excitement shoots around my entire body – we're going to the kitchen. Maybe now I will feel more at ease. It is difficult not to run to our destination, knowing vaguely where it must be. Only etiquette stays my feet.

My mouth hangs wide open as Kiera leads me into the largest kitchen I have ever seen.

"We have solar panels, so there is enough electricity to run a few things such as fridges," she explains.

"Yes, I am familiar with those," I confirm, slowly nodding and blowing out a loud puff.

"Is that a good huff?"

"Oh, yes, it most certainly is."

I slowly walk around, my fingers trailing along shiny metal surfaces. It is a cook's dream – so much so that I pinch my arm.

Kiera giggles behind me. "It's all real, Hassan, I assure you."

"Oh, my goddess."

"Come this way. I think there should be some hard-boiled eggs left in here," she says, opening a fridge.

I silently obey.

"Ah, here we are. You want?" She asks, offering out the bowl.

I take two, peeled, cold eggs.

"And over here, there should be some bread. Do you want to toast it?"

I shake my head. "No, I thank you. Just as is."

I unravel my beloved knives from their leather housing, caressing each in turn. I select one and slice the eggs with it. Another cuts through the loaf of bread Kiera kindly brought over.

"Now, let me see. What else? Leftover bacon? Some sort of sauce? Oh, your spices are over here," she says, opening a larder.

"Do you perhaps have some tomatoes, please?"

"Of course. Here," she says, showing me.

Slicing one up, it joins the egg in a makeshift sandwich. I'm hungry and I don't overly care. A little salt and pepper are all that adorn the fillings. Eagerly, I shove the meagre meal in my mouth, chewing as politely as possible.

"Oh, your poor dear. You barely ate yesterday. I should have brought you something to your room. I'm so sorry."

I chuckle. "Elan told me off for apologising too much. I fear I may need to do the same," I tell her with a wink.

Her hand covers her mouth. "Oh, dear. But please know it's only because I want to make a good impression. We all want this to be your new home. If you want, that is."

I chomp down my mouthful before catching her gaze and holding one of her hands. "I cannot express how grateful I am of the amazing welcome. It is…overwhelming to be shown so much attention and kindness."

She bites her lower lip. "Too much?"

Pinching my finger and thumb close together, I tell her, "Just a little."

"Can I say sorry one last time?"

"Just the one. Then we're even," I say with another wink before finishing off my sandwich.

"Right. Well then, I'll leave you to familiarise yourself with things here, if you would like?"

"I do not mean to sound ungrateful for your company. You have shown me great honour. But, please, I would like very much to acquaint myself with everything here."

"Of course. No problem. You have the place to yourself. The others will show up later. Feel free to ask them any questions. I'm sure they'll all be queueing up to help. But, if I may…a word of caution?"

Inclining my head, I grant her request with a, "Please."

"I know your cuisine is very different, and you're excited to show us. But please take the time to learn ours too. And remember, we are not used to hot, spicy flavours. Yet," she adds with a wink of her own.

Holding up a hand, I allay her fears. "Please, do not trouble yourself. I would hate for someone to come into my kitchen and ignore my expertise. I shall honour your cooks as I would seek to be honoured."

She smiles. "I have no doubt. Thank you, Hassan."

"It is I who must thank you."

Once alone, I put on a pot of coffee then open every door and admire each pot, pan and utensil at my disposal. There is a sink at the rear, so I wash up my knives and place them back where they belong, as well as the board and plate from the kitchen.

I'm leaning on the counter, sipping my third cup of coffee trying to absorb this reality when several other people enter the kitchen in a clamour.

"Hello, you must be Hassan," the first female says, shaking my hand.

"Greetings," I say, waving shyly at them all.

A chorus of welcomes echoes in my ears. I will never remember all those names - I didn't even hear them all. There is a plethora of scents and images sent my way. Planting my feet, I try to steady myself.

Once the noise quietens down, one of the males asks me, "So, what are we making tonight?"

My hand flies to my chest. "You're asking me? I should be asking you. Dai, is it?"

He waves my comment off. "Pah, it's a plant day. You, my new friend, are our excuse for breaking the rules today. And yes, I'm Dai."

We both chuckle. "Well, don't let me stand in the way of good meat. Are you sure you're ready for Arabian cuisine?"

"Ready? My friend, we have been cooking the same dishes for far too long. We are beyond ready. And, thanks to your clan, we have a whole cupboard of spices ready to be used. Please, show us."

"How can I refuse?"

"You can't," one of the others says, giggling.

Rubbing my chin, I ponder. "Hmm...well, you have plenty of chicken."

"Oh yes, we rear our own."

"So I saw on my tour yesterday. Very handy."

She grins. "It certainly is."

"And not too challenging...let's try a *kabsa*."

"Great. What is it?"

I smile. "Simply, rice and chicken."

"Oh."

Many disappointed faces look at me.

"With spices, of course."

That brightens them a little. I list off the main ingredients required, sending them in a flurry of activity to fetch them all. I go and collect the spices.

With everything on the side, I start to prepare the spice mix, telling my onlookers the quantities as I add the saffron, ground green cardamoms, ground cinnamon, ground allspice, white pepper and ground dried limes. The rice is put in to soak.

"Impressive," I comment as the others show off their knife skills whilst chopping onions and chicken pieces.

These people hang on my every word and follow each instruction without question. A sense of pride warms me more than the heat rising from the pans. Collectively, we sauté and boil everything together.

Large platters of fragrant rice topped with juicy, browned chicken as well as toasted, flaked almonds and raisins get taken out to the servery. The smell is making my mouth water.

"Chef's privilege," one of the males declares, handing me a plate.

I already know it tastes good, of course. Nothing goes out without testing along the way. Yet, delighted mm's escape as I tuck into my favourite comfort food. Tears prick my eyes as my fellow cooks do likewise. They like it!

"Hassan, come here," one of the females urges, pulling my hand. Emily, I think.

Peering around the corner outside, I see my new clan tucking into *my* food.

"My fork can't scoop fast enough," one of the nearby folk says.

"Oh, my goddess, this is delicious."

Appreciation echoes around the dining area. It's too much. I have to wipe away the tear trickling down my cheek. My companion squeezes around my shoulders.

"Well done, Hassan. Well done."

"My gratitude," I whisper.

We weren't quiet enough, though. One of the clan has spotted us.

"Hassan," he cheers, getting to his feet and clapping.

I can't move. Their reaction to what to me is a simple rice and chicken meal is staggering.

One by one, my new clan members all rise and cheer my name. The hand covering my gaping mouth gets tugged on.

"Come and take a bow," Elan tells me, appearing at my side.

Shaking my head violently, I stand my ground. "Oh, no. Don't ask me. No. I can't."

"Hassan!" is still echoing around.

Emily shoves my back as Elan yanks my arm, and against my will, I'm in full view of the clan. I take a bow, biting my lip.

The area erupts in cheers and applause. I wave again and run back into the kitchen.

"Please, LET ME BE," I growl at Elan when he comes after me.

"I'm sorry," he stammers with pain in his eyes before rapidly departing.

"Hassan! I'm surprised at you. What the hell just happened?" Emily chastises.

I hang my head. Although surprised by a female speaking so, I fully recognise she is justified. "It is…difficult for me."

"Difficult? To accept praise?"

Drawing my arms around my waist, I simply say, "Yes."

"Oh, dear." To my shame, I see pity in her eyes.

"That may be the saddest thing I ever heard," one of the others says, approaching us.

"I am unused to it," I try to explain.

"Now, *that* is the saddest thing I ever heard," yet another exclaims.

Dai joins in. "Well, you'd best start getting used to it pronto."

I frown. "Pronto?"

"Fast."

"Ah, my thanks." I sigh. "I'm not sure I'll ever get used to it. I cook, they eat, it is just as it should be."

Patting my shoulder, he comments, "Pah, of course, you will. By the end of the week, you won't be able to get out of the kitchen, your head will have swelled so much."

Giggles erupt.

"Aye, we'll shower you with praise," one of the females says.

"I...I don't know what to say."

"*Twp*! No need to say anything, is there?"

"Is that another Kiera word?"

"Oh, no. Certainly not. *Twp* is all Welsh. Means fool but in the nicest possible way."

I chuckle. "Thank you?"

"You're welcome," she says, grinning.

We get back to making more *kabsa*. There is another team who comes in during the small hours to bake bread. However, I pledge to show my new friends how to make my flatbreads, so that they can take it easier some days. By the end of service, I am the best kind of exhausted.

However, getting back to my room, I realise that the level of exhaustion is not enough.

Chapter 12 – Wow!
~ Elan

I know everyone's always telling me I'm an idiot, but sometimes I excel in the stupidity ranks. I was so happy for Hassan that I forgot his timidity. I literally pushed him out in front of the crowd. In all fairness, they were very enthusiastic. Maybe they too felt the need to make him feel welcomed and appreciated.

Having beaten myself up over this for hours, I have arrived at his den ready with profuse apologies. I need his forgiveness. Knocking on his door, I await his permission to enter, which doesn't come. I knock again. But still no answer. Washing my hand down my face, I blow out hot air. There's no towel outside, so I slowly open his door.

"Hello," I call.

But the scene that is revealed shatters my heart into a million pieces. Quickly shutting the door behind me, I kneel beside his bed. Hassan is curled into a ball, sobbing. What have I done?

"Hassan, I am so so sorry," I tell him, rubbing his bare upper arm – his robe is discarded in a crumpled pile on the floor. He's naked, with the bed sheets partially covering his lower half.

His face is buried in his pillow, muffling his reply. "Not your fault."

"So why do I feel like it is? I should never have forced you out there. I'm so sorry." My voice cracks.

I only get more sobs in return.

"Hey, hey," I soothe.

Adding my waistcoat to his clothing pile, I walk around and lie down behind him. Wrapping an arm around his middle and pulling the sheets down a little, I hold his back to my bare chest.

"No funny business, I swear. Look, I kept my trousers on," I tell him.

He doesn't move an inch, but his sobs die down. Breath by breath, he relaxes in my arms. Goddess help me for being a selfish bastard, but it does all kinds of things to my ego, knowing I can help him like this.

"You don't have to say a word, but please know you can tell me anything. I may play the joker but I'm a good listener underneath all of that. I promise."

Wiping the tears away, he finally pulls his face free of the pillow and lays his head down on it. Wriggling, I adjust until he's comfortable.

"My gratitude."

Augh! Two simple words, but ones which bring tears to my own eyes. Breathing deep, I keep them within. This male needs me to be strong.

"Are you that unhappy here?" Every muscle in me clenches, not sure I want to hear the answer.

But he huffs. "No. The opposite if anything." He sniffs.

"Let me get you a tissue," I say, peeling up off the bed.

The box of tissues is on his vanity unit – sweet how they're not already next to his bed like every other person I know. Since I'm there, I pour him a glass of water too and take both items to him. His reddened, puffy eyes never leave me.

"Here," I say, offering what he needs.

Propping himself up on his side, he takes a sip of water and places the glass on his bedside cabinet. Then blows his nose, discarding the tissue in the nearby bin.

"You must think I'm a sullen maniac."

Perching on the edge of the bed, my fingers sweep back the hair clinging to his fuzzy cheek. "I think no such thing. You want to know what is on my mind?"

He winces. "I'm not sure. I cannot possibly have improved myself in your estimation."

My hand strokes his hair as he lies back down. "I see someone who has endured a lot. I see an incredibly strong male who must've been bottling up far too much pain for far too long. I see a resilient survivor."

"You see all that?"

"And feel it, *Habibi*."

A momentary smile passes his lips. "I like hearing you say that."

"I like saying it."

Our gazes lock until his lids grow too heavy and close. Bending down, I kiss my forehead to his. "I mean it. I'm here."

I almost yelp as he pulls me down next to him and into a sudden hug. The movement was so fast and unexpected, it caught me off guard.

Shuffling back, he makes way for me to lie down to face him properly. His sleepy eyes bore into my soul. "There is much I would tell you. But for now, it is too much. Allow me merely to say that everything I have ever known, my entire life until now has been obliterated by the love and generosity shown me here in a single day. I had not been unhappy. At least, I did not realise it until you showed me what happiness truly could be."

"Wow! Is that all?" I quip.

There is a hint of light back in his eyes. "For now."

I sigh. "Well, I can't wait to hear more than a lifechanging epiphany."

"You really are crazy," he says with a rueful smile.

Shrugging, I tell him, "Maybe."

That gets me a wider smile.

"Do you want me to go? Let you have some time to overthink?" I ask, leaning away.

He snuffles. "No. If I asked, would you stay?"

"Of course."

"Not for sex."

"Hassan, I am not in the habit of *shagging* anyone who's upset. I'm not that kind of male."

"*Shagging*?"

"Oh, dear goddess. You know, fucking."

"Oh. Welsh or Kiera-speak?"

"Neither. Just English."

He chuckles. "You're so multi-lingual."

"I sure am, *Habibi*," I admit, emphasising the Arabic word.

His smile reaches his eyes.

Kissing the tip of his nose, I praise, "That's better."

"Well, it's all your own doing, of course."

"I know," I say smugly. "So, no sex, huh? I'm not your type?"

"Hey, you do not get to learn all of my secrets at once, my friend."

I roll my eyes and tsk dramatically. And he smiles back.

"Elan...would you mind holding me like before?"

"You like it from behind?" I ask, waggling my eyebrows.

"Yes, would you hug my back, please?"

"You want me to sleep that way?"

He nods, biting his lip.

"Alright then. But only because you asked so nicely."

I rub cheek-to-cheek before resuming the requested position. We're just wriggling to get comfy when the door opens. I sit up in a flash.

"Well, that didn't take you long. You could've at least put a towel out," Arwyn seethes.

"Ever hear of knocking? And why are you so put out anyway?"

"I did knock. Argh! Whatever. I'll leave you to it. I only wanted Hassan to know he had a friend here, but he's got more than he needs, I see."

He grabs a towel and shoves it on the handle on his way out. The door slams behind him.

"Oh, no. I've upset your friend," Hassan says, having already rolled over.

Pawing the air, I dismiss his concern. "Don't you worry about Arwyn. He'll be fine. I'll speak to him tomorrow when he's simmered down. Goddess knows what bit his arse."

Hassan chuckles. "The things you come out with."

"There's more where that came from. But right now, you need rest. Come on, lay that pretty head of yours back down and close your eyes," I cajole, pulling his shoulder gently as I collapse back onto the bed.

Arwyn is unreasonably upset. There's no use trying to talk to him in that kind of mood. Besides, Hassan needs me more right now. Yet, I'm itching to run after my friend. I hate to see him like that. But no, I must remain here for now.

Humming a calming tune, I stroke Hassan's hair. Well, my fingers need something to do to stop them travelling any further south. This male is pure temptation. But I meant it when I said no funny business. If and when we hook up, it'll be when we both have our heads screwed on straight, and we can both fully enjoy what promises to be a fantastic exchange.

Hassan's breathing slows. Dear goddess, thank you for sending this male here. His long, dark lashes flutter against his lightly tanned cheeks. Finally, he sleeps, and I roll onto my back, looking up at the ceiling as if all the answers are written up there.

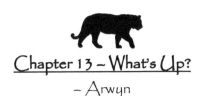

Chapter 13 – What's Up?

~ Arwyn

Fair play, they're two grown males. Very attractive ones. What did I think was going to happen? It's not any great shock. And yet my world has been shaken to its core. I feel sick to my stomach.

Slamming the door to my den, I throw myself onto the bed. What the hell is wrong with me? I was just caught by surprise, that's all. They could've put a bloody towel on the door, for goddess' sake. Or at least yelled out when I knocked. Too wrapped up in each other to notice, no doubt. And doesn't that just twist the knife in my gut a little more?

I had been in such a good mood. Elan and I had conducted our shift together, and I had gone to Cerys to deliver the flowers we'd collected for her. I swear the witch had tears in her eyes at our offering of gratitude. Elan and I had done that together; made our witch happy.

But now all that feels washed away in a torrent of torment. I'm not the only one he does such things with, apparently. And he had left me to deliver the present alone. For him.

At evening meal, Elan had nudged Hassan out to receive his accolade. And then…I can't bear to think of those two lying together. It shouldn't bother me. How many others has he been with? But it's always been just sex, carried out in the Den of Sin. This…this is more intimate. And with Hassan.

Oh, for fuck's sake, I need to get a grip. Jealousy isn't a good look on me. Not that I've ever truly felt it before. Not like this. Holding my head in my hands, I admit to myself that this feels like I'm losing him. Elan's slipping away. And if I try to stop him, it'll only make it worse. Not that he's mine to start with. I have no claim on him. No right. My hand rubs my belly; surely it's bleeding with all this knife twisting.

The harder I try to sleep, the more the cyclical argument revolves around in my head. What's the bloody point? Elan is a free elinefae. And, at the end of the day, I want him to be happy.

When he ran up to Hassan at dinner, my heart broke. He left my side to run to another male. There is finally someone more important than me in his life. It was bound to happen. I just thought it'd be when he found his mate, is all. Not...whatever this is. He's my friend. Mine!

Stop! There is no use in this way of thinking. Let's just see what happens. Maybe there's still room in his life for his old friend. It's not like he's running away to Saudi Arabia. Shit! He wouldn't, would he?

My head hits my pillow as I slam into it. "Aaaargh, enough!"

I'd like to say I calmed down and slept like a contented youngling. But it'd be an outright lie. I barely slept, if at all. As a male who needs his sleep, this does not bode well for a good day.

I skulk to the dining area, trying to brace myself for the sight of two delightfully happy males at our table. I almost bypass morning meal altogether. But adding no food or coffee to my poor sleep could spell disaster for the clan – nobody needs that much anger around them.

My feet stop, as I'm pretty sure my heart does too. There is my usual plate of food on the table next to Elan, at an empty space. My heart restarts in a double thumpity-thump.

"No Hassan?" I ask, taking *my* place.

"No, he's preparing the food," Elan replies.

"Of course," I mutter, taking a bite.

"Well, nobody asked him to. Just doing the dinners is work enough," Kiera comments.

"He's maybe a little too eager to please."

"Arwyn, it wasn't what it looked like," Elan argues.

Pryderi and Kiera look inquisitively, but I ignore them.

"I've heard that before," I grumble, chewing my food viciously.

"Not from me, you haven't. And I mean it. Arwyn, you should've seen him. I went to apologise and —"

Raising a hand, I stop him. "I don't need the sordid details, thank you very much."

Elan pinches my ear as he holds it out and shouts into it, "WILL YOU BLOODY LISTEN, you pig-headed idiot?"

I flinch away from the deafening noise.

He continues, quieter, "And he was crying. Actually crying. He's hurting."

"So, you thought slipping him one would cheer him up, did you?"

"Oh, for fuck's sake, I can't talk to you when you're like this," Elan growls as he launches himself up and stalks away.

"*What the actual fuck*?" Kiera asks in English.

"Not now. I'm not in the mood."

"The Peacekeeper asked you a question, Arwyn," Pryderi rumbles, glaring daggers.

"Pah! She's the one who brought him here," I say, chucking my half-eaten bread onto the plate.

Grabbing my coffee cup, I storm off. The only surprise is that Pryderi doesn't give chase and pin me to the ground. Honestly, I deserve it, speaking to them that way.

As I get further away from everyone, my thoughts begin to calm. In the cold light of day, I know I'm being unreasonable. If those two shagged last night or will do in the future, that's all it can be. Just one in a long line of males who aren't me. It's not something to get all het up over, is it?

It's a bright day, and the sun warms my spirits as it glimmers through the canopy. I breathe in the comforting scents of the forest.

"*Oh, it's your unlucky day*," I think as a rabbit crosses my path, stopping in shock as it notices my presence.

Before it can get its tiny brain into gear, I've pounced on the stupid creature. Its trickle of blood running

138

down my throat is a balm to my soul. Enriching goodness fills my stomach as I munch down on my prey. Thank the goddess for putting it in my path.

An inviting fallen tree calls to me. In dappled sunlight, I recline along its length and bask in the warmth, sated. My breaths are forcibly long and slow.

A kiss on my mouth has me sitting up faster than lightning, almost headbutting Elan. Fortunately, he has enough sense to step back.

"What the fuck?"

"Seemed the best way to awaken the sleeping beauty," he says with a shrug, smirking.

Wiping my mouth, I exclaim, "Shit! How long was I asleep for?"

"I don't know. But I've been here a while, Watching over you," he says with a wink.

"That's the creepy kind of Watcher, Brother." My hands ruffle through my hair.

"Nah, it was more a case of letting sleeping dogs lie."

"Did you just call me a dog?"

"If the bark fits."

"Fine. I may deserve that. I'm sorry for the way I reacted."

He sits down next to me. "I don't understand. Nothing happened. But even if it did, it shouldn't concern you."

I shake my head. "True. I don't know what's gotten into me."

"Well, you're forgiven. But only because I can't ever stay cross with you for long," he says, nudging my shoulder with his.

"Truly, nothing happened?"

Winking, he confides, "Well, no sex anyway. Honestly, the guy was upset. I was only cuddling him. He needed calming. It's all been a bit of a culture shock."

"Yeah, fair play. From what I've heard and seen, it's very different here from what he's used to."

"Not that I'm gossiping, but I believe his exact words were that everything he has ever known has been obliterated by the love and generosity shown to him here in a single day."

"Wow! That's a lot."

"I probably shouldn't have told you that. But, I don't know, it felt like you needed to know. Please don't say anything. I'd hate him to think I broke his trust. I don't think that's something he takes lightly."

"Of course not. Thanks, though. You're right. I think I did need to know. Not that you gave me any details, so it should be fine."

He huffs. "He didn't really tell me more than that."

"Huh."

"What 'huh'?"

"Don't people usually spill their guts to you?"

He chuckles. "Yeah, people tend to confide in me. Give him time."

"Elan, can you do one thing for me?"

"Anything."

"Just...don't forget me."

He slaps the side of my head. "*Twp!* As if I could ever do that. Come on, let's finish this shift together."

"Sounds good to me," I agree, standing and brushing off any loose bark from my clothes.

Walking side by side in comfortable silence, it feels like everything is right in my world again. What was I making a fuss about?

Dinner is a plant-based one today. Our cooks usually do a good job of making delicious treats from the produce of our land. But this? There is a background aromatic flavour which has me gobbling up the food quicker than ever. It's like Hassan has taken our cuisine and enhanced it.

Guilt weighs my head down. I still have not made him feel welcome here. This is not me. I'm not the elinefae I've shamefully become. I must do better.

Sneaking away from our group, I go and talk to one of the other Watchers before stepping into the kitchen.

"Knock, knock," I call out.

The cooks are all bustling about and don't even seem to hear me. None but Hassan, that is. Beaming, he's making his way between scurrying bodies to approach me.

"Arwyn, it is good to see you. But we are still a little busy."

"I understand and shan't keep you long. I wanted to ask you to accompany me on my shift tomorrow."

Cocking his head, he asks, "Really? That is kind, but Elan already shown me around."

"Ah, correction. He showed you the area we patrol."

"You have me curious. I thought I had seen all."

"No, there is still much I would show you."

"Very well. After morning meal service?"

Shaking my head vigorously, I tell him, "No. You will eat with us. Kiera only expects you to cook evening meals."

"She said this?"

"Yes."

"Oh. I did not…Alright, I shall be honoured to eat with you in the morning."

The way he inclines his head shows just how much he appreciates it. He shouldn't. This is normal. It should be expected. Again, my heart sinks for this beautiful, generous male.

Forcing a smile on my face, I hold my hand to my heart. "In the morning, then."

If formality is what makes him feel comfortable then he shall have it.

Chapter 14 – A World of Wonders

– Hassan

Arwyn certainly surprised me, both with his appearance in the kitchen and his offer. So far, he has been distant. But I find myself excited by the prospect of seeing more of this compound and spending time getting to know him better.

Why did Kiera not tell me herself of her expectations, though? She said to prepare evening meal only for now, but I felt ready for more so got on with it. Is this yet another thing that is normal for this clan and not mine? Back in Saudi Arabia, I would prepare both meals in my little section of the kitchen. If only they could see me now, chopping ingredients alongside females and males.

Nobody has come into our clan from others. My recipes go back generations with little change. It is pleasing to know that none have brought my particular flavour combinations to this clan. I have something of value to give. Most seem to have come here from within the British Isles until now. It's beyond exciting to think of all the new meals we can create together.

My shift ends, and satisfaction radiates through me as I head out.

"Oh!" I yelp, jumping back from the exit.

"My greetings to you too," Elan says, smiling wryly.

"Pardon. You startled me. Is everything alright?"

"Never better. I just thought you'd like an escort home?"

"That really is too kind of you, *Habibi*."

"Ah, too much?"

Pinching my finger and thumb close to each other, I admit, "Just a little. But it is lovely all the same. I thank you."

Holding out the crook of my elbow, I offer him to take hold. Having his hand through my arm feels comforting. A smile spreads across my lips as we walk along.

"That's better," Elan tells me.

I cock my head at him.

"You look happy," he adds.

Closing my eyes briefly, I allow the feeling to develop and warm my insides. "Yes. I truly am."

Rubbing his hand along my arm, he simply says, "Good."

Looking at him, Elan seems more content too. More relaxed. A selfish part of me hopes it is my influence which brings this to him.

No words are required as we make our way to our dens. It is a comfortable silence that we share. And I am grateful for the time to rein in my emotions. That this Watcher thought so much of me is beyond humbling. My heart is overflowing, and it's threatening to fill my eyes. However, this male has seen far too many of my tears already. Even if these are born of happiness, I do not wish them to spill before him.

"My gratitude," I whisper as we reach my door.

"You are welcome. I shall leave you alone to your thoughts."

I peek up at him. "You do not have to."

"You wish me to come in?"

Biting my lip, I venture, "Like last night."

"For cuddles only?"

"If that is alright?"

Cupping my head through my gutrah, he asks, "Oh, honey. Who hurt you?" Then pulls me in for a hug.

"Is that a yes?" I mumble into his neck.

"If that is all you want from me, then yes, that is all I shall give."

"Thank you."

I open my door and lead us in. "It's just that I—"

Holding up his hand, he interrupts, "Only provide explanation when you are ready, my friend."

Taking hold of that hand and lowering it, I say around the lump in my throat, "Many thanks."

"Daft male," he mutters, pulling me into another hug.

Being held by Elan feels like all my pieces are being glued back together. I know he wants more from me, but I'm not ready yet. His patience itself is soul-meltingly endearing.

We both use my washbasin to cleanse ourselves.

"This is not right," I comment.

"What?"

"Well, without my thobe, I am fully naked. But here you stand in your trousers."

"I didn't think you wanted..?"

Rolling my eyes, I clarify, "I may not want to have sex yet, but I am not shocked by a naked body, Elan."

"No, right. Why would you be?" He chuckles as he removes his clothing.

One of my eyebrows rises. "And you should not be ashamed of showing that off," I tell him, looking pointedly at his magnificent, erect *zib*.

I can't help but laugh as he places his hands on his hips and waves his manhood about, declaring, "Behold my delightful dick."

I lick my lips. "Oh, I'm beholding."

His face turns serious as he steps towards me. Thumbing my chin, he states, "So, it's not that you're not interested in males, then."

My *zib* has makes that abundantly clear. "No, I'm definitely interested."

"Well, that's a relief." And with that, he climbs onto my bed.

I lay down facing him and chew my lip. "I'm re-learning a lot."

His fingers brush my cheek. "I know."

"In Saudi Arabia, it is illegal for males to have sex."

His eyes widen in horror as he gasps.

"And, as my clan have a great deal of human interaction, we have to be seen to be abiding by their laws."

"Monstrous!"

"It makes things…difficult."

"I bet."

I snigger. "Not impossible, though. There have been snatched moments when alone with males, away from prying eyes."

"Oh, Hassan," he says in a whisper, pulling me close.

Drawing back, I catch his gaze. My voice is so low I'm not sure he can hear me. "Even…humans."

He gasps. "But clan law?"

"I know. But males are not going to breed."

"Well, there is that."

"And our need builds."

"Undoubtedly. But it's against their law, you said. That makes it a double no-no."

Nodding against the pillow, I elaborate, "Yes. But some of their males like to lie only with males."

"I see."

"Do you? Elan, the things I have done. Some of the wealthy men, they requested me to cook for private functions after visiting with us. They paid—" I can say nothing more as the lump in my throat has cut all further words off.

"Good goddess, Hassan. They forced you?"

Steeling myself, I tell him, "No force was necessary. My need was such that I did not care what they looked like or who they were."

His arms wrap tightly around me. "Oh, honey. Never again. Never. I vow it."

His tears match my own as we lie entangled together.

Wiping away the salty traces, I take a deep breath. "The last human…he was…surprisingly well-endowed. And he was kind. Goddess forgive me, but when he requested a second visit, I went, craving his attention."

I'm sure I'm blushing as I stop for breath. Elan remains silent, urging me on with both the look in his eyes and the stroking of his hand through my hair.

"He bought me the most luxurious outfit I have ever owned. This beautiful, powerful male not only noticed but also valued me. It was intoxicating. Even though I knew it was wrong on every level, I kept going back. My Leader was more than happy as the man paid well. My clan benefited too."

Elan's lips pout as he frowns. I close my eyes against such disapproval.

"It was not love. Not for me. But he seemed to develop feelings. He wanted more and asked me to become his live-in chef. Oh, Elan, part of me wanted to say yes. I could not fully explain how bad an idea it was. I had to rely on the law putting us both in danger, that it would be too much temptation, that it was only a matter of time before we would get caught if I were to remain with him."

Elan snorts.

"But he is a rich man of influence whom people do not say no to. He grew angry at my refusal. I did not use the right words. We fought. He told me if I persisted in denying him, he would report me to the authorities, telling them I tried to force myself upon him."

Elan growls long and loud. "Arsehole!"

"Shh, *Habibi*. It is alright. I yelled and ran away, back to clan. But he made good on his promise and reported me."

"He WHAT?"

"I cannot truly regret this, for it is why I am here. My clan would never have allowed one of us to stray away otherwise."

Rising up to a sitting position, Elan hisses a breath in and out, pinching the bridge of his nose whilst scrunching his eyes. The next growl from him is more of a rumble. I can see he is trying to calm himself, but words again fail me. What can I say? My shame is out there, and this male is deciding whether to report me too. I have angered him, and he is in the right. I am responsible. And now my life hangs in the balance, as it should.

His hands wipe over his face. "What the fuck, Hassan?"

I sit up too. Remaining silent, my head droops down. "It is alright, Sir. You should go."

His head reels back. "Is that what you want?"

"It is what is right. Go and report me to your Leader. He should not have to keep a male here with such low morals. Leader Rhion was kind enough to invite me here, but my truth must have been kept from him. He should know so he may choose to send me back. Or declare the execution order himself."

"What the fuck are you going on about now? Send you back? Low morals? Execution? Hassan, look, I cannot pretend not to be shocked."

"You are justified in your anger. It was my choice, Sir."

He huffs. "I am angry at others, not you. And stop calling me Sir. Your clan created this whole bloody situation. If you were free to live your life naturally, this would never have happened. And as to accepting money for…well, it's beyond disgraceful, isn't it? The human is the worst of all, though. Buying you pretty things, declaring his love then promptly betraying you as soon as you stand up for yourself. No. Just no. That is not right."

"But I—"

"No, Hassan. You take too much on yourself. I won't hear it. Yes, you made choices. I can't say they were good ones. But they're understandable."

I stare at him, dumbfounded.

He shakes his head. "It's a mess. But you're not the one at fault. Not really. Can you not see the reality?"

I consider his words. "I see that I was eager for affection. That I offered myself willingly to a human who has thrown me to the wolves. But yes, maybe, if things had been different, I would not have acted so."

Taking a deep breath and pulling me close, Elan tells me, "My friend. You should not die for the want of appreciation. He never deserved you. You're too good for the likes of him. You are safe now. You're here. We…I will protect you."

"I…" Sighing and nestling into his smooth chest, I murmur, "My gratitude."

"No. My honour."

Wrapped in his embrace, I feel the power of Elan's words. I have no doubt of his sincerity. It is a relief that he is not reviled by my revelation. But he goes beyond that. This astonishing male pardons my transgressions and accepts me for all that I am. With the guarantee of his protection, I relax and eventually fall asleep.

A contented sigh hums out of me as I wriggle my backside against the hardness there.

"Good morning," Elan greets, kissing the back of my head.

"Hmm, good morning," I return, giving a more definite wiggle.

"Feeling frisky?"

"Just enjoying the attention." Sleepiness fills my voice with hoarseness.

"*Snuggle slut!*"

"Huh?"

"Kiera says it means someone who enjoys cuddles a lot. But they're usually the post-coital kind, I think."

"Hmm."

"Maybe I didn't use it right." I feel him shrug.

Pulling my shoulder, he encourages me to roll over onto my back. Staring up into kind, violet eyes, there is no other place I'd rather be. His sleek black hair falls forwards, over his shoulders.

"Thank you, for what you told me last night. I need you to know I won't tell anyone. But I do think you should tell Kiera, at least. She won't judge you. But there are things in your clan which need to be addressed."

I shake my head. "It's not what you think. I wanted to. My Leader just monetised it. Well, accepted what was offered for the good of the clan. Officially, my cooking skills were all that were being purchased. That human just got too involved. I shouldn't have gone back."

Elan sneers and hisses. "You know that is not the whole truth."

Sitting up, I re-iterate, "It was my choice."

"But they encouraged you, Hassan. Even condoning sexual activity with humans is against clan law."

"But—"

"No! Do not tell me again how it's about not breeding. That is not the sole purpose of the law. Humans turned against us, Hassan. They're a threat. We're supposed to avoid contact as much as possible.

And you have experienced why," he says through clenched, bared teeth.

My voice rises in return. "Maybe here, but it's a matter of survival there."

"Everywhere, it's the law. To protect us."

Launching up from the bed, I stride towards the washbasin. "You try living my life for a day, Elan, and see what you do. We do not have the same resources you do. Our witch can only spell our water source so much. You cannot know how fortunate you are. There, life is a constant battle for survival."

I viciously scrubbed my body whilst launching my diatribe, but Elan now approaches and lowers my hand.

His voice is softer. "You're right. I don't understand. But there must be other ways. Elinefae are all one. We would all help. All this human interaction, it's not safe." His voice dips. "You've seen yourself how dangerous it is. I hate that you found yourself in that situation."

I huff out a sigh. "And I love how protective you are. Look, things happened. But I cannot truly be sorry for them, for without those events, I would not be here now. Besides, Kiera…" I stop myself from finishing the sentence, not wishing to disclose secrets which shouldn't be shared.

"Kiera what?"

"Never mind. Just, please don't be angry."

Smiling, he brings his forehead to mine and holds the back of my head. "Know that my anger comes from my need to protect. And I hate what you've had to endure. When you're ready, you pick out whoever you want and I'll invite them to the Den of Sin for you."

I chuckle. "And that makes you better than my Leader how? It is a kind offer, but I can find my own partners, my friend."

He blushes and coughs. "Right. Of course, you can. I just thought you might feel shy is all."

"Come on, get ready. I don't know about you, but I'm hungry."

"Ooh, I like it when you get bossy," he says, grabbing a washcloth.

"Hmmm, duly noted."

He gawps but says nothing. Opening my wardrobe, I find a woollen top with a note.

Dear Hassan,

I thought this cardigan may help whilst you acclimatise to our weather.

Love Pryderi (& Kiera)

xx

"Aww, that's sweet," I exclaim.

Elan cocks his head. "What is?"

I hold up the caramel-coloured *cardigan* and the note.

He smiles. "Ha, that's Pryderi alright. To be honest, I should've thought of it. Try it on then."

Pulling my arms through the sleeves, I shrug into the soft warmth. There is a deep 'v' at the neck, so some of my chest is still visible, but it's cosy.

Stroking my chest hair, Elan admires, "Mmm…I like how furry you are."

"Funny. I like how smooth you are," I reply, running my hand over his pecs.

Clearing his throat, he announces, "Right, well, we'd best quickly stop at my den so I can dress in clean clothing."

Smiling, I nod and follow him out, picking up the wastewater on the way.

Elan grins. "You're such a good boy!"

My stomach does fifty flips at that, but I try not to show any hint of the spike of lust which shoots through me. I don't want him to think I'm there yet. The bulge fighting my leather trousers is arguing that point, however.

We finally make it to the dining area. Elan grabs items seemingly without thinking, loading up two plates. I take time pondering my selection but end up choosing berries and yoghurt. The coffee available is far weaker than what I'm used to, but I help myself to a cup anyway. I'm just glad they have it at all.

Within moments of us taking our place at the table, Arwyn joins us. It's as though he felt our presence. Either that, or he was lurking in wait. We sit on either side of Elan, as seems to be our place now.

"Alright?" he checks, I think with us both.

"Never better," Elan replies.

"I am well, I thank you. And yourself?" I respond at the same time.

Arwyn grins. "Oh, I'm well enough. Nice *cardi*!"

I frown for a moment before realising he's looking at my new top. "A present from Pryderi. Thank you, my friend," I say to the approaching male himself.

"I'm glad to see you wearing it. You don't have to. Your old clothing is fine if you prefer." He winces as Kiera nudges his ribs.

"This is warmer. You are correct. I am adapted for hot weather."

"Well, there's a shock, coming from the desert 'n all," Arwyn mocks.

"I would have you know it gets cold at night."

"My friend, I suspect you don't know the meaning of the world cold. But have no fear, we'll keep you warm in winter," he says with a wink that sets my internal fires on full blast.

"My gratitude," I reply with a cheeky smirk.

Elan is licking his lips.

"You always have honey on your bread," I note.

He accentuates the movement of his tongue. "My favourite!"

I am so tempted to lick the dewdrop of honey from the corner of his mouth. But no matter how liberal this clan are, I am certain such an indecent public display would be beyond their acceptance. Instead, I focus my gaze onto my spoon as I stir the berries around with it.

"That's not much of a breakfast. Here, try this," he says, holding out a rasher of crisp bacon.

I close my eyes. It smells delicious. Of course, such things are not permitted where I come from. Somehow, that spurs me on. I open my mouth and take a bite from Elan's hand.

"Auugh!" I groan.

"Good?"

"How have I missed out on this my whole life?"

"What? You've never had bacon?" Arwyn asks.

I shake my head.

"Hassan's clan mingle human laws with their own," Elan explains for me, making me frown.

"Well, it's not a law so much. More frowned upon."

"Their loss," Arwyn says with a shrug, tucking into his own.

Elan shoves the rest of the rasher into my mouth and lets go. I happily munch it all. I know what I'll be eating tomorrow morning.

We finish our meal amongst idle chatter. Kiera hasn't spoken much but keeps looking at me with an odd mix of approval and inquisitiveness. I think about telling her my story, as Elan said I should, but now does not feel like the time. Besides, Arwyn demands my attention as soon as we've eaten.

"Alright, Hassan. Ready for an adventure?" he asks.

With an eager nod, I agree, "Lead the way."

Waving goodbye to our friends, a slight pang of regret strikes my heart. I'm a grown male. Surely I don't need Elan to hold my hand the entire day. Yet I miss him already.

Arwyn leads us in the opposite direction I was taken on my first day. As the sun peaks from behind the clouds, I'm grateful that it's not raining. Breathing in, I marvel at all the scents of this place – the forest, the earth, the cooking, the flowers, the plants...there is a wondrous array with each inhalation.

"Nice, eh?" Arwyn asks at my side, smiling.

"It's all so...green," I marvel.

"Aye, that's home. I'm glad you like it."

"How could anyone not?"

"My thoughts exactly. This way," he says veering up a side path through trees.

We keep climbing upwards until the trees thin out. Before coming here, I never knew trees could grow in such abundance. But, as we reach a stony outcropping, my breath is utterly taken away. Down the steep slope lies field after field of vegetables, I think.

"This is where we grow our food," Arwyn informs me, "You get a better view from up here."

My jaw is silently working.

"Ha, you should see the look on your face. Classic!"

"There's...so much!"

"I'm pleased that size impresses you."

I startle at his words, an echo of my own to Elan.

"Too lewd?"

Shaking my head, I chuckle. "Not at all. Honestly, you and Elan do like to think I'm a precious flower petal."

"Well, you did seem pretty timid."

I hold up my hand. "I know how I must have seemed. Your clan is more extensive than mine in every way. I was nervous. And more than a bit shocked. And the surprises keep coming."

"Well, as long as they're all good surprises, we're doing alright."

"Beyond my wildest dreams." The words are out of my mouth before I can stop them.

He just jerks his head upwards "Tidy!"

The ground at my feet is suddenly fascinating.

"Right, well, over there, are the vegetable plots. Potatoes, carrots and cabbage-type stuff. And then there's the salads, your lettuce leaf things. See those tunnels? We grow tomatoes, courgettes and strawberries in there, I think. And then there's the fruit trees."

My gaze follows his finger as he points to each section. "Wow!"

"I thought you might like it."

"Like it? Oh, my goddess, I love it. Thank you Arwyn." I pull him into a quick hug.

"I think if either of us had known you're a cook, Elan would have brought you here on day one," he says against my head.

"Oh, I think I would have passed out. It would have been too much. Now is perfect. At least I'm more mentally prepared. It's…staggering."

"Want a closer look?"

"Just try to stop me!"

"Right you are then. There's a path down here but mind your footing. It's a bit slippery. There's a better path the other way, but I really wanted you to see it in all its glory."

"For the view, I'm happy to risk it. Thank you again."

"Come along then. No dillydallying."

We carefully pick our way down the hillside. Or is it a mountain? I'm not sure.

"Your accent, it is stronger than Elan's," I note, trying to make conversation.

"Ah, well, you see, my family made me learn Welsh as well as English. Elan speaks it a bit, but my family, well, we tend to be the ones sent on errands, so we practice a bit more. That's the accent you hear, probably."

"I like it. It sounds…cheerful." Phew, I almost said sexy.

"Hmph!" He shrugs. "It is what it is, I suppose."

Tugging on his waistcoat, I ask, "Please. What is the purpose of this? It doesn't seem to offer much cover."

He chuckles. "Ah, well now, things are not always as they appear. You see, the leather is protective, especially when spelled as it is. Our vital organs are covered. And it's warm enough. Although, in the coldest weather or when it rains, we wear overcoats."

"Huh. My thanks."

Embarrassed at how badly my fingers wanted to explore under his garment, I walk on in silence, trying to quell my growing desire. I've never before felt this way. Since arriving here, it is as if my hormones have gone into overdrive. And I'm not sure how to cope.

"So, how come we've never seen you at any sabbats? We just celebrated Litha. I'm sure I would've noticed you there," he asks.

Oh, my. He would have noticed me? This is not helping calm me at all. In fact, I have to clear my throat before I can answer. And my voice still sounds squeaky, even so. "Umm...well, my clan...not all get to attend such events. But do you mind if we don't talk about them at the moment, please?"

"Of course. Don't mind my nosiness."

"Oh, I mean no disrespect. I'm just too happy absorbing all of our surroundings."

"Right you are, then."

His respect is so humbling. He holds his tongue, even though I can see there are more questions bursting to get out of him. Honestly, it is a struggle to take my eyes off him, even with such a landscape to admire. But I force myself to look away. Whoever thought there was such wonder in the world?

Upon reaching our destination, Arwyn introduces me to the people who are farming the produce, and they're able to tell me more about what is grown. I'm even given some samples to taste as we walk around.

"Have you a list, please?" I ask once we've almost completed the circuit.

"Hmph. Not written down, I don't think, no."

"Oh."

"But I'm sure we can create one if it'll help?"

"Oh, only if it is not too much trouble. All this has got me thinking about what I can cook."

"Well, if it's anything like that chicken dinner you made, we're more than happy to support you in any way we can. If there is anything you especially need, I'm sure we can try to grow it for you."

Placing a hand on the lady's arm, I tell her, "You are most kind. My gratitude."

"My pleasure," she says, grinning.

My head is already brimming with ideas as we walk away. There is a variety of things I've not seen before. But also, some familiar fayre is on offer.

"That's our outer boundary there," Arwyn points out, jerking me out of my thoughts.

"How do you keep all of this hidden from humans?"

"Ah, well, there are hills there which form a natural barrier, you see?"

I nod.

"And then there are the magick wards which stop anyone crossing through. And there may be a slight glamour over this area. We're in a remote location. Not many come this way. But even if they did, all they would see is a steep slope of trees."

"Clever."

He shrugs. "Right, after all that excitement, would you like to go back to your room on your own until you need to cook us up something tasty?"

"That sounds good to me. I can't thank you enough for this. I don't know what to say."

"Aww, come here, you dafty," he says, gathering me into a firm hug. "You're very welcome."

I linger, inhaling his delicious orange and clove scent which seems to have strengthened. It must be my imagination. Before the hug can be considered too long, I step back.

"Well, thank you again, my friend."

He pouts. "Aww, all that doesn't earn me a *Habibi*?"

I laugh. "I was not aware you craved it. I thought maybe it was not welcomed. But, learning otherwise, I offer you my gratitude, *Habibi*," I say, inclining my head.

He chortles whilst ruffling my hair. "Ha, thank you too, *Habibi*. Yes, I like this word."

With that, he departs, leaving me to find my den. I certainly have a lot to think about.

Chapter 15 – WTF?
~ Elan

The aroma of cooking pizza hits my nose as I approach the dining area, making my stomach growl. Augh, but that smells delicious. My pace quickens close to a jog as I hurry towards the source.

Many kinds of cured meats are on the slices I grab before making my way to our table. The others are already there. Except Hassan, my mind whimpers.

"Elan, I can't believe you weren't the first one here for pizza night," Arwyn teases as I take my seat next to him.

"I was busy." Yeah, busy getting nailed in the Den of Sin so I can cope if Hassan wants another night of only snuggles.

I don't mind, but a male has needs which build up. Hassan is all kinds of tempting at the best of times, let alone when he's lying naked next to me; it's like asking me not to devour this pizza. Which I do. As though I've not eaten for days, I wolf down the cheesy, tomatoey, meaty goodness.

"Watch your fingers," Pryderi cajoles.

I pull a face before continuing the devouring.

"You'll give yourself heartburn, *Habibi*."

Immediately, I stop mid-chew as my head swivels towards the voice.

"Hewwo," I say around a mouthful of food.

His beautiful face fills with disgust. "Manners, please." But he laughs.

Chomping and swallowing as quickly as elinefaely possible, I try again. "Hello. What are you doing here?"

He raises an eyebrow. "That's still not exactly polite," he tells me, nudging my cheek with his as he sits.

"Aren't you cooking?"

"Ah, so you do believe my place is in the kitchen," he teases. The glint in his eyes is devilish.

"Alright. Who are you? And what did you do with Hassan?"

He laughs. "I'm not allowed to tease back?"

I catch his gaze. "Oh, you absolutely are."

The heat between us is unmistakeable. But for once, it's me who looks away first. I pretend it's so I can pick up another pizza slice off my plate. But Hassan intercepts it before it reaches my mouth – he actually takes a bite. What else can I do but growl?

"Hassan, you are either supremely brave or extremely foolish. Nobody gets between this one and food," Arwyn says.

Hassan pouts at me. "Aww, you wouldn't truly be angry at me, would you?"

Dropping my pizza back on the plate, I catch Hassan in a head lock and knuckle the top of his head. "Maybe not, but don't test me."

"Eww, greasy cheese hands!" he cries, wiping at his hair.

"Ha, serves you right."

I take the opportunity to finish my pizza slice whilst he continues to brush at his hair. Dramatic much?

"So, really, why are you not hiding in the kitchen?" Arwyn asks.

"Oh, everything's all prepped. We can't all fit around the pizza ovens, so I'm free to sit with my friends and enjoy the product of my hard work." His smile is dazzling.

"Something's cheered you up," I comment.

He nods. "Yes. Arwyn took me to see the farming area. Oh, my goddess, Elan, it's amazing."

I smile as he rabbits on at ninety miles per hour about all the ingredients he saw. He's so excited, and doesn't that just fill my heart with joy? He's radiant. But also too distracted to eat. So, I pick up a piece of pizza from his plate and bite a piece off.

"Hey!" he cries.

"*You want it, you come get it,*" I tell him mind-to-mind, my mouth closed firmly around the tasty morsel.

To my amazement, he painstakingly slowly brings his face close to mine, his hands crawling along the bench. His head dips as if stalking prey. His eyes narrow.

"You don't think I will?" he quizzes.

I slowly shake my head. And he brings his face right up close to mine. He licks his plump lips. Long eyelashes flutter enticingly at me.

Instead of grabbing the pizza, his head languorously bobs right, across my face, his eyes not leaving mine for a second. He begins to hum an enchanting melody as his fingers trail down my left cheek. My eyes close of their own accord as he twists my hair between his fingers, still humming that tune.

My eyes shoot open as the pizza is snatched from my teeth. Hassan sits proudly dangling his pizza from his mouth like a tongue, pulling back from me. Despite the recent session, my dick is twitching already. I'm left looking dumbly at this brave, enticing male.

"*Sweet baby Jesus,*" Kiera exclaims.

"Aher, anyone for more pizza?" Arwyn asks, getting up.

"Not for me, thanks," I murmur.

Without asking, I pick up Hassan's remaining slices of pizza. "You, follow me."

His breath hitching, he complies.

The walk back to my den is the longest in all eternity, but we eventually get there, albeit with a slightly lopsided hobble. I place the pizza down on my table and a towel on my door handle before closing it.

I cough. "Correct me if I'm wrong, but—"

He doesn't even permit me to finish my question. Goddess bless him, his lips are on mine. My tongue laps at his, tasting the spicy hints of pizza but also honey and cinnamon.

"Mmmm…you do taste good," I mumble.

"Shh, *Habibi*. No words. Not now," he instructs, placing a finger on my lips.

His hips nudge my groin, backing me up against a wall. With one hand by my head, his other grabs my side. He claims my mouth in a burst of fiery passion. Our mouths slide and collide, our breaths heaving thick and fast. His body writhing against mine. Holy fuck, that's good.

He starts humming that tune again as he kisses a trail down my neck. He tugs my waistcoat off so it doesn't stop his descent down my chest. His rough tongue licks down my navel and dances around it in a circle. Oh, good goddess, then it delves into my belly button. His hands explore above his head, tracing circles around my pecs, then squeezing a nipple as his tongue explores…no, he gently nips my side.

"Gonna come," I warn.

"Oh no, *Habibi*. Not yet."

His ministrations are swiftly removed, and I'm left bereft. What the..? My hair's clinging to my face, but I peek through it and down at him. He's looking up at me with glowing blue eyes.

"Goddess, you're beautiful," I whimper, reaching down to stroke his hair.

He swats my hand away. "Shh, no words, Elan. And no touching."

This male is going to kill me with lust. And I can't think of a better way to go. Willingly, I give my life to him.

He struggles with the laces on my trousers. "Stupid invention. This is why thobes are easier," he mutters.

I bite back a laugh, not wanting to kill the moment. Instead, I help him. At last, he manages to pull my trousers down to my knees. My dick springs free. Hassan sniffs along its length, not touching it. Damn, that's enticing. Gritting my teeth, I resist the urge to direct myself into his mouth.

"Please, Hassan," I cry as he sniffs along the other side.

"Patience."

But the tip of his tongue slides up one side and then down the other. Fuck, I'm throbbing here. My dick is jumping in anticipation. One of Hassan's hands grabs hold of the base. Then his evil tongue teases my engorged, darkened tip - only around the head.

"Argh!"

"You like, *ya amar*?"

"Yesss," I hiss.

I mewl as his tongue laps another circuit. And then howl as his finger presses into my slit. Nobody has ever teased me so…fucking delightfully.

"Need," I whimper.

He plants a chaste kiss on my tip.

"*Bastard*," I exclaim.

He snickers. Fucker!

"Alright. I know what you want, my horny friend."

Sweat is beading on my brow. "Would you mind giving it, then?" I ask between clenched teeth.

The little shit actually withdraws further. "Ooh, tsk tsk. I said no words. Disobedience should not be rewarded."

"Heeeuuuurgh!" I cry out to the ceiling, my fists clenched against the wall.

"Aww, poor Elan."

He licks up my shaft once. Once! "Arrrgh!"

My almost silence is rewarded with another lick. Seriously, this male is going to have my cock rammed down his throat in a minute if he doesn't help me out here.

"Nnnaaaauuugh!" His mouth descends, plunging me all the way in in one swift gulp.

"Oh fuck, oh fuck, oh fuck."

He chuckles around my dick but brings his head back to slide up and then mercifully back down. And up.

"Auuugh!" The suction is exquisite.

His head bobs forward and back, never relenting in his sucking. Hands grip onto my buttocks, and my hips are bucking into his mouth. As he cups my balls I explode like a geyser into his mouth with an almighty roar. He swallows every last drop.

Collapsing onto the floor in front of him, I kiss him, tasting myself on him; apple and vanilla mixing with honey and cinnamon. Delicious!

"You're amazing," I say between breathy pants.

"Your *zib* is tasty," he replies with a smirk.

"I assume that means penis."

"Dick, actually, but yes, *ya amar*."

I cock my head.

"Literally, my moon."

"Aww."

"It's intended use is more like most beautiful. But for you, I see the moon in your eyes when they glow."

I cast my gaze down. "They glow the same violet as my normal colour."

"No, *ya amar*, you are wrong. They shine like the moon, with the power of a thousand stars. Not at all like your daylight eyes."

Hell, I'm so emotional after that blowjob that I actually shed tears. "Nobody has ever said anything more wonderful to me, honey."

Grabbing me into a hug on the floor, he whispers in my ear, "I like my honey on your tongue."

I chuckle. "Is that a request?"

"Oh, not today. I'm nowhere near done with you yet."

"What? There's more? Honey, I think you drained me."

"There is drinking water there," he says, nodding towards the table.

I crawl towards it and gulp down water like I'd just crept out of his desert.

"Better?" he checks.

I shrug. I'm unconvinced but will do my best to please him any way I can after that.

"Trousers fully off. Then on the bed," he commands.

I obey, pulling myself onto all fours on my bed.

I watch over my shoulder as he removes his trousers. Somewhere along the way to my climax, he'd removed his *cardigan*, I only now realise. This male is good!

Just one solitary finger draws up my crack. Oh good, we're back to the teasing, I think sarcastically.

"Good boy," he purrs.

I almost leap off the bed as his tongue travels the same path as his finger. I just about manage to contain myself to a yowl.

"Good?"

I nod silently and get another lick.

"So juicy for me already. You want my *zib* in you, *ya amar*?"

I nod more vehemently, biting my lip. Oh, yes, please! I shuffle back closer to the edge of the bed, inviting him.

"No. Not this way," he says.

I glance back at him, concern furrowing my brow.

"I want to see you."

I let out a sigh of relief and move so I'm lying against my pillow. He raises my legs and our gazes lock – blue flames dance towards me.

Inch by inch, he slides inside my slick hole, taking his sweet time. His eyes close and it's like someone stole the sun.

"Open your eyes, gorgeous," I plead.

Holy goddess, I almost ask him to close them again. Relief and gratitude are shining through his tears.

"Fuck! Honey, come here, come here. We don't have to."

He shakes his head. "Oh, no way am I stopping now."

Gently, he pulls himself back before diving back in. It's an agonisingly unhurried pace but I don't press him for more. This clearly has to be set at his speed. I'm just enjoying the ride.

"Feels…so…good," he says between gasps.

"Lean down for me, honey."

Surprisingly, I'm not reprimanded for my non-silence. He lowers himself for me and I kiss him for all I'm worth. I need to show this male just how much I adore him and how special he is. His whimpers send tingles all through me. Then his movements increase in speed.

Gathering momentum, he raises back up. With stretched arms either side of my head, he bucks into me.

"Aurgh, goddess, yeah, like that," I cry.

Spurred on, he speeds up more.

"Augh, fuck me, honey!"

His dick is pounding against my sweet spot with every forward surge, and oh, it feels so good.

"Hass…Hass….Hasaaaaaan," I yell as my climax soars through me.

My teeth latch onto his shoulder as it draws close, and I bite down.

"Elaaaaaaaan," he screams before biting back in turn.

Hot squirts shoot inside me. My cum coats our stomachs between us, and he collapses down.

My arms wrap around him. His shoulders start quaking.

"Shhh, it's OK," I tell him, rubbing his back.

"Elan, please shut up."

"What?"

He rolls to one side, and I see his face. He's not crying but laughing. I can't help but feel a little hurt.

"What's so funny?"

"Really? Elan, what just happened?"

"Other than the amazing sex?"

"Do you truly not feel it?" His mouth forms an 'o' as he frowns.

"You have to help me. My head is a million places at once."

He nods. "Yeeees. And your soul is...?"

"Holy fuck! I wasn't hallucinating? That whole cosmic stardust explosion thing? No."

"Apparently so."

"But you're male."

"As are you, as I think we both know."

"But what? How? You can't be..."

His laughter is almost hysterical. "Who knew? I didn't think it was possible either...**mate**!"

"Holy fuck!" I start laughing too – there's nothing else for it.

What the hell is going on? Two males as a soul-matched mated pair? Is that even possible? I mean, clearly it is, yes. But...what the ever loving...? What?

I roll into my mate and hold him tightly to me, nuzzling his cheeks, his neck, his hair, his forehead, anywhere I can reach, marking him with my scent. I can't help it. I have to. And it seems he has the urge too as he buries his head wherever he can. It smells like an apple pie in my room, and I love it.

"Mine," I snarl.

"Mine," he snarls right back.

Grabbing his face in my hands, I kiss him with all the emotions of my heart before telling him, "I honestly love you. This attraction between us, I'd felt it. But now I *feel* it. Does that make sense? Or am I crazy?"

"Only if I'm crazy as well. I love you too." He rubs his hand over his heart. "I feel it. I think maybe I always did but denied it, thinking it was impossible. However, there's a connection I can no longer deny. From the first moment I met you I felt...home."

"Holy fuck!"

I'm too exhausted to go anywhere. I can't move a muscle. Goddess bless him, Hassan drags a washcloth over my sticky body and his. Then collapses back down next to me, his back to my front again. This is why I love his slightly softer body – my hands wander over his torso, luxuriating in snuggly bliss.

I chuckle. "So, you're only bossy during?"

"Apparently so," he says with a shrug.

"You…you'd never topped before, had you?"

"No," he says with a sad sigh.

"Do me a favour?"

"What?"

"Never introduce me to your former clan."

"Why?"

"Because I'll rip their fucking heads off."

He shrugs as he sleepily replies, "You do what you have to do, *ya amar*."

I chuckle into his neck.

"Now, shh! I'm very tired," he mumbles.

Before long, my mate is nestled in my arms, snoring peacefully. His sleep purrs are the most gorgeous thing ever – he's safe, happy and content. With me. My mate!

Hassan's eyes flutter open. At some point, he'd rolled over to face me. And damn if it's not the best view first thing.

"Good morning," I whisper, planting a kiss on his full, peach lips.

"Good morning," he replies groggily, palming those sleepy green eyes.

Sweeping his hair back from his face, I tell him, "You really are the most stunning male I've ever encountered, you know that?"

He gives me a nervous laugh.

"I mean it."

His loving look turns me to mush. "Thank you. And, so you know, I feel the same way."

"Mmmm…you don't know how much I want to stay in bed with you all day."

"Oh, I think I do." Mischief glimmers in his eyes.

Still stroking his enticingly soft hair, I add, "But I have questions."

Twisting his mouth, he admits, "Me too."

"We shall seek them together. But first, my mate, I need to make sure you're fed."

He chuckles. "No, *ya amar*, I need to make sure you are."

My hand travels down his chest to his stomach as if I can rub away the growl. "I guess that works both ways."

We share a deep, loving kiss before trying to roll apart.

"Well, I do enjoy the taste of honey first thing," I quip.

"I cannot ask…"

"It wasn't a question, gorgeous."

He bites his lip but doesn't stop my head as it starts trailing kisses down his lithe, sculpted body. His abs may not be as deeply defined as mine, but my tongue still travels smoothly through his grooves.

"Mmm!" I moan.

I don't tease like he did. With just a quick lap of the dewdrop already glistening on his dark, peach tip, I sink my mouth over his dick. He's already so hard. For me. Mine. A deep rumble purrs through my chest as he gasps.

"*Ya amar,*" he groans.

If I were a betting man, I'd stake all I own on him never having received such pleasure before. Another first I get to give him. My chest swells.

"*Mine,*" I think at him.

"Yours. Mine," he whimpers as I draw my cheeks in to pull harder on my upward draw.

Slurping, sucking noises fill my den as I work him enthusiastically. I truly do love honey for morning meal, but when cinnamon's added…best treat ever. I add a hand to his base, rubbing in unison with my mouth.

His entire body quakes in response to me, making him writhe.

"*That's it, give yourself to me,*" I urge in his head with an image of what I'm doing.

His fists clutch the sheets as his hips buck. His motions grow more frantic as he grunts. His whole body clenches. Gripping my lips tighter, I hold on, ready for his release which soon spurts into my mouth. In response, my own climax shoots out.

"Fuuck," I cry out with the sudden surge.

We both draw ragged breaths.

Kissing my way back up to his face, I murmur, "Delicious."

"Mmmm…" he moans in a sated haze.

Wrapping my whole body around his, I hold him whilst he climbs back down from his high.

"I got you, mate."

"Hmmm…I should've known you meant more than friends the first time you called me that." He sniggers.

"I think part of me did know, it just didn't tell the rest of me."

His stomach growls again.

"Aww, honey, you've not eaten yet."

"As much as I'd like to return the favour—"

I kiss him. "Shh, *Habibi*. I meant actual food."

Biting his lip, a grin forms. Augh, can he look any more tantalising? His bashful ways will be my undoing. What am I saying? He's already undone me entirely.

Cleaning up, we get ready.

"This is sweet," he comments, holding up a framed photo of Pryderi, Arwyn and me.

"Yeah, Kiera gave me that as a birthday gift. Sort of contraband, being a modern technology thing, but, well, some rules can be bent when you're friends with the Peacekeeper."

He nods knowingly.

Once we're both dressed in clean clothes, we head towards the dining area. Hassan had another *cardigan* in his wardrobe which he happily put on, preening a bit in all honesty. I nudge his arm playfully as I notice him piling three rashers of bacon along with scrambled eggs onto his plate.

"I have to keep my strength up," he whispers, his eyes heated.

How is a male ever supposed to walk straight once he's got a mate? I'll have to ask Pryderi. Talking of, we head to the table where the happy couple is already seated, silly grins plastered across their faces.

"What?" I ask, feigning innocence.

I put Arwyn's plate down, but he's still not turned up yet. My heart stalls. I can't sense him nearby.

"Have a good night, did we?" Kiera asks.

Poor Hassan blushes wildly and tries to avoid answering by filling his mouth with food. He's too irresistible – I plant a swift kiss on his cheek.

I, having no such qualms, wink at my friends. "The best. Do you want details?"

Kiera holds up her hands. "Eww, no. Not at morning meal."

"Then don't ask," I say with another wink, shovelling food into my mouth.

Arwyn's food is getting cold. Where is he? I've finished eating in record time, even for me.

"Look, I was going to ask Arwyn to cover for me. But as he's a no-show, is there any chance..?"

"Why? Where are you going?" Pryderi asks.

"To find Cerys, actually."

He looks at me quizzically.

"You'll find her in the cottage," Kiera supplies.

"What? Why?" Pryderi questions, but winces.

"Shh, I'll tell you later," she whispers but not quietly enough.

My breath catches. "You knew, didn't you?" I accuse, glowering.

"I may have had an inkling," she replies, looking all too smug.

"I don't like being toyed with, Kiera," I snap, launching up from the table.

Grabbing Hassan's hand, I pull. "Come, Hassan."

He steels himself against me. "I am not a dog," he sneers.

Letting go of his hand, I wipe my forehead. "No, I know you're not. But please, I need to go. Now."

He shrugs towards our friends and follows as I walk off.

Raking my hands through my hair, I begin, "I'm sorry. I didn't mean—"

But he takes hold of my hand and squeezes. "It's OK. I understand. But please, do not take it out on me. I've been kept in the dark too."

"I'm sickened. How could she have known? And not tell me? We're supposed to be friends." My footsteps fall with greater speed with each stride.

"I don't know. I don't understand any of this," he replies, struggling to keep up.

I come to an abrupt halt. Running my fingers through my hair again and looking to the sky, I declare, "Neither do I."

He pulls me in for a hug, my chin resting against his cheek. We both sigh heavily.

Kissing his forehead, I suggest, "Come on, we won't find answers standing here. Let's get to Cerys."

He nods and falls into step alongside me as I deliberately slow the pace. Running is probably not encouraged in his clan either – he seems unused to so much as rapid walking.

"Brace yourself," I instruct as we reach the boundary line in silence.

"For what?"

"For this," I tell him, walking through.

We both shiver.

"Brrrr, what was that?"

"The magick barrier."

"We are outside your encampment?"

"Yes," I confirm with a nod, "We're not at home anymore."

His eyes widen.

I ruffle his hair. "Not to worry, honey. It's perfectly safe. There's a hidden trail to Cerys' cottage."

Bless, he tries to smile but Hassan clearly remains unsure. Holding his hand, I walk us further towards our destination, chattering over everything and nothing in the hopes it'll distract him.

"Down," I bawl, squatting behind a hedge.

He has no choice but to do the same as our hands are still firmly clasped together.

"What are we hiding from?" he silently asks.

"Car," I whisper.

A few seconds later, the said vehicle whooshes by on the other side of the hedge.

"Perfectly safe, eh?" he asks with a wry smile.

"Yes. As long as we take precautions."

Shaking his head, he picks his way along the path.

"Not much further," I singsong at him.

The hedges thin and then thicken again along our route. Finally, we come to Cerys' cottage on the outskirts of the village. It stands proudly on its own corner, guarded by conifers with no other houses in sight.

The scent of azaleas drifts along with that of bougainvillaea which now grows. Until recently, Cerys had been unable to grow the flowers of her true name, so azaleas had been planted as a substitute. My lip curls at the usually sweet fragrance as it puts me in mind of my traitorous friend, Kiera – it's her scent.

Checking the way is all clear, I pull us out from behind the hedges and cross the road, disappearing swiftly into the conifers. I know Cerys has alarm chimes in place, but I still bang on her door anyway, trying to vent some frustration.

"Alright, alright," the witch grumbles, opening her door.

"Cerys," I greet with a nod, striding in.

Holding out her arm, she says, "Come on in, why don't you?"

Plunging myself onto one of her soft sofas, my knee starts bouncing immediately. Hassan shrugs an apology to Cerys as he moves to join me.

"Tea, I think," she muses, walking to the kitchen.

"I have questions," I yell out.

There's a pause and the click of the kettle going on.

Poking her head around the corner, she answers, "I'm sure you do, but not until you're calmer, young Elan."

We clan members always know when she's enforcing her superiority when she puts 'young' in front of our names. I shrink into myself, planting my head in my hands, elbows balancing on my knees. I stare at the carpet with a huff.

My shoulders relax a little as Hassan rubs my back.

"My gratitude," I whisper.

"It'll be OK," he soothes in hushed tones.

Great! Now he's the one reassuring me? Aren't I supposed to be *his* guide? I couldn't feel any worse right now. He places a kiss on my ear. Twisting, I offer him a weak smile. OK, I can do this. Hassan is my mate. I'm OK with that. It's apparently possible. We just need to find out what that entails.

Chen comes into the room, his usual cheerful self. "Hello."

"Greetings," I reply automatically.

"My greetings, Chen. Sorry, we're a bit on edge," Hassan says.

"Ah."

"Come give me a hand with these mugs, Chen," Cerys calls from the kitchen.

Four steaming mugs of herbal tea get placed on the table between us as the other pair sit opposite.

"So —"

"Uh-huh! Sip first. Questions after," Cerys reminds me.

Rolling my eyes, I pick up a mug. It's already the perfect drinking temperature. I don't know why she bothers with a kettle – she only spells the water cooler anyway. She'd once told me it was a comforting habit when I asked.

"There. Alright now?" I ask through clenched teeth once I've gulped down my drink.

"Oh dear, you are in a state," she replies.

"Cerys, please," I urge, squinting at the ceiling.

"You'd think uniting with your mate would make you a lot happier."

"What?" My head jerks in her direction.

"That is what happened, is it not?"

"You knew too? Of course, you bloody did. Was the whole clan in on it? Let's have a good laugh at Elan. He's so stupid he won't know males can be soul-matched mated pairs. Oh, how funny."

"You're being hysterical," she points out, taking another sip of tea.

"Really? And this surprises you why? How did I not know? Why did nobody warn me?"

She shrugs. "I would've thought you of all people would've known."

"What's that supposed to mean? You know what? No. Forget it. I can't do this," I gripe, standing up, my hands gripping my head.

"Elan. Take a breath," she commands.

But even her authority can't keep me here. I run out into the garden.

Chapter 16 – Stay

– Hassan

My bum plants itself back on the sofa as Cerys commands me to, "STAY!"

I growl. "Why does everyone talk to me like a dog? I thought you were supposed to be better."

"Oh, Hassan, I was just trying to stop you chasing after that no-better-than-a-youngling-fool."

"That MALE is my MATE," I tell her, my lip curling.

"Alright. We all need to take a moment. Relax," Chen urges, hands drawing down through the air in front of him.

"With your forgiveness, I am not sure I can, Sir. I have a mate and he's male. Neither he nor I knew such a thing could happen. Yet, those Elan trusted most knew and have kept this from him. This I can expect and accept from my clan, but yours? No, it is too much. I must beg leave to check my mate is alright after such betrayal."

Chen continues to waft his hands. "I hear what you're saying. But truly, we did not realise he was unaware of the possibility."

I scowl at him.

"There are things that need to be said. Given his history, Cerys and I are both shocked at his obliviousness."

Cerys puffs out her cheeks as she blows out. "It would appear that poor elinefae has indeed been kept in the dark about many things. Things he should have learned of a long time ago. I'll have a word with him when he's ready to listen. Now is clearly not that time."

"I am free to go?"

I feel her ward being released. "Of course. But maybe you should remain here a moment? Elan has always been a hothead. It is best to let him simmer down on his own, I find."

I bite my lip as indecision tears at me. I do not wish to make him feel worse. But if anyone can soothe Elan, surely it's his mate?

"I'll make you some *jiānbǐng*," Chen coaxes.

"What is this, please?"

"Chinese pancakes, simply put."

"Normally, I'd be tempted..."

"But your mate is in distress."

"I can feel him," I say, rubbing my middle.

"Alright. Go and check on him. I wouldn't want to upset either of you more. But if he's either alright or too feisty, come back. You won't regret it."

His smile is so warm, I feel some of my tension ease. "I thank you."

Getting up, I exit out the same door Elan had. Following the invisible rope between us, I feel his turmoil all the more as I get closer. He's at the far end of the garden, behind some trees, chopping logs.

I watch a moment, admiring his muscles as each contracts, readying to make a blow. Sweat is already making his skin glisten in the early morning light. It's like looking upon a dream.

"Are you alright?" I quietly ask, drawing cautiously closer – the male has an axe in his hand.

"Yes. No. I don't know." He throws the axe into some timber and leaves it there.

"Want to talk?"

His hands wash over his face. "I don't think I can at the moment, gorgeous. I'm not mad at you, though. You know that, right?"

I nod. "Just everyone else."

He snickers. "That about covers it. These are my people. My friends."

"In all fairness, Cerys and Chen seem genuinely surprised at your...unawareness." I stop myself from saying ignorance – that seems to place the blame on him which is entirely unfair.

"They do?"

"Cerys says she would like to talk with you when you are receptive. She understands now is not the best time. But she is more than willing to tell you things you supposedly should have been told of."

He winces. "Sounds ominous."

"Tssaryar! Think of it as enlightening."

Scrubbing his face, he moans, "I'm so confused."

"I know, *ya amar*, I know. But you have me now. Is that so bad?"

"I'd be lying if I said it was."

"How hard are you going to make me work? Come here, you ball of fluff."

"Ball of fluff?" He half-laughs, but steps closer.

Wrapping him in my arms at last, I whisper, "Yes, you're very fluffy."

"This coming from a male with fur on his face, chest and legs?"

"Aww, not physically. You have fluff in your head, I think."

He slaps my back, not breaking away from my embrace. "Now you're calling me stupid too?"

"No, *Habibi*. It just stops you from listening sometimes."

He chuckles, the reverberations travelling through my entire being.

"That is a better noise," I tell him.

"I can think of better ones you can bring out."

"Now, Elan?"

He laughs. "Maybe not right now."

"Good, because Chen wants to cook me some pancakes. Come with me?"

He shakes his head. "Not even for *jiānbǐng*. But I imagine you want to try them?"

"I can wait."

He sighs. "Come, let me quickly check something."

He guides me back into the house.

Ignoring Cerys, he asks, "Chen, can you see he gets home safely if Hassan stays for your tasty food?"

"Of course. Will you not stay, though?"

Elan shakes his head. "I need to be on my own, I think."

"I understand," he says, bowing his head.

"My gratitude."

Turning to me, he checks, "You alright here on your own?"

I nod.

"OK. I'll see you later then." With a quick kiss, he leaves.

My heart is aching for him. But my mind is whirling. Maybe it is best to distance ourselves to stop the emotion exchange which seems to be ping-ponging between us. Maybe then I can think more clearly.

Ignoring the ache from our separation, I turn my attention to Chen. "So, what are these pancakes?"

"*Jiānbǐng*. Pronounced jeeyan-bing," he repeats more slowly.

"Show me?"

"My pleasure."

"I'll be off to the shop then, shall I?" Cerys interjects.

"Uh, if that's alright, dearest light of my life?"

She scowls but breaks into a grin. "Oooh, you! Well, I suppose it's in the name of a good cause. See you later, Hassan, dear."

"Shop?" I ask Chen once she's gone.

"It helps integrate with the locals a bit and makes some money so we can buy in goods for the clan. It's a metaphysical store."

I cock my head.

"Err, it sells items of a mystical nature like crystals, runes and tarot cards."

"Ah, I understand."

"Let's get these *jiānbǐng* started. I know you're going to love them."

He makes a batter and slices some spring onions. After frying wonton wrappers, an egg gets cracked onto the frying crepe, then some black sesame seeds and the spring onions. It all gets flipped and then spread with bean pastes.

"The humans add coriander, but elinefae don't like that herb much as it tastes like soap to you lot," he tells me as he adds the crispy crackers and folds the pancake into layers.

My mouth is watering at the aroma rising from the pan.

Turning it all out on a plate, Chen offers it out, "Try this."

"Oh, my goddess," I mumble around soft and chewy yet crispy deliciousness. "I have to make these for clan."

"I was hoping you'd say that. I've not had a chance to talk with any of the cooks yet, but all the elinefae who come here love these. You can add different fillings. It doesn't have to be only a morning meal dish."

"Thank you so much."

Chen is busy making a *jiānbǐng* for himself but smiles across at me. "You are most welcome. I bet you feel a bit better too. Am I right?"

I peer at him. "Did you enchant this?"

"Ha, no. They bring comfort all on their own. Would you like more tea?"

"Yes, please. I think I would like that very much."

There is something about this witch which calms me. He is so open and friendly.

Once we are seated and sipping our drinks, I venture, "Chen. You are from a different clan outside Great Britain?"

"Yes. China."

"Is it very different where you are from?"

"Ah! Hmm, well, not really. Except for the food. But then maybe Cerys rubbed off on me in my youth? I don't know. I think we've always tried to keep our traditions."

My lips pull into a tight line.

"Are you asking if there are others like yours?" he queries.

"Yes, I suppose I am."

"I have not pried. But from the little I have heard, yours seem to be more integrated with humans than any other I know."

"I see."

"I say this without judgement. It is not necessarily a bad thing."

"It is."

He looks worried. "It is?"

"We seem more governed by humans than our own kind. I see that now. Here, it feels right. Back there, we have to hide too much of ourselves, I think."

He puts a hand on mine. "Thank you for sharing that. I see you, Hassan."

"It is not easy to openly criticise what I have always known. But I fear there is harm being done to us."

"I hear you. We, that is, Cerys, Kiera and I have already sensed as much. It was her concern for your welfare that made her request your stay with us."

"It was?"

"Mm-hmm. I think she was surprised at how easily they granted her request. Know that she never intended to infer anything by her method. You weren't part of the deal. Having noticed your distress, she pitched the idea of you experiencing life here. She only wanted you to have an opportunity to escape so you could find happiness. Although, I suspect she sensed something of your potential match. Kiera is highly intuitive."

"It would have been nice to have been informed."

"I agree. But she must have had her reasons."

"I suppose. But maybe it is best not to talk too much about that. I was just beginning to feel happy."

"Why so upset, though?"

"Apart from the deceit and betrayal?"

"Harsh words, Hassan."

"Maybe. But they are what Elan feels. And to some extent, so do I."

"I appreciate single-sex soul-matched pairs are not commonplace."

"Try unheard of."

He baulks. "None?"

"Not in a country where homosexuality is illegal. It is punishable by death."

"Ah. Hmph, too governed by humans. I see. But I wonder…no. That avenue is to be explored later. But even Elan was unaware. There haven't been any such pairings here for a while, I understand, but…perhaps it is best not to explore that at the moment either. If you reach out, can you sense Elan?"

Closing my eyes, I try to tap into that invisible thread between us. It's faint. "Unsettled."

"Let us get you back to him. Newly formed mates shouldn't be apart for too long."

We wander into the garden where there is a small pond at the side of the house. Chen whistles, and a familiar red nose surfaces.

"Hello, Shui, Sir," I greet as the dragon comes onto land.

He chirrups, so I stroke his head.

"He told me you had already met."

"He did, huh?" I ask, peering at my little friend.

I swear he smiles. I step back as he starts to grow bigger.

"Woah," I exclaim.

"Ready for a flight?"

"On Shui?"

"Yes. He says he'd be happy to."

"Err...alright?"

Chen chuckles. Shui goes down on his haunches.

"Up here, like this," Chen says, climbing onto a leg and then up onto Shui's neck. "Get up behind me and hold tight. It's an odd sensation until you get used to it."

I do as instructed. I can't stop my scream as Shui launches into the air.

"I did try to warn you," Chen says.

I cling around Chen's waist as tightly as possible as we climb higher into the sky with weird snake-like movements. The air around us seems to pop.

"That's the realm shift," Chen shouts over the noise of the wind.

"Uh-huh!"

Forcing my eyes open, I marvel at the luscious green landscape below as we pop back, presumably to our realm a few minutes later. Dizziness makes my head swim as we spiral down to the ground and land with a thump in a clearing. I'm not entirely certain my food will stay down as we come to a bumpy stop.

Chen slides down Shui's side, so I copy him.

"Thank you, Sir," I say to Shui, patting his massive leg, not entirely sure I'm all that grateful.

"Don't worry. You'll feel fine again in a couple of minutes," Chen assures me.

He stays with me whilst the world stops spinning too fast. Once I'm feeling better, Chen grabs my shoulders and gradually turns me. "That way," he says.

"My gratitude."

"It will get easier if and when you want to try again."

I smile as I watch Chen climb back onto his familiar. It's certainly quicker than walking. I watch as the pair ascend into the sky and vanish. Huh, so that's what it looks like. No wonder it was so disorienting.

The sun shimmers through the trees as I head towards the encampment. Taking my time, I revel in the warmth and the serenity emanating from the ancient trees around me. Reaching out across our link, I can sense where Elan is and head in that direction.

"Well, someone's feeling better," he says as I approach, not even looking behind him.

"Hm, that's going to take some getting used to."

"Cool though, right?" Oh, I missed that mischievous grin.

"You're happier too," I note, pulling him towards me.

"All the better for being with you," he says, nuzzling my cheek.

"Shui flew me home. I think I need to go and lie down."

"Say no more," he replies, wiggling his eyebrows.

"You are insatiable."

"Don't pretend like you're not."

"Ha, maybe. But please, I do need to wait a minute. That flight was something else."

"Pryderi told me it's bewildering."

"You've not flown yourself?"

"No. No, thank you."

I laugh. "I didn't think my mate was a wimp."

His lip curls, but his eyes give him away. "Watch who you call wimp."

"Wimp!" I challenge, staring him down but grinning.

"Tease!"

"Oh, you know I am."

The gleam in his eye sends flames through me. I wonder if I can feel better in the time it takes us to get back to my den. Or his. I'm not fussy.

It turns out to be his. We've still not got inside but he's pinned me against his door, our hands and mouths exploring every available inch. I'm breathless and almost fall backwards as he opens the door.

<u>Chapter 17 –Discussion</u>
~ Arwyn

"Holy goddess, can't you give it a rest?" I moan.

Elan growls at me where I'm sitting on his bed. "Not a good time, Brother."

Standing at my full height, I demand, "Now is exactly the time. Elan. A word. Alone."

I move towards his door. They both stare at me.

"Later," Elan tries to delay, holding onto his mate with one arm.

I growl. "No. Outside. NOW," I command, shoving him away from Hassan.

"Don't push me, Arwyn."

"Don't deny me. Not now."

"You should go," Hassan timidly suggests.

"For fuck's sake. Fine," Elan grumbles but follows me out.

My fury builds as I take us to the edge of the forest, away from prying ears.

"So, are you going to tell me what the hell is so important you'd pull me away from my mate?" Elan says through clenched teeth, his fists balled.

"How could you do this?"

"Do what?"

"Don't play dumb. You're not thick. Mate with Hassan, if I really must spell it out."

"In case you hadn't noticed, I didn't exactly have a choice. I'm just as shocked as you are."

"Sure."

"Can't you just be happy for me?"

"No. I can't. Not about this," I confess, tearing my pained gaze away from him.

"What…what are you saying?"

My heart is thundering in my ribcage. "I…argh, what's the use?"

He shoves my chest. "No. You cannot back down now. I won't let you. Say it."

Raising my head, I meet his stare. "You know."

"Say the words, Arwyn."

"Brother…Elan…I…"

"SAY IT!"

"I love you. I want to claim you as my own. If you were to claim a male it should've been me. Have I not waited my entire life for you? What did I do wrong?"

"Do you not think I've thought about that all day? That I've not been questioning why him and not you? I love you too."

My breath is caught in my throat, and I'm frozen to the spot. Those precious words linger between us. How long have I waited to hear them? And now here they are. And I have no fucking clue what to say.

Elan and I stare at one another. His look begs me to say something, anything.

With fury firing from his eyes, he's the first to break the silence. "And you thought you'd tell me this now? NOW? Fuck you, Arwyn. How long have you known? How many years have you had to declare this?"

"Right back at you."

But the wind just got taken out of me? How long have I had feelings towards my clan brother? Worked and played by his side, hiding my truth.

"I'm a coward," I declare, shoulders slumping, my head turned towards the ground I wish would swallow me up.

A hand cups my cheek, bringing my face back up, but I can't look at him. "No, Arwyn. No. You are the bravest male I have ever met."

I snort.

"Look at me," he commands.

I obey.

"Truly. You are no more a coward than I. We were oath sworn never to get involved. It is only honour which has held my tongue, as apparently, it has yours."

I close my eyes, drawing in a deep breath. My eyes turn heavenwards as if the goddess herself will come to my aid.

Firm arms wrap around my shoulders, drawing me near. Oh sweet, torturous body contact. How many times have we held one another like this? How many times have I silently urged him to bring me to this place?

I melt into his embrace, finally sinking into the meaningful hug I have craved for far too long. A tear trickles down my cheek which nestles against his neck.

Another tear breaks free, no longer contained by the dam I had carefully built. And another. Before I know it, my entire reserves burst forth, making my body convulse as I unleash the full force of my pent-up frustration. Sobs wrack my chest and shoulders.

Heaving for breath, I barely notice hands rubbing up and down my shoulders. But once I do, I cry all the harder. Elan is my rock as always, providing a safe haven for my meltdown.

Drawing a ragged breath, I try to stop the flow. "I love you," I finally manage to whisper.

Only then do I notice Elan's shoulders shaking.

Pulling my head back far enough to look at my lifelong friend, I whisper, "Babe." And clutch him to me once again.

Time stands still as we console one another through this…grief. I cry for the lost years, for the bad timing of this declaration, for the love I have already lost.

His lusciously dark pink, lips are suddenly, finally on mine, smashing against me in the most heated, passionate kiss of my life. Having needed this for so long, I give into it. Our hands are everywhere, holding on for the anchor we sorely need.

Feeling his bulge through our trousers, my lust fires up all the hotter. Shoving Elan against a tree, I rub my groin to his, needing to get more.

I feel a burst of utter fury, and my body is pulled away with such force, it must be a dragon at my back.

"GET OFF MY MATE!" Hassan yells like a banshee.

"FUCK YOU. HE WAS MINE BEFORE HE WAS YOURS," I yell, shoving his shoulders, my teeth elongated to match his.

His claws descend as he slices across my cheek. "MINE!"

I match his blow, drawing a trail of blood across that all too pretty face.

Elan does the unthinkable and punches me, right across the jaw. I see stars!

"What the fuck?" On instinct, I strike back.

I'm not even sure who's hitting who in the flurry of fists, feet and snarls.

"YOU WILL STOP THIS!" a female voice screams into the fray.

Damn Kiera, but my entire body is frozen still. But so are the others, I notice. All three of us stand panting, bloodied and bruised.

"CERYS!" she calls.

Oooh, we're in trouble. Our Peacekeeper just magickally pulled our witch to her.

"What in the goddess' name did you do that for?" Cerys grumbles.

Pointing with her open palm, Kiera tells her, "This!"

"And what am I supposed to do with this?"

"Look at them, Cerys. They were fighting."

"Pah! Have you gone soft? I'd barely call it a scrap."

"A SCRAP?"

"Do you *see* any broken bones or gaping wounds?"

"Well, no."

"That's right, dear. The bleeding's stopped already. Honestly, I was in my shop. What if someone had seen me just vanish into thin air? And for what? A catfight?"

"But…"

"I'm disappointed, Kiera. I thought you had learned more of elinefae ways than to panic at such trivialities."

I stifle a snicker. Elan's in my eye line and looks like he'll wet himself with the effort of not laughing. Hassan seems stunned. We're all still frozen in our stance. I cough.

"I hate to disturb a good dressing down, but would someone be good enough to release us?" I ask.

"Only if you promise not to start beating the crap out of each other the moment I do. I don't care what Cerys says, this amount of damage is not what should happen between—"

"You three," Cerys finishes off.

Kiera waves off her spell, and we all sag in relief.

"Now," Cerys says, "Will you boys require any of my healing for your owies, or are you alright to lick one another's wounds?"

My head shoots in her direction at the same time as Elan and Hassan's do.

"How can you be so insulting?" Hassan asks, "And will someone tell *him* to stay the hell away from my mate?" He points his thumb in my direction.

"You sure you want me to do that?" Cerys quizzes.

"What are you talking about, witch?" I sneer. Now is not the time for her games.

Rolling her eyes and sighing, she gives in. "Oh, very well."

She approaches Elan and pinches his earpoint.

"Ow!" he complains as she uses it to pull him away.

"Don't be such a youngling. You, sit there," she orders.

"You, over there," she directs me.

I do as instructed, eager to avoid her gruff ear-pulling.

"Hassan, just sit where you are, dumpling."

He frowns but also complies, glowering at me from a safer distance.

A log hovers from among the forest to behind her feet. She sits on it.

"Kiera, won't you join me?" she asks, patting the space next to her.

"Right, are we all sitting comfortably?" she asks, sarcasm lacing every word.

"Start talking," I demand.

"Then let me begin. Sometimes people love each other very much."

"Cerys, make sense or I'm leaving," Elan interrupts.

"Sometimes, those people are of the same sex," she continues in a slow, deliberate, frankly patronising tone.

"We've worked out that much, thanks for not warning us," Elan says.

"Really, dear, do shut up and listen. Those who behave like younglings get treated like them. This seems to be the only way you will hear what I have to say."

"Do not blame us for not knowing that which was deliberately kept from us. We are grown males, and it's about time people started treating us as such," I tell her.

"Fine. But it's more palatable my way," she continues in her normal voice, "Where was I? Right, so you know that same-sex soul-matched mates are a thing."

"Apparently," we chime in unison.

"But there can be no babies. How can they be considered mates?" I ask.

"Wait. I can't become pregnant, can I? Shit! I'm not going to grow some sort of birthing pouch, am I?" Hassan asks.

The poor guy is visibly sweating.

"No, Hassan, you're not," Cerys assuages.

All three of us puff out a relieved breath. That sounds painful.

Cerys looks to the heavens before continuing, "Mates are not always about procreation. However, there are options. But I think that's a whole other conversation. We have more pressing matters at hand."

I nod.

"Nor is it always pairs."

I'm pretty sure we all peer at her inquisitively.

"Yes, well, there are triads. That's three people," she adds, reverting to her patronising ways.

"Three?" I check.

"Yeees, three. That's right. Have a cookie. Oh wait, I don't have any."

Elan, Hassan and I look from one to the other, confused.

"One, two, three," she counts, pointing at each of us.

Seriously, how frustrating can she be?

Fortunately, she turns serious again. "Although, there hasn't been a triad here since...well, your parents, Elan."

"Wait. What?" he asks, aghast.

"Yes, we come to why I was surprised you didn't know about any of this. I suppose it makes sense. Poor Elwyn."

"Elwyn. As in my father's friend, Elwyn?"

Making air quotes, Cerys confirms, "Friend."

"Well, I did hear they'd shagged after my parents mated. I thought it was weird."

"Yes, it would have been. Elan, dear, your father, mother and Elwyn were a triad."

"But...but he didn't live with us."

"No, dear, he didn't. It's all very sad. He insisted that your parents must be the true match. He too put the importance of breeding at the pinnacle of such things. But that's not the case. Not naturally. To be fair, procreation rose in importance after the Time of Battles when so many elinefae were killed. Maybe we all lost sight of the other aspects."

She stops to go over and hold Elan's hand. "I know this comes as a shock to you. For that, I'm sorry. If I'd only known..."

"No. They argued. Cerys, he tore my parents apart. And where was he when we needed him? He ran off when my father was killed."

"No, he didn't, dear. Elwyn, like most mates, passed into spirit when his soul-match died."

"But...that's the reason Arwyn and I stayed platonic. My father and Elwyn...their sexual encounters poisoned their friendship and ultimately ended with my parents' death."

I can't bear the look of agony on his face. I go over and hold him at the same time Hassan does. Shuffling, we take a side each, both of us holding...our mate, I suppose, together.

"All this time," he mutters.

"Oh, Elan, love. Is that what was stopping you? Oh, you poor fool youngling," Cerys croons, rubbing the hand she's not let go of.

Kiera adds her hug from Elan's back, holding all three of us males. "That's awful."

"Understatement," Elan replies, shaking his head.

"Fuck," I murmur.

"Not now, eh?" he says with a half-laugh.

"Always the joker."

"Arwyn, I'm so sorry. I fucked things up between us for nothing."

Squeezing him tighter, I correct, "No, baby, no. Delayed. And it seems we needed to wait for this one anyway." I look across at Hassan.

We break apart from the group hug, but none of us goes far.

"The power of suggestion is great, but the power of denial is equal if not stronger," Cerys states, "Besides, you're correct, Arwyn."

"I am?"

"You have always been a three, you, Elan and Pryderi. Only, Pryderi wasn't your third in the triad sense. When he found his mate, I think it triggered your need for that connection. It had been hidden in friendship until then."

"Aye, I see the truth in that."

"And when Kiera, a member of our clan made contact with that third mate, I'm guessing you two felt the beginnings of that connection."

Rubbing my stomach, I confirm, "Yes." Looking at Elan, I add, "We've been sort of antsy since…Kiera went away. Shit!"

Cerys nods, smiling kindly. "Nothing was certain until you met. And then, well, sex does tend to cement the bond."

Hassan laughs hysterically.

"Hey, honey, hey. You OK?" Elan checks.

But Hassan can barely breathe let alone reply. I look to Kiera and Cerys for help.

Bending down in front of him, Kiera waves her hands in an arc then rubs his upper arm. "Hey, Hassan. Just breathe for me, OK?"

He draws in a shuddering breath.

"Good boy. And another. Come on. Phhhwwww…" she instructs, breathing in herself.

Wiping tears away from his eyes, he manages to say, "Sorry. But just this morning, I was shocked to my core that I have a male mate. But now it appears I have two. Oh, my goddess, they'd never believe this in my old clan."

"No, I don't suppose they would," Elan admits, chuckling.

"Well, it is kind of funny," I admit.

Instead of stopping Hassan's hysteria, we all fall into uncontrolled laughter.

"Holy fuck," Elan exclaims. After pondering a moment, he looks at me and adds, "But I'm sort of relieved. It explains the overwhelming emotions I've been experiencing. I was a bit confused for a while there."

Stroking his cheek, I admit, "Me too, babe."

"Hmmm...this could be fun," Hassan muses.

"Mmm...very. But right now, I think Elan and I are overdue."

But Elan shakes his head, making my stomach clench. "I don't want him to feel left out."

"I can work with that."

Hassan graciously concedes, "No, please. You should be together. It's OK. Truly. I understand. You deserve this moment."

Kicking my chin up at him, I reply, "You're not going to be trouble, are you, little mate? I believe this one just told us what he wants. It'd be rude to ignore him."

"Well, I would not like to be rude," he says, leaning in to kiss my cheek.

But I turn my face so his lips meet mine. It's a tentative brushing of mouths as we seek the truth of this crazy day. For my part, I like it – there is a rightness to us.

"Well, that will be my cue to leave. Do attempt to get to a den...oh blast!" And off Kiera goes, Cerys following.

Chapter 18 – Exploration
~ Elan

Curiously, there isn't a shred of jealousy as I watch Arwyn kiss Hassan. They're both being very careful with one another. Hardly surprising after our scrap, I suppose. Part of me is getting turned on whilst another is trying to wrap my head around everything that just happened.

Two pairs of eyes are staring at me.

"You alright, Elan?" Arwyn asks first.

"Yes. I think so," I tell him with a shrug.

"Aww, you want one too?"

Before I can reply, his mouth is on mine. What was I thinking? All thoughts seem to have flown away as I'm engulfed by…holy goddess, by Arwyn kissing me. It's Arwyn. My friend.

"Disappointed?" he checks as I back off.

The hurt in his eyes makes me want to kiss him back, but instead, I tell him, "Of course not. My head took over. I mean, after all these years, here we were…playing tonsil tennis."

"Well, there is only one thing to do in such circumstances," Hassan interjects.

We both look at him.

"Fuck, of course." He's grinning like the cat who got the cream.

"And this is your deep, insightful input, is it?" I enquire.

"It's not a bad idea," Arwyn adds, pulling me to a stand and rubbing his body against mine.

"Well, if you insist."

All three of us jog back towards the dens, our bodies already mostly healed. Reaching Arwyn's first, that's the one we pile into. Hassan pushes on our shoulders, encouraging Arwyn and me down onto our knees once we've all torn our clothes off.

"Oooh, I like this angle," I comment, wiggling my eyebrows – Hassan's dick is invitingly close, making me lick my lips.

"No, *ya amar*. Today, you only have eyes for Arwyn."

It's on the tip of my tongue to argue the point, but I think better of it. Hassan guides my hands to Arwyn's shoulders.

"Look," he whispers, "Look into the eyes of your mate."

I try but have to look away.

He bends down and pecks my lips. "Try again, Elan."

His hand tenderly pushes my head back towards Arwyn. "Just look."

This time, I gaze deep into those pale blue eyes. The ones I've known for an eternity but always avoided close inspection of. Now, I see and feel the love coming back to me. And the longing.

"Good. Now, hold hands," Hassan commands.

"Bossy, this one, isn't he?" Arwyn remarks, chuckling.

"Ooh, you'll find out and some," I inform him.

"Mmm…we'll see."

Our fingers interlock either side of us.

"Breathe each other in," Arwyn instructs further.

I can't resist. The need has revved up and is taking control. Hungrily, I mash my mouth to his. Our hands part only to move up and down each other's backs. His dick is so ready. Wait. Who goes where?

I must have stopped kissing as Hassan's hand is on the back of my head, coaxing it back to where it should be.

"No overthinking, *Habibi*."

Wait. Whose hand..? Hassan. Oh, my goddess, Hassan has his hand around my dick and Arwyn's, joining them together. It feels too good to ask 'what the hell?' My shaft gets stroked up and down, grinding against Arwyn's. Holy fuck!

Our kiss ignites to a whole new level. Arwyn seems as frantic as me to get more purchase.

"On your back, Elan. Let him in," Hassan encourages.

I eagerly comply.

"Aaaaauuugh!" Arwyn and I cry out in unison as he glides in all the way home.

Without taking his eyes off me, Arwyn pumps in and out. And nothing ever felt so right in my life. Grabbing his butt, I pull him, spurring us both on. He's rock hard as he surges over my sweet spot, striking it exactly how I need. As my moans grow louder, he goes faster.

"More," I yelp. There will never be enough of Arwyn.

Fiery friction builds, all my muscles flex-rigid. My hands grab on anywhere they can, using Arwyn as my anchor.

"Can't…hold…back," Arwyn chokes out.

"Then don't," I tell him between gasps.

A few more thrusts and Arwyn launches forwards and down, his teeth piercing my shoulder. He comes, filling me with his seed and scent of orangey clove. He is all over and in me. My very soul shatters, only to merge back with his like a million stars in the night sky pouring into a moon. As soon as his teeth are released, mine sink into his taut trapezius. My orgasm rips through me, spilling between us.

"You're delicious," Arwyn comments, pulling back to lick my sticky stomach.

A towel gets chucked between us.

"You're both hot," Hassan murmurs, looking down at the towel on his own groin.

"Like that, did you?" Arwyn asks with a wink, wiping us both down.

Pinching his forefinger and thumb together, he answers, "Just a little bit."

Arwyn gets up and walks over and holds him close. "Dirty boy!"

"Mmm…if that is dirty, may I never be clean."

"Thank you," Arwyn tells him, kissing his cheek.

"You are very welcome. I am pleased to have been of assistance. I will see you at morning meal."

But I jump in front of the door as Arwyn pulls on his hand. "And where do you think you're going, sweetheart?"

"My den. We will not all fit on your mattress, Arwyn. And you two should have some time alone. I think it must be more shocking for you two, discovering you are mates."

Wrapping him up in his arms, Arwyn tells him, "You really are a cutie, aren't you? But, in case you have forgotten already, you too are my mate. Apparently, I am a greedy greedy male."

He laughs. "Me too. But I think we are all done for the night."

"Hmph! Not everything is about sex, Hassan."

Turning to me, Arwyn says, "Elan, make sure our mate doesn't leave. Use any means necessary. I will be right back."

"Any means necessary, eh?" I check, pinning Hassan to a wall with my body as soon as he's released from Arwyn's hold.

He simply chuckles and nuzzles my neck. Arwyn makes his escape.

"In the romance books Kiera lends me, I think they would call you a cinnamon roll," I note.

Hassan laughs. "Sounds appropriate."

"Ha, so it does. Hmm...smells like cinnamon, tastes like cinnamon," I confirm, licking his neck, "Yes, must be a cinnamon roll."

"What does that mean? I presume not the pastry."

"Ooh, do you know how to make them?"

"Of course. But stop avoiding the question."

"Well, it means someone very sweet." I kiss his cheek. "And innocent." His other cheek gets kissed. "And kind." I peck his lips. "And deserves better than the bad things that have happened to him."

He stares at me. "Truly?"

"Mm-hmm. Truly."

"I don't believe."

I mock gasp. "You question my honesty? It's true. You can ask Kiera. But maybe not right now."

A scraping, sliding noise interrupts our cuddling.

"Where did you get a spare mattress from, might I ask?"

"Oh, Elan, it's yours, of course."

"What?"

He lets it fall to the floor with a bang and drags the bedsheet off his shoulder, dumping that on top. Then drags his mattress and covers off the bed and plonks them next to it.

Shrugging, he tells us, "Hassan was right. These beds can barely fit two."

"And you'd know this how?"

"So, I've heard."

"Uh-huh."

"Anyway, now we can all stay close together. For warmth."

"Oh yes, for warmth. It's so cold in here." I fake shiver.

He play-punches my shoulder.

"Thank you."

"All three together, right?"

We stand together in a three-way hug, rubbing cheeks and purring. Switching the lights off, I head to the pile.

"Oh, from blue to orange," Hassan comments.

"Aye. Which is funny as your eyes glow blue," Arwyn replies.

"Must be fate."

"Mmm…must be."

I don't know if it's some sort of pecking order or natural height selection, but Hassan lies down at the front. I happily snuggle up behind him. With Arwyn at my rear. We let out a joint sigh of contentment. Arwyn kisses my ear. And I pay it forward. Holding my hand up, Hassan kisses that.

At long last, there is a wholeness. The missing pieces have all slotted into place. I feel complete.

Waking up, the opposite is true. My arms are cold and empty.

"Hassan?" I call into the darkness, my eyes adjusting.

"Shh! Don't panic. It's OK, babe."

"Arwyn?"

"You were expecting Pryderi, maybe?" he jokes, squeezing my middle.

"Arse!"

"Was that a request?"

"Oh, my goddess, you're going to be insatiable."

"I have many years to make up for."

But the panic still hasn't vanished. "Where is he?"

"Our resident sweetie has gone to get us some food."

"Aww. He didn't have to do that."

I feel Arwyn's shrug. "I think he did. Must be a mate thing."

He nuzzles my neck.

"Mmmm…I could get used to this."

"I have every intention of never waking up any other way."

"How does this work? Can we have a quickie whilst we wait for Hassan? It doesn't feel right."

"Relax. I had no intention of fucking you alone. Not yet, at least. Can a male not just enjoy a cuddle?"

Running a hand down my face, I moan, "I have so many questions."

"Huh, and I thought I was supposed to be the thinker. Aren't you supposed to be the fun one? Come on, do something funny." He jostles me.

"Stop it! Arwyn. I mean it," I gripe, rolling away.

The noise of the door opening cuts off my snarl.

"I leave you two alone for the briefest of moments, and already you're bickering," Hassan comments, rolling his eyes.

"Ha, not really. Arwyn's just teasing me before I've eaten."

"Foolish mate."

"Are you two ganging up on me?" Arwyn asks, hand on his chest.

Nudging that hand away with my nose, I murmur, "Would you like us to?"

"Maybe after you've been fed, oh *hangry* one."

"*Hangry*?" Hassan asks, putting a plateful of bacon sandwiches on the floor.

"Kiera word. It is a mixture of *hungry* and *angry*," I tell him then translate those two words into Eline.

"Uh. I think I get this too," he admits.

"Then eat," Arwyn suggests, shoving a sandwich into his mouth.

Hassan pours coffee from a flask into three cups.

"Organised. I like," Arwyn admires.

"Yes. We definitely appreciate someone with some sense," I tell him with a wink.

My head gets a soft whack from Arwyn. "Cheeky!"

"Tell me it's not true."

"Fine. But still…"

Hassan sits grinning at us around his food.

"What?" I ask.

"Nothing. It's just nice."

"What, sweetie?" Arwyn asks, pulling him into his side and kissing his nose.

"You two. You joke all the time. But it is how you show love, I think."

"Of course. We never mean anything by it."

"No, not nothing. Love."

"Huh!"

"Huh," I echo.

Arwyn and I have always shared banter. But maybe it did always have a deeper meaning behind it. We don't tease Pryderi half as much. Our mate is very observant. Is that a good thing? I feel seen. And maybe bare.

Our pilfered meal finished, I crawl towards Hassan who is still sat under Arwyn's arm.

Licking my lips, I comment, "Mmm…I need something sweet after that salty snack."

Arwyn holds Hassan's arms as I remove his trousers. His dick springs free, gloriously dark peach and hard already.

"Unless, Arwyn, you're feeling peckish?" I ask.

"Now that you mention it, I am a bit."

Hassan wiggles, but I think it's more in anticipation than trying to run away.

"Or do you have any objection? Or preference, come to think of it?" I check with him.

Our cinnamon roll just shrugs and replies, "Whatever makes you happy."

"Oooh, but this morning is all about making you happy, sweetheart," Arwyn croons, repositioning himself.

"Really?"

"Mm hm, really."

"If this is the case, Elan needs to be here too."

I raise an eyebrow at him but kneel down to kiss him. "What do you want, gorgeous?"

He bites his lip before quietly telling me, "Your cock in my mouth, please. But I need you both."

"Like a daisy chain, honey?"

"I do not know what that is."

"Let me show you."

Lying down, I position myself so Hassan can get his request granted, and also so that Arwyn's dick is within my reach. We form more of a triangle than a circle.

"Ooh, that's creative," Arwyn comments, curling round so he can reach Hassan.

"Augh! Yes, like that." Hassan gasps as Arwyn's mouth descends.

"I like how furry you are."

"That's nice," Hassan replies to him in a daze.

Before I can enjoy the view too much, Hassan licks my tip. Oh yeah, I'm supposed to be doing something here too. I copy every lick and suck performed on me, applying them to Arwyn.

I soon lose track, though. The dual sensation would be heady enough, but when my mates' emotions flood our link and I see Arwyn's head bobbing up and down Hassan's dick…I'm lost. I float away until sensations fill me entirely. I'm sucking and being sucked until I don't know which is which.

Darkness fills my mind as my eyes close. Everything becomes one as my balls tighten and buttocks clench. Blood thunders through my ears as heartbeats echo. Moans bounce between us. Flames lick up my core, consuming every inch of me. I am filled with fire…until I burst. As Hassan greedily holds onto my dick, my mouth is filled by Arwyn.

"Fuck, that was intense," Arwyn cries, collapsing onto his stomach.

Dragging his way over to me, Hassan whispers croakily, "Show me what he tastes like." And kisses me deeply, his tongue delving in.

Licking his lips, he groans, "Mmmm…!"

"You do realise you've just added my vanilla to his orange, right?"

His half-lidded eyes still manage to glimmer. "Uh-huh. Yummy. Apple, vanilla, orange and clove."

"Nnnaaaugh," Arwyn groans.

"Aww, you missing out?" I tease, crawling up his body and licking his tongue with mine.

"Mmm...honey and cinnamon add the perfect finish," I tell them.

"It's like an apple pie at Yule," Arwyn mumbles.

"Sounds like something I'll have to make," Hassan comments, snuggling up to my back.

"I think you already did."

We all chuckle before falling silent. If I could freeze time, this is the moment I'd choose. Utterly satisfied, I could happily live like this forever.

Eventually, Arwyn breaks the silence whilst stroking my hair. "Is it weird?"

"No, your dick is wonderful, darling," I tease.

"Phh! No, this. Us. It's not like I've slept with many females. But I have two mates and they're *both* male."

"Is that a complaint?"

"Yeah, are we not good enough, Arwyn?" Hassan asks, leaning over us.

"Of course, you are. I couldn't be happier. But...I don't know. We're males."

"Well observed," Hassan remarks with a wink.

"And there are three of us."

"Oh, and he can count," I add.

Swiping through his hair, Arwyn tries again, "Will you two be serious?"

Hassan shrugs. "What can we do? Fate has spoken."

I look Arwyn in the eyes. "You are happy, aren't you?"

"Yes," he replies, stroking a hand down my cheek.

Rubbing my middle then his, I tell him, "I sense it. Here. Now I know what this is, and I've accepted we're all mates, it just feels right. Like I've opened a door and you both walked through. What I already felt has been recognised, so it can be fully embraced. I'm sure there will be a learning curve as we explore our relationship more. But we have each other."

Nuzzling each of us, Hassan confirms, "Yes. We will help one another."

Arwyn wraps his arms around us both and kisses our noses. "You're right. I know you are. It's just unexpected."

"And yet welcome?" Hassan checks.

"Yes. I'm overthinking. I have to admit it *feels* right."

"Good," I tell him, digging my fingers into his ribs.

Backing away from the attack, he roars and laughs. But then launches his counterattack. I almost squish Hassan as I roll onto my back, yelping. He hurls himself at Arwyn though, clearly leaping to my defence.

"Oh, so that's the way, is it? On his side, are you?" Arwyn quizzes whilst pinning Hassan to the floor with tickles.

The poor male is helpless, kicking his legs and struggling for breath.

"Submit, Hassan."

"I submit, I submit," he cries, wriggling and laughing.

Arwyn immediately stops and pecks his cheek. "There. Wasn't so difficult, was it?"

Hassan pokes his tongue out at him as he stands up.

"Use it or lose it."

"Again? Already?"

"Good goddess, who are you?"

Enveloping Hassan in my arms from behind, I supply, "What I think we have here, Arwyn, is a dark jaguar. Timid shy-boy to all, fearsome beast in the bedroom."

Enclosing Hassan between us and smiling, Arwyn replies, "I'm definitely not complaining."

"Oh, I almost forgot. I saw Kiera when I got our food. She said to find her once we were done making the beast with two or three backs. Her words, not mine."

"I presume she won't mind if we have a quick shower first."

"I'm not sure he's keen on showers. Are you, honey?" I add.

"Err…I…"

"Eww. You've not had a shower before?"

"Be nice, Arwyn. In a clan with little water, quick washdowns are essential. Am I right?"

He nods.

"We'll show you. It's nice. Come on."

We don't bother putting clothes on. It's not far and nobody cares. And I'm not at risk of saluting anyone on the way. Huh, I suppose I won't ever again. Arwyn and Hassan are, in theory, the only ones who will make my body react that way now. Wait, they've not bitten each other. Can they still stray? We need more love bites between us, and soon.

Hassan is pulled under a showerhead with Arwyn. "See, you just pull this cord."

Water cascades down on them both. Hassan yowls and jumps away.

"Here, here" I soothe, wrapping a towel around his shivering form.

"So cold," he cries through chattering teeth.

"Aww, honey, I'm sorry. We should've considered that. It's not cold to us," I apologise, rubbing his limbs through the large towel.

Turning to a stunned Arwyn, I direct, "You finish up here. I'll take him back to his room for a wash."

Arwyn gawps but nods.

By the time he joins us, Hassan is clean, dry and in fresh clothes.

"My apologies," Arwyn says, gazing at the floor as he enters.

"You did not do it on purpose. It is OK."

"Let's see if we can get you some hot chocolate on the way to find Kiera, eh?"

"I'll catch up," I tell them, nipping into my room to get clean clothes of my own.

We've been so preoccupied that I have no idea what time it is. But I'm pretty sure we're late for duty. My heart lurches, realising that means not being with my mates. What are we supposed to do?

With a million questions rolling through my mind, I find Hassan and Arwyn sitting at our usual table, three cups of steaming hot chocolate in front of them. Hassan's nostrils flare as he breathes in the rich aroma. Kissing his cheek, I settle down by his side.

"I thought you would've grabbed these and gone to seek our Peacekeeper with cups in hand," I comment.

"Aye, but it's so peaceful here. There's hardly anyone about. We thought we'd take a minute to compose ourselves," Arwyn replies, cupping Hassan's shoulder, who smiles and nods.

Rubbing my cheek, I admit, "Yeah, it's been a whirlwind, huh?"

"Besides, I've barely spent any time alone with Hassan. You've been hogging him."

"Hardly. But I take your point."

He shakes his head. "I'm mated to a male I barely know."

"And one you know very well," I add, wiggling my eyebrows. "Anyway, I think we all need to get to know one another better."

"Fate, it is a curious thing," Hassan muses, "Some choices are made for us, yet it remains our decision what to do in the circumstances in which we find ourselves."

My eyebrows almost shoot off my head. "That's very profound."

"Aye. Too deep for this time of day," Arwyn puts in.

"There you all are," Kiera hails, approaching.

We all wave.

"I thought I said to come find me, not make me go in search of you."

"Agreed. But there was…an incident with the cold shower. Arwyn was trying to warm me up," Hassan tells her.

"I don't know where to begin with that. I'll forego mentioning there are better ways for new mates to warm one another up, and merely promise to show you a secret later."

We all mutter our disapproval.

Rolling her eyes, she explains, "Not like that. Please! Eurgh, you three, get your minds out of the gutter. And don't let Pryderi catch you insinuating smutty things at me."

"Pph! I only have eyes for these two now," I inform her.

She grins. "I know. Marvellous, isn't it?"

"It's not bad," Arwyn retorts, nuzzling Hassan.

"Better now we know what's going on," I mumble.

"Don't any of you expect me to apologise. It's not my fault you were all so utterly clueless. Besides, didn't I bring you together? I would've thought some thanks would be in order, if anything. Anyway, I have a surprise when you're done with your choccie woccies."

"Is it a nice surprise?" Arwyn checks. I can't blame him for his scepticism as I'm feeling it too, to be honest.

"Oh, poo! Of course, it's something nice. And very much needed, I think," she says with a high and mighty glance.

"Hassan, love, how are you apart from cold?" she asks.

"More spoiled than I've ever been my entire life."

"Oh, well, that's lovely, isn't it? As long as you're settling in. Ooh, remind me *cardis* a bit later too."

"Oookaaay. Tell me, please, this clan, most of you are asleep at this time?"

"Ah, you noticed that? Yes, I'm given to understand that elinefae are nocturnal by nature. Given your own unusual circadian rhythm, I'd say you hit the jackpot with day-dwelling mates, eh?"

"You mean I am lucky? Yes, I am the luckiest male who ever lived."

"Aww," Arwyn and I chorus, nuzzling into him.

"But you are wrong, honey. I'm the lucky one," I murmur.

"No. You're both wrong, I am," Arwyn argues.

"Good grief! There's no need for a competition over it, guys. Was I this bad when I first joined with Pryderi?"

"No, of course not," I reply.

She gives a self-satisfied smile.

"You were far worse," I add, breaking into cackles.

She shoves my arm. "Hey, cheeky! Easy or I'll change my mind about my surprise."

We gulp down what's left of our drinks and place the cups in the wash-up.

"Right, you'd better show us this amazing thing before we turn in for duty."

Kiera chuckles. "Don't you think it's a little late for that? Where do you think Pryderi is, eh? *Twp*! Neither of us thought you'd manage to crawl out of your den at all today, so we have you covered. And the next two days you were due off anyway. Goes for you too, Hassan, love."

Holy shit! I think an actual crack just ruptured across my heart. If I hadn't guessed already, one look at Hassan's eyes would've told me where that distress originated.

"What?" I croak at him.

"Please, no. Kiera, I am certain you mean well. But, please, let me cook." His fingers clench and unclench as he talks.

My chest feels tight.

"Of course, if it means that much. Hassan, I only wanted to give you time with your mates. I know how intense these first feelings can be."

"What the fuck?" Arwyn asks before I can.

Hassan shakes his head. "Do not misunderstand. I need to be with you both. I do. But cooking…it has been my refuge. My safe place. And right now, I feel overwhelmed. I…"

Putting a finger to his lips, I tell him, "Shh! Honey, it's OK. It's OK. You do what you need to do."

Arwyn wraps an arm around him. "Just don't expect to do it alone."

"Huh?"

"We are absolutely coming with you. Isn't that right?"

"Wild horses couldn't keep us away," I confirm.

"But do you know how to cook?"

"Oh, no, baby, no. But we are very good at *Watching*."

Even I groan at his pun.

"But honestly, you will watch me cook?"

"Honey, I'm looking forward to it," I say with a lascivious grin.

"Goddess, spare me! Can we go now?" Kiera snips.

Chapter 19 – My New Home
~ Hassan

We follow Kiera to the mated couples' living area, as Elan explains to me. But we pass all the doors and straight outside through a rear exit. We go past shrubs and trees, up to a wooden hut which has been concealed.

"I thought I'd better show you this first," Kiera says, "But tell anyone else and I'll have to do horrible things to you. This is for you alone, Hassan, and only because you have my sympathy. You see, I was brought up with the blessing of hot showers literally on tap. I didn't take too well to what these heathens call a shower."

"Hey," Elan exclaims.

Ignoring him, she continues, "So, I had this one rigged up. It doesn't hold much water, so you have to be quick. No loitering or sexy time showers. But…" Reaching in, she pulls a cord and quickly brings her arm away.

"Go on, put your hand in," she instructs.

Obeying, I gawk. "It's warm!"

"Exactly. Warm. Not piping hot. But it does the job."

"And I can use this?"

"So long as it remains our little secret. The rest of the clan a) don't need it and b) would use up all my precious warm water before I get a look in."

"Your secret is safe with me."

"I knew it would be. Now, come," she says, stopping the shower and walking back inside.

"That's Kiera and Pryderi's den," Arwyn points out as we walk past.

"That's weird," Elan comments.

"What?" I ask.

"Arwyn, do you smell anything?"

"No."

"Exactly. Shouldn't you, though?"

Kiera giggles. "You know, Pryderi said the same thing. Apparently, we stop detecting, err, certain smells when we're mated."

"Oooh, that's why the mated live in one area?" Elan checks.

"Well, that and the noise, I suppose," Arwyn adds, chuckling.

"Aher, yes, well. This one's yours," Kiera says, opening a den door.

"What?" we ask as one.

"Aww, you guys are so cute, all synced up and everything. Welcome to your new den."

"Sorry, what?" Elan asks again.

"You're mates now, right? I'm presuming you want to share a bed?" Kiera responds.

Looking in, I see a large, ornately carved wooden bed with a plush mattress and teal sheets.

"Wow," I murmur, walking in, trying to take it all in.

There are three large wardrobes which match the bed; one has a full-length mirror built into the door. A comfy seating area. A triple washbowl unit. Shelves – books are stacked on some of them. The picture of my mates and their friend stands proudly on a small table next to the bed. An abstract painting filled with green, violet and blue hangs on a wall. Stepping closer, I see Kiera has signed it - she must have painted this especially for us.

"This room was…well, it was intended for a triad once. The bedframe was already here. I forgot to get the new mattress moved in. I asked Pryderi to lend me a hand getting it all nice for you last night."

"You bloody knew, didn't you? Were we so much a certainty that you ordered all this finery? How long ago, Kiera? How long have you been aware of our mate and kept him secret?" Arwyn growls.

She has the decency to blush. "Um, well, Hassan's clan witch contacted me a few months ago seeking assistance. And maybe there was a vague hint of a notion. I may have got over-excited and ordered this stuff just in case what I thought came to fruition. I didn't know for sure. The feeling got stronger when I met you in person, Hassan. But please believe me, there were no guarantees. Not until you all acted on instinct. I didn't want to build anyone's hopes up if I was wrong."

Arwyn is glaring daggers, hissing. But Elan pulls an arm around Kiera's shoulders, guiding her towards the door.

"Give him time. He'll be fine. I'll talk to him. Honestly, I understand," he tells her.

Pride swells in my chest. This caring, protective male; I get to call him mine. He was so angry before. But now he's had time to calm down and think, he's clearly made sense of all this already, and is even defending Kiera. Which is more than I've managed, to be honest.

Shutting the door, Elan approaches the still-seething Arwyn. I'm not completely calm myself. Months? I feel manipulated. Arwyn's agitation is only adding to my own. But surrounding that is Elan's blanket of calm.

Rubbing Arwyn's arm, he soothes, "It's alright, hissy. We're all together now. That's what counts, right? You, me and him." His head jerks in my direction.

Arwyn huffs out a huge breath but reaches an arm out my way whilst still looking at the floor.

"He's right, you know," I admit, tucking myself under that muscular appendage.

Cheeks nuzzle side to side as we all huddle up.

"I know, but..." Arwyn starts.

"The only but I want is your butt, handsome," Elan says, giving it a squeeze.

"Tart!"

"You love it."

"Yeah. I do," he whispers.

"Time to try out this magnificent bed?"

In reply, Arwyn picks Elan up and chucks him onto it. "Damn right."

"So soft," Elan croons, stroking the sheets as he bounces.

"And such a pretty colour," I add.

They both turn their heads towards me, their unasked question pinching their brows.

I roll my eyes. "Remember the colour wheel? Blue, violet and green?"

"Yeeees," Elan replies.

"Wouldn't they create teal?"

Elan's face scrunches. "More like a dark grey. Lavender, at best."

"Well, I like it. It feels very us," Arwyn says, pawing the sheets.

"Teal symbolises trustworthiness, calm, protection, devotion and support. Very us. Well, maybe except for the calm," I agree, approaching my mates.

"Come here, sweetie," Arwyn commands, pulling my hand.

I fall onto the bed, and we lie face up, side-by-side.

Arwyn swipes his hands over his head. "Argh, what a day!"

Elan rubs his cheek on the shoulder closest to him. "Yeah, but we have each other. And a swanky new den."

Arwyn chortles. "Hmm, yeah."

We all start nuzzling and cuddling on our sides until I start dozing off. Arwyn strokes my hair, making me purr.

"I could listen to that all day," he whispers.

"Mmm...make me," I reply, adding extra rumbles.

My eyes are closed, but I hear the coffee machine percolating away. When the bed dipped, it must've been Elan getting up.

"Did you put enough coffee in?" I try to sit up as I ask, but Arwyn's arm keeps me down.

"Uh huh, no moving. I like you exactly where you are," he tells me.

Elan calls across, "And no, probably not, to answer your question. But then, you could stand a spoon up in your coffee. However, I hope it's a compromise as I put more in than I usually would. I'm just grateful to have a machine now. Mates need to keep their strength up."

"So, none of us will be happy with this brew?" Arwyn remarks.

"Compromise being the word, Arwyn."

"Hmph!"

Poking his ribs, I warn, "Don't be grumpy. It's a nice gesture. Thank you, Elan. It's nice of you to make a change for once."

Arwyn boops my nose. "*Smartass*! I suppose mating up isn't a big enough change, hm?"

"Well, have you moved halfway across the globe? Started to dress, talk and behave differently? Got cold? Changed what you eat?"

"Ah, now, you see, yes actually. You've changed our food already. Ha!"

I grin. "Oh, poor you."

"It wasn't a complaint."

Raising my eyebrows, I shoot back, "It better not be."

Leaning down, he kisses my mouth as I stretch up. "Definitely not."

The plip-plop-whooshing of the coffee machine stops. Elan pours it into three cups and brings them over. Nudging my legs, he sits next to me.

"Goddess, I feel spoiled," I exclaim.

"That's the idea. But, just so you don't get the wrong idea, we do expect you to return the favour at some point," Arwyn cautions.

Elan jostles me as he reaches across and slaps Arwyn's arm. "Don't spoil it!"

"What? We can't have him thinking it's always going to be this way."

"*He* is still here," I remind them.

Ignoring me, Elan replies, "Today, we can spoil him." And rubs my legs.

"In that case, you can go lower," I tell him, cheekily raising my foot and waggling it at him.

"Really?"

"Actually, I was joking."

But Elan is already sidling down and taking my foot in his deft hands, massaging it.

"Aww, you made him purr again," Arwyn comments as his fingers drift to rub the patch of fur behind my ear; bliss. His other hand travels down and rubs my belly.

"I'm in the afterlife," I murmur, leaning my head further into his touch.

"You had better not be."

Arwyn's hand slides up and over my shoulder then down to my upper arm. His fingers trace my clan mark. "So, a red eagle, huh?"

"Not quite, *Habibi*. It is a roc. A bird of prey so large that it can carry an elephant in its talons."

"Sounds terrifying."

"Is that not the purpose of clan marks? To show our might? You have not one but three green dragon heads in yours."

"True."

"I think it's fabulous," Elan comments.

With a kiss on my head, Arwyn returns to smoothing my hair and I'm purring again.

I groan when the coffee cools and my mates stop their ministrations to pick up their cups, forcing me to sit up and do the same. Not that I can complain, considering I must be the luckiest elinefae to have ever lived. Who would have thought such burly Watchers could be so tender, loving and caring? And mine.

<u>Chapter 20 – Torment</u>
– Arwyn

Hassan had told me of his bad experience with the human – I was livid. But now, pride overfills my heart as Hassan relaxes under my touch. I hate what he's had to endure yet am so very grateful I can give him so much better. With Elan.

Sipping my coffee, I shake my head at the surreal situation. It's amazing yet unimaginable. But here we three are.

"It's not that bad, is it?" Elan checks.

"Don't be daft. I was just thinking about how wonderfully unusual all this is. But since you're asking, I've had better coffee." I add a wink, hoping to soften the blow.

"It's not that bad," Hassan affirms. His wincing gives him away, though.

Scrunching up his face, even Elan has to admit, "Maybe an acquired taste. I'm sure we'll get used to it."

"Nothing a bit of honey and vanilla can't cure," I say, winking again.

"Oh, my goddess. Do you never think above your waist?" Hassan exclaims.

"Not if I can help it," I reply, moving in for a slow lap of his tongue.

"Hm, what do you know? Orangey clove does help," he admits.

"You're so sweet."

"In every way," Elan adds, getting his own kiss from Hassan.

As their kiss deepens, my cock hardens.

"Like what you see?" Hassan asks when I groan.

"Fuck, yeah."

His eyes smoulder. "Or would you prefer to swap places?"

I nod, not even sure which one he means I should trade positions with – I just want in. Hassan leans in towards me and strokes my tongue with his, providing an answer without me asking.

Our mouths hungrily mash together. Reaching down, I rub through Hassan's trousers where he's pleasingly solid too.

"You want something, baby?" I check.

"Uuuh-huuuh."

"Tell me, sweetheart. How can I please you?" I ask, sucking at his throat.

"Want...you." He pants.

My hand rubs harder. "Where? Tell me where."

All I get in response is a whimper as his hips grind forwards against my hand.

"This should be interesting. Two bossy males," Elan muses, gazing intently between us.

My hand keeps working at Hassan's groin whilst I lean across to kiss Elan. "Couldn't it just?"

I swiftly untie Hassan's trousers and tug them down and away. His lithe body is laid out in full view; his tanned, softly rippled gorgeousness in all its glory. My gaze travels down the trail peppered with fur from his chest to the dark nest framing his proud cock like a target marker, and my eyes are zeroing in.

Elan's removing his clothing – eager bunny. Not wanting to be left out, I quickly get up to whisk mine off too.

"Come here, gorgeous," I command him.

We stand together, hands wandering over what was forbidden for so long, kissing and nipping, breathing one another in.

"It's so good to hold you like this," I whisper.

"Right back at you."

His body is a firm rock against mine as we devour one another. A whimper comes from the bed.

"Don't worry, I haven't forgotten you," I tell Hassan who's touching himself.

"Let me do that for you," Elan urges, sitting next to him, taking over.

"Augh! That's too good."

At my tap on his shoulder, Elan's hand abandons our mate, Hassan's cock bouncing with the sudden loss.

"What…?"

I lie down on my back behind Hassan. "Hey, Mr Bossy, want to come this way?"

"Me?" Hassan asks, pointing at himself.

Oh, my goddess, he's so adorable. "Yes, you, sweetness. Come here."

"And I'm the bossy one?" he quips, crawling up my reclined form as soon as I nod.

"I want inside," I whisper into his ear, making him shudder. "Mmm…you like that idea, huh?"

Biting his lip, he nods.

"Then what are you waiting for? I'm all yours."

The disobedient sod scooches down and sucks my cock tip instead. I'm too busy moaning to tell him off, though. Good goddess, he's skilled with his mouth.

Grinning at me, he finally makes his way back up my torso. Ah, he just had to do it his way. I'm good with that. His descent onto my throbbing cock is tantalisingly slow. I gasp and grunt, entirely at his mercy. Elan has moved close to our side and rubs Hassan's leg.

"Who's in control now?" he teases, clearly taking too much enjoyment from this.

"Hassan," I confess.

"Good boy," he commends, leaning in for a kiss.

"Auugh," I yelp as Hassan rises and slams down, "Fuck!"

Green eyes shimmer love towards me as he takes his time riding me like a cowboy. Uuuup and…

"Augh!" Down in one swift move.

My hands grip onto his hips, trying to control his movements. He stops completely and glares with a tsk. Only once I release my hold does he begin to move again. Elan chuckles in my ear before kissing my cheek.

Kneeling, he kisses Hassan. His cock is temptingly close to my mouth as he pulls back and away. Elan shuffles and holds Hassan's erection as he continues to thrust. Augh!

We're all connected. And Hassan only increases his furious pace, building frantic friction. The combination of our arousal whirls through me. So intense. So…

"Going to come," I warn.

Elan chuckles. "So are we."

Oh, my goddess, Elan's wanking himself at the same time. Hassan's continuing his rapid rhythm, pounding himself onto me. Faster, harder. More.

"Fuck me, sweetheart. Oh yeah, like that," I call out.

Elan's breathing is as hissed and shallow as mine. My eyes widen as I gaze at him, tugging off two beautiful cocks at once. And Hassan's tight arse clenches around mine more.

"Aw, augh, AUUUGGGH!" I yowl, firing my load into Hassan.

Hot jets squirt onto my torso from both my mates. But then, fuck, teeth are in my shoulder and Hassan's still going. The friction rebuilds and doubles, no, triples. How? My balls are impossibly tight again already as Hassan rocks and sucks.

Rearing up, he yells his release, my blood dripping down his chin.

"Oh, fuck, come here quick, sweetness," I plead.

He bends down as my hips buck. Licking my way up the red trail, my tongue delves into his mouth. Bless him, he's spent but still rocking for me.

"You're so fucking gorgeous," I grind out.

Mmm's echo between us with increasing intensity. My teeth elongate and bite into the soft flesh at his shoulder and I come like a fountain.

"Mine," Hassan declares.

"Mine," I declare.

He collapses onto my chest, and I'm so fucking happy to hold him there. A head gets nuzzled up to us.

"You good?" I ask Elan.

"More than good. I'm just glad we all got our love bites."

"Worried, were you?"

Holding his thumb and finger close together, he says, "Maybe a little."

Hassan shoves him, sending Elan reeling back.

"Shit! Sorry, I didn't mean to be so rough," he quickly apologises, pulling up from me.

But my arm brings him back down against the vibrations in my chest. "If he can't defend himself better, that's his problem."

Elan's laughing face comes close. "He's got a point," he says, kissing us each on the cheek.

He disappears, but I'm too snuggled into Hassan to focus on why. Until a towel hits my hand, anyway.

"More coffee?" Elan asks, looking far too amused.

Hassan leaps up. "I'll make it," he hollers, wiping himself down as he sprints towards the machine.

Elan and I are both left laughing.

"Hey, you sure you're OK?" I check with him, feeling guilty that we left him out a bit.

"You're joking, aren't you? That was amazing."

I peck his swollen, even darker than normal pink lips. "Well, you did seem to enjoy the show."

"I enjoy us." He purrs as he brushes noses with me. "All of us."

We cuddle up as Hassan makes the drinks.

"Here you are, *njūmiyy*," he says, smiling, putting a cup in my hands as I sit up.

"Uh oh, what's *njūmiyy*?"

"My stars," he explains, brushing his thumb over my cheek.

"Wow!"

"Aww, *ya amar* and *njūmiyy*, how very astral," Elan remarks, going doe-eyed.

"Eh?"

"*Ya amar* is my moon. What I call him," Hassan elaborates.

"Why?"

"It shines in his eyes. And you? You make me see stars." He bites his lip and looks away.

"Aww, you really are the sweetest. Come here," I encourage, putting my cup down and pulling his hand.

Tugging harder, he lands across my lap, his legs dangling off the edge of the bed, so I can kiss him.

"I'll get my own then, shall I?" Elan grumbles, getting up. I pat his arse as he manoeuvres, though.

"Cheeky," he snips.

"Aww, don't be grumpy, moonshine."

"That's *ya amar* to you," he replies and soon saunters back with his cup.

"So, Hassan, what do we call you, then?" I ask.

Twisting his mouth, he ponders. "*Ya shamsi?*"

"Enlighten me."

"Haha, too true. It means my sun."

Pecking his mouth again, I tell him, "Perfect."

Elan starts singing the weird song "You Are My Sunshine" – goddess give me strength! Sometimes, I wish Kiera had kept her music to herself. What's worse is that Hassan starts swaying side to side in my arms.

"And fate decided this was a good idea?" I mumble.

"Oh, who's being grumpy now, star boy?" Elan teases before finishing the whole damned song.

"Hm, well, you can be in charge of coffee making, sunshine," I tell Hassan, sipping my coffee carefully amidst his, err, lap dance.

"I added extra cream and sugar for the cute kitties," he taunts.

I put my cup back down. "Right, that does it," I tease, tickling him until he falls off my lap and onto the floor.

"That wasn't very nice," he says, launching himself to tickle me back.

I try to evade him, but Elan's on the case already and pins me down so Hassan can commit death by tickling. He doesn't stop, despite my kicking feet, until I'm breathless and tears are streaming down my cheeks, decrying, "OK, you win. You win. I'm sorry."

We all sit back down like normal elinefae beings. I slant my eyes at Elan though.

"Don't think I didn't notice whose side you were on. Again."

"I am merely on the side of the righteous in any quarrel," he defends haughtily.

"The righteous, eh? You hear that, Hassan?"

He shrugs. "You expect me to disagree, *njūmiyy*?" He flutters his long, dark eyelashes.

I hold his gaze for a breath. "No," I whisper, cupping his cheek, "I expect you to claim your victory."

"Victory? Of what?"

"Our hearts."

"Love is not a battle to be won or lost, *njūmiyy*. It is to be felt, treasured and shared."

After another round or two of exploring each other's bodies between naps, we are all collapsed on our backs on the cushy bed.

Stretching and sighing, Hassan says, "I suppose I ought to head to the kitchen."

I can't help but chuckle. "The dining area, perhaps. The kitchen, no."

"What?" He yelps, sitting up.

Elan is the first to raise himself up to put a reassuring arm around him. "Sorry, honey. My stomach is telling me it's time to eat."

"What time is it?"

"Evening mealtime?" I suggest.

"Argh! You need a clock."

"Hey, is this not your room too?"

"Fine. *We* need a clock."

"You use such things?"

"Don't you?"

"Why? The sun and our stomachs tell us all we need to know."

"That's another thing. The light changes so it cannot be artificial. How does the sun get in here when we are underground?"

"That, I can tell you," Elan replies, getting up and beckoning Hassan.

Pointing up to the round spot in the ceiling, he explains, "This is not a light but a sun tunnel. It captures sunlight, reflects it off mirrors and diffuses it into each room. So, we only need to turn the lights on when the sun sets."

"This is clever."

"In the old days, we used to rely on our night vision alone. But as most people are awake during the dark hours, they wanted to read and stuff. Lights make that easier. What did your old clan do?"

"We did not need this. Daylight dwellers, remember?"

"Oh, yeah. Of course."

"When you two have finished, can we go in search of food?" I interject, my stomach rumbling as I stand.

"Aww, is poor Arwyn hungry?" Elan chides, approaching to rub my belly.

I push him down onto the bed. "Well, you're welcome to stay here."

I've made the mistake of turning my back. He leaps from the bed onto me. "No way. Come, take us to the food," he calls, kicking his feet.

Hassan is clothing himself, shaking his head and laughing. With Elan still on my back, I canter up to Hassan and nuzzle cheeks.

"You're not angry we kept you away from your sanctuary, are you?" I check.

"How can I be angry with such pleasing distractions?" he answers with a kiss.

"Me too, me too," Elan cries from my back, and gets a peck as well.

"Come on, then. I thought you were hungry," Hassan says to us both.

"I am. We're going like this," Elan tells him.

Plonking him down onto his feet, I point at his cock. "See this? Only we get to see it now. I don't want anyone else looking at my mate's package."

He pouts. "Shouldn't that be my decision?"

I fix a glare at him. "You want other people to look?"

"As long as it's in admiration."

"Of course, it would be. Well, if you're game I'm game." I take a step towards the door, naked.

"Oh, no. No, you don't."

"Ahh, different rules, babe?"

"Fine. I get your point," he replies, shrugging on his trousers at the same time I do.

"Funny, you both seem to have green eyes in this light," Hassan comments.

"Only outshone by yours, oh sun of my life," Elan chimes.

We finally manage to get out of our den and head towards the dining area. To be fair, it's even later than I imagined. Many others are already eating.

Sniffing, Hassan points and asks, "What is this, please? Smells like onion and cheese."

Clapping him on the back, I inform him, "Those, sweetheart, are Glamorgan sausages. And you need to try them. Leeks, breadcrumbs and cheese, deliciously fried."

I place a few on a plate and slap on a good helping of mashed potatoes, runner beans and carrots and hand it to him. "Here. All yours."

"Err...thanks?"

I load up two more plates whilst Elan gets cups of blood for us.

"I hear congratulations are in order, handsome" Gethin says, reaching out to clap my upper arm.

Hassan's lip curls as Gethin leans forwards to whisper, "I sort of wish it had been me, but I'm truly happy for you all the same."

He must have overheard as a growl rumbles from Hassan. Elan's not looking wildly happy either.

Taking a strategic step back from my former playmate, I tell him, "Thank you."

He takes the hint. "Alright. Well, all the best, handsome," he says before walking away.

Hassan glowers after him.

"Steady, sweetheart. It's OK. He won't expect sexy times from me ever again. You're safe. We're mated."

He snorts. "He called you handsome. Twice."

"Oh, that? You mustn't mind that."

"And why must I not?"

"Yeah, that's sort of my fault," Elan admits, "When we were younglings, I discovered Arwyn's name means handsome. I called him it as a joke, but others

257

overheard and it caught on. And stuck." He has the good grace to look sheepish as he confesses.

Hassan looks dumbstruck. "No! Awryn, it means handsome?"

I grin. "Yes. Don't you think it suits me?"

"Yes, of course. But you do not know, I think. Hassan, it means the same."

"Oh, my goddess. Are you serious? Talk about fate."

We all laugh as we walk towards our table.

"Oh, you've surfaced then," Pryderi teases as we approach. There is an empty plate in front of him.

"Couldn't wait for us, Brother?" I chide.

"Well, we didn't know whether you'd be here at all."

Getting up, he walks around the table and hugs each of us in turn. "Congratulations, you three."

"Thanks. Where's…never mind," Elan starts to ask but is interrupted by the distant squawking of a baby dragon.

"It's like having your very own youngling," I observe.

"Aye. A fire-breathing, temperamental, youngling."

"Shui is a baby?" Hassan asks.

"Oh, shit. No. Sorry, honey. I forgot you've not met our other friend yet."

"Another dragon?"

Pryderi nods and smiles. "My mate has a dragon familiar too. But a green, earth one. Delivered as an egg by a dragon lord himself. It was quite the shock to all of us."

"Wow!"

"Eat up and I'll take you to meet Terrah after. Sounds like she's getting snacks, so her hanger should've subsided. Honestly, never let a dragon get hungry, it's not good."

"I will bear it in mind." Hassan's smirk is sexy as fuck.

"But tell me what you think of these, first," I demand, lifting a fork of mash and Glamorgan sausage to his mouth.

His mouth encloses around the fork as he slowly pulls his head back, his eyes blazing. Would anyone mind if I jumped his bones here and now? Hmph, probably not the best table manners. Best not.

"Mmmm…" he moans dramatically.

Elan nudges him. "Stop that. Seriously, do you like them?"

"Yes, I seriously do. Is that mustard I taste? And…parsley?"

"What do I bloody look like, a cook?" I jest.

"Ha, alright. I will ask my friends in the kitchen tomorrow."

"Oh, you think you're working tomorrow, do you?"

"Yes."

"Hmph!"

"Haha, you're bickering like a long-mated couple already," Pryderi says, chortling.

Hassan eagerly forks more food into his gob. I wish I was that fork!

Arms wrap around me from behind. "Arwyn, there you are. I've been looking for you."

Hassan growls.

"Down boy! This is Megan. She's like a sister to me. Megan, this is my mate, Hassan."

Her arms leave me and land on him instead. Kissing the back of his head, she cheers, "Hello and congratulations, Hassan. I can't believe Arwyn hasn't introduced us already. Oh, this is so exciting."

"And what am I, chopped liver?" Elan grumbles.

"Aww, is poor *dwt* Elan jealous? Congratulations to you too. Oh, I can't believe we have our very own triad. Although, Elan, it's about bloody time, isn't it?" she says, pinching his cheeky chops.

Shrinking out of her grasp, he tells her, "It's not like it's my fault, is it?"

"Really? And how do you work that one out, then? There was him and there was you. I didn't see anyone else stopping you."

"Leave off him, Megan. We've all had a shock, haven't we?" I caution.

"You used to be fun before you were mated."

"Give over. You joining us?"

"Not likely. Some of us have work to do."

"It was nice to meet you, Megan," Hassan says.

"Ooh, I do like him. So polite. Pay attention you two, you may learn something from your mate here."

I playfully smack her retreating arse. "So could you."

She merely raises a middle finger, continuing to walk away.

"She is your sister?" Hassan asks.

Shaking my head, I explain, "No. My family brought her in when she lost hers. So, we grew up together. So, like a sister but not one."

"Huh. Weird, as I see a resemblance."

"You do? Well, she is my mum's sister's daughter, so we are sort of related, I suppose."

"Or maybe growing up in the same household just rubbed off on the poor girl," Elan adds, picking a runner bean off Hassan's plate and chomping it.

"I'm right here, you know."

"Are they always like this?" Hassan asks Pryderi.

"Afraid so."

"Oh, goody."

Jabbing his ribs, I tease, "Complaining, mate?"

"I wouldn't dare."

"Goddess help you," Pryderi sympathises with Hassan.

"The goddess has obviously blessed him," I correct.

Smiling, Elan adds, "Twice." Then seductively sucks and bites on another runner bean.

"Enjoying those, are you?"

"Ooh, yeees."

I kiss those perfectly plump lips. "Tease!"

He smiles but his eyes say, 'take me now'. I have always heard tales of the intensity of matings, yet it's still a surprise to be subjected to such unrelenting lust. It's a wonder we even managed to get out of the den to eat.

We're busy shovelling food when my head shoots up as tingles run through me. "Uh oh!"

A familiar voice shrills, "Arwyn, what do you mean by neglecting us? Why did I have to learn about such momentous news from someone else, eh? I didn't bring you up to be so rude."

I flinch at the scolding. "Sorry, Mother. But we only just…"

"Don't you give me any of that. I don't want your excuses."

Elan intercedes. "Honestly, we were sort of side-tracked. And shocked. And, well, it was daytime."

"Hmmm…"

"Come on, love. Surely you remember what it's like for new mates?"

My mother actually blushes at my father's words. "Well, it was embarrassing being told by someone else as they congratulated me on something I had no idea about."

"My apologies," I supply, "I would have preferred to have told you myself first, obviously."

"I've not even been introduced, have I?"

"Mother, this is Elan."

She lightly slaps the side of my head. "I know you know I didn't mean him, Arwyn."

Looking up, I see she's smiling though. I grin at her. "Mother, Father, this is Hassan. Hassan, this is my mother and father."

"Hello, Hassan. It's a pleasure to meet you at last."

"The honour is mine," he says, getting up to bow to her. "My apologies for not meeting with you sooner."

"Well, the least said about it the better, I say. My, the rumours did not do you justice, young Hassan, love."

"You are night dwellers, ma'am?"

"Aye, and that will be why our paths have not crossed, I suppose. But call me Branwen. And this here is my mate, Perceval."

"I am humbled, Sir," he replies with another bow.

My heart swells once more. My mate is so charming.

My father inclines his head. "It's good to meet you, Hassan."

"And congratulations to you too, Elan," my mother tells him, rubbing his arm, leaning down for a hug.

"Ohhh, I told you we'd be late." Another voice carries over to us.

Pryderi's mother rushes across. "Elan, love. Arwyn. Congratulations. Although, I won't pretend to be overly surprised. And you must be Hassan, welcome, my dear. Welcome." She grabs each of us into a cheek rub.

"Umm…hello. My greetings," Hassan squeaks.

"Hassan, this is Eirlys, Pryderi's mother. And sort of mine. She helped raise me after…" Elan starts.

Hassan strokes our mate's cheek with his thumb, then returns his attention to the woman in front of him and bows. "My gratitude."

"Oh, well, aren't you sweet? It wasn't a difficult task, really. His parents had done the hard work. He's always been a good lad," she says, ruffling Elan's hair.

"Eiiiiirlyyys," he gripes.

"I'm just so happy for you all." Tears well up in her eyes, and her mate is immediately at her side.

"No tears, my love."

Swiping under her eyes, she replies, "They are only happy ones. It's fine."

"Greetings," he says to Hassan, his fist at his heart.

"My greetings, Sir."

"Owen."

"Owen," he repeats.

"So, you're Hassan? I can see why the fates chose you."

"You can?" he asks, his lips falling open.

"Ha, indeed. You might just be in with a small chance of being a calming influence on these two ruffians."

"Hey," I exclaim, squirming away from his hand which ruffles my hair.

"Pah! Tell me it's not so."

"Still, maybe you didn't need to say it, eh?"

Hassan laughs. "What? This was a secret, maybe? I have eyes and ears, Arwyn."

Clapping him on the shoulder, Owen observes, "Yes, a very good mating."

Walking round to his actual son, he rubs cheeks. "And how are you, Pryderi? Well?"

He nods. "Yes. Very."

"Aww, look at you lot. Ahh, Eirlys, isn't young love grand?"

"Truly," she replies.

My mother and father both wipe their eyes, but it is my father who speaks. "Such joy."

We fall into idle chatter as our parents quiz Hassan and repeat their congratulations. Clan means so much. But this is my family, and they mean even more. I wipe a tear from my own eye as I watch how readily they accept Hassan into our midst.

"I saw that," Elan says with a nudge.

I shove him back. "Like you're not weepy."

"Never said I wasn't." He wraps an arm around me and I'm truly, utterly home.

Chapter 21 – Plan of Action
~ Elan

"I should contact my parents," Hassan says to me as we make our goodbyes, his brows furrowed.

"PRYDERI! Wait. Are you or Kiera able to assist Hassan in making contact with his parents?" I call out.

He pivots and returns. "Such things are beyond my power. But of course, Kiera, Cerys or Chen will be happy to help." He turns to Hassan. "You must miss them."

"Not as much as you suspect. I do. But it is another difference to here. We are birthed to parents but as soon as we are weened the entire clan raises us. You stay with your parents until your transition, I think."

"Yes. But the clan do get involved still."

"You are all individuals."

"I suppose you can look at it that way. But we are more individuals as part of a whole. We have our dens for sleeping, our own personal space. But there is always someone around should we wish."

"Where I come from, we eat, sleep and work together. Do you not get lonely?"

"Sometimes, it is nice to be alone with your thoughts. And there is not much chance to feel lonely, not really."

Hassan nods, but the wrinkles on his forehead show he is still wrapping his mind around what Pryderi told him.

Draping an arm around him, I encourage, "Come, let us get that connection made. You must have much to discuss."

He looks up at the darkening sky. "I think maybe not now. They will be asleep. It is later there."

"In the morning then," I reply with a squeeze.

Running a thumb across Hassan's brow, Arwyn notes, "Besides, you seem ready for sleep."

Leaning into his touch, Hassan replies, "You may be right."

"Aww, did we wear you out?" I tease but then yawn myself.

"Ha, look who's talking."

Pryderi interjects, "If you want, you can meet Terrah after your conversation tomorrow. But it's up to you. She won't be offended."

Hassan yawns. "It seems I must be patient, as much as I wish to meet your mate's dragon."

"Come on, sleepyhead," Arwyn coos, picking him up in his arms.

Hassan kicks. "I have legs. I can walk."

"You do, but please permit me to take care of you."

In response, Hassan nestles into the hold, his eyes closing.

"Poor guy. It's all been a lot," I think at Arwyn.

Pryderi makes a heart with his hands then waves as he quietly walks off to seek Kiera.

"*For us all*," Arwyn replies.

We head to our den. Ours. The retreat we are blessed with.

"Was there sleeping potion in his food?" I whisper, tackling the trousers and cardigan off my deeply slumbering mate.

"You don't think there was, do you?" Arwyn's whisper is sharp and not terribly quiet.

Stretching and yawning, I tell him, "No. Don't you feel it too?"

"A weariness I've not felt in many a year?"

"Yes, that."

"I don't know what you mean," he says, rubbing his eyes.

"It's a good kind of tired. One born of being utterly satisfied."

He pulls me close and strokes my hair. "Satisfaction at long last."

Enveloping me in a cuddle, he breathes deeply.

"I never thought…dared to hope," I begin, my voice cracking.

"Shh! Me neither. But we got there."

"I'm so sorry."

"No, you're not, for you have nothing to be sorry for."

A tear trickles a salty path down my face. Gripping Arwyn tighter, I declare, "I love you."

"I love you too. Always have. Always will."

"Always."

We stand there, rubbing one another's backs and sniffling in the dark silence of the den. Relief washes through me. Love banishes angst, sending it into the night.

With a deep sigh, I admit, "I don't want this to end. But I really need to sleep."

"Me too. It's OK. We sleep."

Passing the wash basket, I chuck my trousers in and wander to the bed where Hassan is sleep purring. I hesitate, realising Arwyn has gone to the other side of the bed.

"*He needs us both,*" Arwyn thinks at me.

Twisting my mouth, I ponder. Hassan seems pretty content from here. But maybe he's right. There is so much for Hassan to unlearn and come to trust. Snuggling up to his back, I smile. At least he has us to help him through.

The mattress dips as Arwyn joins us, sliding his hand up next to Hassan's. Without waking, Hassan interlinks fingers with Arwyn. My mate was correct – our presence must be reassuring.

Together, I muse with a contented smile as sleep beckons.

A finger is tracing the grooves of my abs, drawing out a purr. "Mmm…that's nice."

"Good morning," Arwyn chimes.

Patting around us, my eyes open wide as I cry, "Where's Hassan?"

Arwyn's heavy paw keeps me where I am. "Hush, jumpy. He's making coffee. He's here."

Cups clang as Hassan carries them over. "I'm here," he tells me softly.

My hand washes over my face as I close my eyes and sigh, opening myself up to the reassuring connection. When did I become so needy? I panicked at the very thought of Hassan not being near.

Lying back next to me, Hassan's hand follows in the wake of my own. "It's OK. We have coffee, *ya amar*. It will help." His nose rubs mine.

I sigh. "My gratitude. Did you sleep well?"

"Better than I ever have."

Arwyn joins in, "Me too. Hey, you don't suppose there really was sleeping potion, do you?"

"*Twp*! No, I do not. I think it's a mating thing."

He shrugs. "Meh. Makes sense."

Reaching around me, Hassan pokes Arwyn's arm. "You know it does. The joining of our souls is a strenuous act. Let alone all the joining of bodies we got up to."

"Mmm…talking of…" Arwyn trails off as he nuzzles my neck.

My forearm slumps across my eyes. "Meurgh, Arwyyyyyn. Not before coffee."

"Huh, is this a rule?"

"Yes. A hard one."

"Talking of hard ones."

"Arwyn, I mean it. I'm not even awake."

"Tell that to Little Elan," he quips, palming me through the sheets, making me wriggle.

Hassan jostles the bed as he smacks Arwyn's hand away. "He said no. Behave. And you know morning wood doesn't count."

Peeking from under my arm, I see Arwyn holding his hands up. "I was only teasing, little mate."

"And that's another thing. Stop saying little. Elan's *zib* is no such thing and neither am I."

Arwyn swipes a hand down his face. "Oh, goddess help me. Two mates and neither one has a sense of humour before coffee."

Worried this may escalate, and really not being in the mood for a squabble, I sit up a little and brush Arwyn's cheek with my thumb. "I know you were not serious. Not really, anyway. But let us be mindful, eh? Hassan is still getting to know us. Gently, Arwyn."

His eyes go wide. There's a pause. His gaze turns to Hassan. "Only with permission. Always. You need to know I would never —"

"I do. I know. It's OK. I need to trust. Can you give me time?"

Arwyn clambers over to Hassan and cradles his face. "You take all the time you need, sweetheart. You hear me? You take your time. We'll give you everything you need." He kisses the tip of Hassan's nose.

Hassan gives a rueful smile. "My gratitude."

My heart swells looking at their interaction. I don't want to say anything to disrupt their moment. Instead, I try to bring my head into the land of the living. It's more of a struggle than it should be to wake up this morning.

"So, this coffee cool enough yet?" Arwyn asks, reaching to pick up a cup.

"Patience, *njūmiyy.*"

Arwyn snorts and passes me the cup. I offer him a smile and a nod as I grip onto the warmth in my hands. Inhaling deeply, the heavenly scent of coffee mixes with the essences of my mates, swirling up my nostrils. I let out a contented moan.

"That's better," Arwyn comments, kissing my cheek, "But I think we need food. Shall I get us some, bring it here?"

I stretch my neck, leaning my head side-to-side. "That sounds good to me."

"OK. You two rest here. I will forage."

"Forage," I scoff, "Hardly. It's all laid out on tables."

Looking down his nose, he replies, "There are different types of foraging, Elan."

I laugh as he scrambles out of bed. "If you say so."

His broad shoulders taper down to his bubble butt. His muscles stretch and skew temptingly as he walks towards his cupboard to grab some clothes. It's almost a crime to cover up such magnificence. His shoulders roll as he stands up, pulling on his trousers.

"Such power," Hassan murmurs at my side.

"Hm, like what you see, sweetheart?" Arwyn calls over.

His answering grin is full of lustful mischief.

"Ah uh uhh. He's not had coffee yet, remember?"

Hassan's pout is almost more than I can bear. But Arwyn's right. We need sustenance.

"No sexy time until I'm back," Arwyn warns as he reaches the door.

He almost stumbles as he walks across the threshold. "What the…?"

"What?" I cry, suddenly wide awake.

"Some idiot left a basket in the way."

"A basket? What's in it?"

"How do I know?" Bending down, he picks it up and sniffs suspiciously. "Hm, Smells like bread."

Lifting the cloth covering, he grins. "And a jar of honey. And some bacon. Hmph, no eggs, though."

"Aww, someone's looking after us."

"But who?" he asks, sniffing at the gift again whilst bringing it over to us.

"Look, there's a note," I say, grabbing it.

Dear Trio,

We thought you may not want to leave your den. Enjoy.

Love Kiera and Pryderi

xx

"Aww, that is so kind," Hassan says.

"They're the best friends."

"Excuse me?" Arwyn checks with mock horror.

"Except us, of course," I add, rolling my eyes.

"Thank you."

"Argh! I need the loo now."

"Good point. Me too."

"Me three," Hassan says.

I laugh. "What? Even going to the latrines is now a three-thing?"

"Seems so," Hassan answers with a shrug.

Calls of nature answered, we scurry back to our bed and basket.

"*Twp*! There *are* eggs, look. They were wrapped up under the bread," I tell Arwyn, holding one up.

"Huh, so there is. Ooh, still warm," he comments, taking it from me. "But where to put the shell?" He looks around.

"Tsk. It's like you were raised in a barn. Here," I cajole, getting up and bringing the bin over.

He grins. "Thank you, mate. You have your uses."

I playfully smack his arm. "Many of them."

"Scooch over," he commands Hassan who complies.

I get back into the soft cosiness of our bed as we unpack our meal. We tuck in, all seemingly famished. Plates have been provided, and we carefully try to catch any crumbs. Especially Hassan, who has made a makeshift bacon sandwich.

"Don't you get that honey everywhere," Arwyn cautions me as I spoon some onto a piece of bread.

"Hmm…where would you like it to go?"

"Did Kiera spell this food? That's a quick turnaround. You were barely conscious not so long ago."

"I slurped some coffee," I tell him with a shrug.

An impish look passes across his face but falls. "No. I just can't. Too sticky."

I gasp. "You even thought about it? Oh, my goddess."

"One has to be open to trying new things."

"But honey?"

"What can I say? I've developed a taste for it," he says, waggling his eyebrows.

"Have you? I'm happy to help with that," Hassan pipes up.

"That's a very kind offer. I might even take you up on it after our food's gone down. If you're lucky."

Hassan and I chuckle.

"How gallant," I tease.

"I thought so," Arwyn replies.

Silence descends, our munching the only sound in the room. My eyes close as I savour the delectable, honeyed bread. I lick my lips to catch a stray strand of goo. Arywn growls, but I ignore his lust for now. It's evident I must build up my energy for the day ahead.

Hassan brushes his hands over his plate, shedding a few leftover crumbs. "Delicious!"

His satisfied grin makes my stomach flip. This is the look he should always have. And I intend to keep it there.

Arwyn and I finish our morning meal soon after. All three of us slurp down the rest of our coffee. Plates and cups then get piled up on our side table as I stretch my legs straight out under the covers.

"There's a contented kitty," Arwyn murmurs, wrapping an arm around my waist and nuzzling my neck.

"Mmmm…" I moan before purring whilst nestling into his embrace.

His strawberry tinted lips trail kisses up to my jaw. His nose gently nudges my face, urging me to turn towards him. With us both lying on our sides, facing one another, Arwyn's lips hover at my mouth, questioning. In answer, I bring myself the rest of the way, kissing him lazily, taking my time.

His tongue laps mine, and he lets out a breathy chuckle. "So tasty."

My hand rakes through his soft, dark hair as I lap back. Cupping the back of his head, I glide in further, our tongues entwining, our mouths opening wider, my eyes closing. Arwyn's hands clutch my buttocks, and our erections harden against one another.

"I need in," I break off to mutter, looking into his fiery blue gaze.

His eyes widen. He says nothing.

Moving my hand to his cheek, I ask, "What? You don't do that? You don't want me inside you?"

He grimaces. "It's just...it wasn't good when I did."

"OK. We don't have to."

My disappointment must show because he replies, "If I would with anyone it would be with you."

I don't want to ask what happened. But by the way his erection's softening against me, it must've been bad. And I had no idea.

"I'm sorry," I whisper, stroking his hair.

"You tried only once, though?" Hassan asks, wrapping around Arwyn's back.

I'd been so immersed in Arwyn, I'd sort of forgotten Hassan was there. And now I feel even worse.

"Yeah. It put me off for life."

A disapproving groan comes out of Hassan's pout as he pulls himself up and over to look at us. "That is no good, *Habibi*. But, if the only coffee I had ever drunk was the first cup I had here in this clan, I may never have drunk it again. And then I would have missed out on a world of flavour, nutrition and pleasure."

"It was that bad?"

He nods. "Sorry to say it, but yes."

"Huh."

"But maybe you would like Elan's flavour of topping, I think? You trust him, do you not?"

"Of course."

"I am not saying you need to try now. But I would ask you to consider it."

Blue eyes search mine like lanterns in the night.

"I promise to go at your own pace. No pressure," I assure him.

"We should. Now."

"Woah! No rush. Don't do anything you don't want to do. Think about it a while."

"No. Hassan's right. I do trust you. It's not fair to let one bad experience keep me from potential pleasure. If we wait, I might talk myself out of it, and I don't want to do that."

"You're sure?"

"Sure."

He reignites our kiss, and I'm left in no uncertainty of his desire.

"I will go for a walk," Hassan mutters, sliding away from us.

But Arwyn spins round and captures him. "Will you *please* stop trying to run off, my jumpy jaguar?"

"But you should have privacy for this."

"Says who? Maybe I want both my mates here with me for this."

"This is your wish? If it helps, I will stay."

Arwyn pecks Hassan's forehead. "Good boy. I know you want to. At least, I think that's what I sense from you? There are lots of emotions flying around right now."

Hassan smiles. "You are correct. So, what do you need, *njūmiyy*?"

"Well, I do remember you offering a taste of honey…"

"You are certain you can cope with that too? At the same time?"

Arwyn's eyes glow orange. "Oh, I think it's the perfect distraction."

I chuckle. "Well, you don't ever do anything by halves, handsome. Come and get spit-roasted."

Patting the mattress as I move to kneel on the edge, I add, "On all fours, right here."

Slowly, he paws his way across and circles around until his beautiful butt orbs are facing me. Unable to resist, I bend down, and with my teeth retracted, I gently nibble. My teeth sink into his firm flesh without breaking the skin. Goddess, I've wanted to do that for the longest time! Arwyn groans.

Hassan passes me the bowl of water and a cloth.

"My thanks. Comfort from the front, will you, please?"

He jogs to his position and strokes Arwyn's hair. "You like that?"

Arwyn purrs.

Hassan kneels up on the mattress, his dick ready and willing, within mouth-reach of Arwyn. I hear Hassan's moan of delight as Arwyn surely takes the bait.

Reaching round, I run my hand up and down Arwyn's shaft. Lapping noises turn to slurps as his head bobs. The pair of them grunt their pleasure.

Arwyn flexes rigid as I drag the wet cloth over his hole. "Sorry. Cold?"

"Uh hngh!"

"My apologies. I'll be quick."

True to my word, I ensure my mate is cleaned in as little time as possible. Bless him, he's already sucking again by the time I'm done.

Taking my opportunity, I duck down and run my tongue through Arwyn's crack. His whimper is muted, his mouth still full. I wait until his shoulders start moving again before repeating my action. He doesn't react, so I do it again. The slurping gets louder.

"Hmm, nice, huh?"

A stifled, "Uungh," is his reply.

Using the tip of my tongue, I trace a star pattern across his hole and surrounding area, up, down, across. He mm's in satisfaction as I then blow a long breath out. Fluid leaks out, telling me he's ready. But I'm not going there yet.

I draw a long, slow lick across his taint. He cries out around Hassan's dick. So, I treat him to another one. And one more for luck since he seems to enjoy it so much.

His bum is wiggling at me.

"Patience," I warn, giving it a playful slap.

He whimpers, but I feel his excitement. Running a finger around his hole, I assure myself of his eagerness, before gradually easing it inside him.

"Augh! I think he likes that," Hassan grits out.

"Yeah?" I ask, gliding my finger in and out.

His muscles clench around me.

"Can't...hold...on...much...longer," Hassan bites out.

"Oops! Sorry, mate."

Arwyn whines as I remove my finger.

"Shh, it's OK, gorgeous. I'm going to give you what you really want. Ready?"

"Mm hngh!" His arse does a little dance.

Kneeling up, my dick rests at his entrance. It's suddenly surreal. How many times have I fantasised about this? And now, here I am.

Arwyn's hips move back an inch, breaking my thoughts apart. I can't deny my mate. This is exactly where we both want to be. Here. Now.

Carefully, I edge my dick inside. Getting nothing but encouragement, I slide in inch by gradual inch until I'm all the way in. Groans erupt from us all.

Steadying myself, I ease back out and glide back in.

"Mmmmngh!"

"You feel so good," I cry.

"Not bad…from here, either," Hassan calls.

Winking at Hassan, I pick up the pace with my next thrust.

"Holy goddess!" he exclaims.

I still, letting Arwyn take up control as he shuttles between us.

"*So much cock!*" I hear him in my head.

"Take it, handsome. Take it all," I urge.

He speeds up, faster and faster. Goddess, he's good. He's sliding along my dick, gripping, pulling, shoving, never relinquishing Hassan from his mouth. His moans are shorter and quicker too. His tone notches up.

Argh, my balls tighten. My whole body tingles. Every sinew is taught. I slam in as he pulls back. Again and again. My head falls back as I roar my release, my cum filling him.

I'm vaguely aware of Hassan and Arwyn's cries. Arwyn's arms collapse down, and I pull out. We all collapse in a breathless heap.

Catching my breath, I crawl up Arwyn's back and hold him to my front and kiss his ear. There's a flash of movement; Hassan pulls away the towel he must've placed under Arwyn earlier. I smile at his forethought. I'd been incapable of such practicalities; too carried away with what lay in store.

"OK?" I check with Arwyn.

"Wouldn't miss that for the world," he slurs.

"See, you can trust me."

"Never doubted…"

Hassan gets up and brings back glasses of water which we gulp eagerly, sitting up on our arms as much as we can.

Placing the empty glass on the floor. I collapse onto my back, my arm over my eyes. "I've never been so spent."

"Me neither," Arwyn mumbles, next to me.

From his other side, Hassan joins in. "Truly magnificent."

"I really really like honey. And we are so doing that again," Arwyn announces.

"No argument from me," I tell them.

"Or me," Hassan agrees.

We lie there, staring up at the ceiling, each of us grinning from ear-to-ear.

Chapter 22 – Replete

~ Hassan

We manage to get out to morning meal on time. I pile my plate up, ravenous after our exertions.

"So, Pryderi says you want to call your parents?" Kiera asks as we dine together.

"If that is permissible, yes, please."

"Of course. You must want to tell them your good news. But, before you do, can I ask you something?"

I frown. "Yes."

"Don't look so worried. I only want to check that you three want to remain here in this clan?"

"Oh, errr…" I look at each of my mates.

Elan coughs. "We've not discussed it."

"I didn't think you would have. Hence my question. Well?"

Arwyn smiles. "What do you think? Can you sacrifice the warmth to be here? I will be with you no matter which clan you choose to call home."

"Me too," Elan adds.

My heart melts. "I think you two will keep me warm."

They both eagerly nod.

"Then there really isn't much of a question, is there?"

"Right, Saudi Arabia, it is," Elan says, laughing.

I tap his arm but chuckle. "I choose here, *ya amar*."

"I thought you might. It was worth checking, though. I'm sure your former clan will want to know," Kiera says.

After we've finished eating, Kiera leads us all to Cerys' den to make the connection. My nerves jangle despite all the power and support around me. I'm glad to be sitting as three faces appear in the mirror. Of course, the Leader would insist on being present with my parents.

It's he who speaks first. "Greetings, Hassan. I trust you are not disgracing yourself there and are representing our clan well."

Elan's hand reaches further behind my back to nudge Arwyn as he growls. But they make me smile; so protective.

"Yes, Sir. But of course. However, it may not be in the way you expect."

He raises a brow. "Ohh?"

I look at Arwyn and Elan on either side of me. "You see…" Two arms squeeze me tighter. "I have met my mates."

"Congratulations!" my mother cries.

But my Leader is glowering. "You surely don't mean..?"

I nod. "Oh, but I do. Leader Babr, Mother, Father, I would please like to introduce you to my mates, Elan and Arwyn," I say, indicating each.

"Greetings," my mates chorus, their hands to their hearts, heads bowing.

"Son, you do not need to do this," my father says, "The authorities have been sent away. Others, human men, came forward, and your human accuser is to be executed without you having to go to court. It is over. Safe."

Growls erupt from both sides of me. Oh, and from myself, apparently. "You think I am mated because I am afraid of a HUMAN?"

"You can come home."

"I AM home."

Three shocked faces stare back.

"He likes it here. It's good for him," Arwyn tries.

"I decide what is best for MY clan. And I say Hassan must return," the Leader says through clenched teeth.

From behind me, Kiera intercedes, "Leader Babr, you were so good as to send Hassan to us. Although, I understand better now, your true reason for doing so. I would point out that our deal has not yet run its course, so Hassan must remain with us."

If looks could kill, Kiera would be writhing on the floor, breathing her last.

Undeterred, she continues, "Furthermore, Hassan has mated. A triad is surely a blessing to any clan. I had believed this call would be only to his parents, otherwise my Leader, Rhion would have also been present. As it is, as Peacekeeper, it falls to me to point out the logistics of such a mating. It would be extremely hazardous to all three males to reside with your clan, so they must all remain here. Together."

My Leader's face has turned red. "You dare instruct me?"

"I do not instruct, Leader Babr. I merely point out what was surely already obvious to someone of your intellect. However, I would point out that I will never condone trying to separate mates."

"Witch!"

"I would thank you not to use that title in such a derogatory fashion, Leader Babr," Cerys interrupts, "Especially when it is inaccurate. Kiera is an elinefae sorceress if we must use titles. Peacekeeper to *all* elinefae."

Kiera takes up the speech, "This has clearly been a shock to you all. We will give you time to absorb this exciting, wondrous news. Good day."

Cerys disconnects the call, and all we see is our own reflections staring back at us.

"Well, that went well," Kiera announces, swiping her hands together.

"Wine?" Cerys asks.

"I think that would be appropriate."

Rearranging the chairs, we sit in a circle. Kiera slumps into her seat. "Eurgh! I'm sorry, Hassan. I had not foreseen that difficult conversation. Really! Cerys had called ahead and asked for your parents. The nerve of that male. What is he so afraid of that he could not allow your family their privacy? Cerys and I were more than happy to simply connect and depart until he intervened."

"Here," Cerys says, nudging the full wineglass into Kiera's hand.

"Please. I had not thought you would expect any less. Leader Babr oversees and controls all. It is his role. As for the rest, he is surely frustrated his plan did not work, that he has lost my cooking skills. I doubt there is any other reason he would wish for my return. There was never much hope of me mating with a female. Perhaps he is angry that my status has been elevated?"

Arwyn growls then hugs me close. "Your status is as it always was. Or should have been. If anything, it is we who are honoured by your presence, mate."

I can't help but go and sit on his lap to preen into him. "You're too kind."

"No."

I don't bother arguing. All three of us pick up the wine glasses from the table and sip. I know I'm trying to gulp down the lump in my throat. My mates probably are too.

"This may not be the best time, but, Hassan, are you still happy to attend my event?" Kiera asks.

Arwyn clutches me tighter. "What's this?"

"It may be…awkward now you're all mated. But I'm hosting what I'm calling a Farmers Market."

Cerys makes a scoffing noise.

"You see, as I've been going about my duties as Peacekeeper, I've been privileged to visit many clans. And it's clear that too many are being forced to interact with humans in order to survive. And, as we know all too well, that's a perilous situation."

"Agreed," Elan says.

"So, I came up with this idea. All clans can send representatives. I've found a space, similar to the one for sabbats, only time works differently there, so everyone from both hemispheres can be there together. When we have surplus produce, we can take it to the Farmers Market and barter with it. Then we get more variety and therefore reducing our reliance on human supplies."

"Riiiiight," Arwyn begrudgingly agrees.

"But as a lot of the food will be new, I realised that demonstrations would be a good idea too. So, I thought I'd use that as my excuse to get Hassan here. He was trialling different cuisine to see how receptive elinefae clans would be."

"You used our mate as a pawn?" Arwyn sneers.

She rolls her eyes. "I'm not playing a game, Arwyn. This is serious. We all need to be more self-sufficient again. Did Hassan tell you how some of his clan went to work in the city? A *human* city!"

"What? No!"

"Exactly. Cerys and I had to infiltrate the office and drag them home by their ears. This is only a start. But I'm hopeful we can inspire more. So, my intention was to have Dai and Hassan prepare some food at the first Farmers Market next week."

"Absolutely not," both my mates roar.

"Of course, we'd have our three best Watchers there too. Each clan will have the same opportunity. Cerys and other witches have seen the venue. We've clearly marked out areas for each clan to set up in. Hopefully, nobody will feel overly territorial. It's neutral ground. A shared space."

"Hmmm...I still don't like it," Arwyn grumbles.

"Why on ever not? There's a whole world of cuisine out there. Trust me, I grew up eating many types of food. This is a good thing."

"You already agreed to this, didn't you?" Elan asks me.

"Before I met you, *Habibi*, yes. Kiera makes a good point. Not so much here, but places like where I grew up, we need this."

"I'll think about it," Arwyn mumbles.

Standing up, I shout, "IT IS NOT YOUR DECISION TO MAKE, ARWYN. Your Leader, Witch and Kiera have already agreed. *I* have already agreed. Other clans have agreed. I will not go back on my word. You will not force me into dishonour."

"I...I....ARGH!" Arwyn yells, then stomps out.

"Oh, for fuck's sake, Arwyn. What's wrong with you now?" Elan calls, chasing after him.

"I don't understand why he's so upset," I mutter at the two ladies.

"In all honesty, neither do I. I just thought that maybe you three would struggle to leave one another alone for a whole day. That's two unexpected turns today. Cerys, is my intuition broken?" Kiera asks, knocking the side of her head.

Cerys shrugs. "You were right about the triad, weren't you?"

"Yes. Of course. It's just…something feels…off."

"Go and get some fresh air. It's been a weird morning."

"That sounds nice, actually. Hassan, join me? Let's leave Arwyn to simmer down whilst you and I meet Terrah."

"Maybe I should go check on him?"

"Pah! He'll be fine. Elan's with him anyway. It's probably best not to get embroiled in his emotions when they're running this high. Elan's used to it and knows what to do. They'll find you when they're ready," Cerys explains.

"Well, if you're certain of this. Alright, take me to Terrah, please, Kiera."

Chapter 23- This Little Piggy Goes to Market
~ Arwyn

I freely admit to having a fiery temper. But this is unreasonable, even for me. Being mated isn't all sunshine and sex, apparently. Who knew? Or maybe the overprotectiveness is worse for Watchers.

Despite numerous conversations with my mates, I can't shake off the feeling deep in my gut that Hassan shouldn't go to the Farmers Market. Even Elan shares my misgivings to some extent but is more easily swayed. The worst thing is I don't have any viable argument against the scheme.

Kiera has found a safe location which the witches have verified. It's actually a good idea – becoming less reliant on humans is surely good for our kind. And, without it, Kiera may not have had an excuse to bring Hassan here. So why do I not want him to go?

Hassan, I know, had been worried about our first impressions. But I've been surly ever since, well, just before his arrival. I hate myself for it. I need him to see my true self. Begrudgingly, I've seen sense; Hassan must honour his agreement. Elan and I will be there as Watchers, so we'll be with him. But it's not stopped me being a grump all week.

You know, I suspect Hassan likes my irritability. The worse it gets, the more he coaxes me into wild orgasms. Maybe he enjoys the challenge. I certainly do! Augh, this male; he is all kinds of delicious. I'm not sure if I deserve such sweet devotion.

Elan hasn't needed any encouragement to try to cheer me up but even he's been caught up in Hassan's boundless...what did Kiera call it..? *Joie de vivre*. He really is our ray of sunshine.

"Come on then, let's get this over with," I say, knuckling Hassan's hair once we're all dressed.

Reaching up, he kisses my cheek and grins. "It will be fine, *njūmiyy*. The team and I have worked hard to create the best dishes for other clans to try. They're going to be trying to raid us just to get our produce."

"And this is supposed to make me feel better, is it?"

"Yes. Now, let's go show off."

All three of us share a kiss. Palming the sword on my back, I take a deep breath and lead the way out of our den to meet up with Kiera, Pryderi and Dai.

"My, don't we look grand?" Kiera chimes as we approach.

Pryderi growls.

I hiss. "Not so very different from any other day. You ready?"

A scowl creases her eyes before she nods. "Right this way."

We pick up the containers piled up on the kitchen side, and head towards the truck which has been pulled up outside. Kiera reassures us this is a small trailer in comparison. There is a sink and room to prepare and serve hot food.

Kiera takes us all through the portal she opens. And yes, as I begin to pull, the mobile kitchen is as heavy as it looks. Pryderi is at my side whilst Elan is relegated to pushing. Fortunately, it doesn't have to move far, just to where our clan's area is marked. Tension has my hairs standing on end; other clans are arriving and making their own preparations. My lip involuntarily curls. Elan is better at hiding his reaction, but I catch sight of it all the same. Neither of us is happy about this. Clans may be able to celebrate together occasionally, but this? This could become very territorial very quickly.

Granted, Kiera has done a fair job of ensuring distance between the marked areas. The marketplace is massive. It's outside, but as I breathe in, my lungs are not filled with the fresh air I'd expected. There's a sour taste lacing the atmosphere.

Hassan claps me on the back, making me jump. "Stop looking so worried. We're all keeping our distance. I think everyone here sees the necessity."

I grimace more than grin at him. Goddess, I hope he's right.

Dai and Hassan excitedly set up our clan's stand. I've been privileged enough to see my mate in his habitat a few times now; cooking truly is his refuge from the world. His smile soothes my anxiety as I watch him sauté the prepared vegetables. And I can tell he's added his own spices to the large pot of venison stew which is warming up; the smell's making my mouth water.

Elan is at my side and subtly rubs my back as we stand guard. I risk a thankful smile at him in between glancing around us. Pryderi steps forwards with Kiera, to a raised platform in the centre.

Her voice echoes around. "Firstly, thank you all for coming here today. I appreciate it's uncomfortable. But with practice, I'm sure it will become easier. What is one day per month, after all? Especially when it is for the greater good."

Murmurs, nods and some head shakes go around the clans. I make a mental note of the perpetrators of the latter.

"Now that all the cooks seem well underway, I would urge the chosen clan representatives to start making their rounds. Do try the food on offer here. I am sure there is much to discover and barter for. We're all aware of the rules. Obey them and have fun." She raises her hands up and out in invitation.

Kiera and Pryderi meet with Rhion as our representatives, and lead by example, going to nearby stands. They chat as well as taste. Rhion soon brings one of the other Leaders to our stand. My heart stops as he approaches. My stomach tightens as the stranger tries my mate's food.

"Wow! Oh, my goddess. Rich, dark, spicy, nourishing. What is this meat?" he asks.

Dai answers, "Venison, Sir. Deer. It is exceedingly good at fortifying. We do syphon blood, but we are not dependant on it as much goodness is contained within the flesh."

"Come with me. You must see what we can tempt you with to exchange for some of this…venison."

Dai looks at Hassan, seeking assurance in his glance, which is offered. With a nod, Elan leaves to accompany him. My claws descend. And my stomach churns until

I think I'm going to be sick. But their safe return saves me that embarrassment. What have I become?

More people come and try our food. Hassan's grin gets wider and wider as more and more offer goods in exchange. Goddess bless my mate, I don't think he could be any happier.

Dai is called off a few times, also ecstatic. There is an increasing buzz as everyone gets more adventurous and discovers a world of flavour. Kiera did this. Our clan member. My friend. I'm fit to burst with pride for her and my mate. But that strange metallic, sour scent grows stronger.

Someone is making an exchange with Hassan when a loud whistle pierces my ears. I grimace against the onslaught but am prepared to do my duty despite the pain. However, before I've even drawn my sword, there's a blinding flash.

That sour note has turned into a stench. Combined with the echoes of the whistle and trying to blink away the spots in my eyes, I feel dazed and queasy. I've jumped into attack stance, but am faced with…

"HE'S GONE!" I scream.

Dashing around the stand, I seek in vain. "HASSAN! HASSAN!" I yell over and over.

Elan runs up. "Where is he? I can't feel him. Arwyn!"

My hand clutches my stomach where our mate link should be, and double over in pain with a yelp. Elan yowls, squatting down.

"HASSAN!" we both cry.

"Oh, my goddess. Oh, my goddess," Kiera murmurs, coming towards us. "Oh, my goddess. What happened?"

My glare burns towards her "YOU! I told you no. You wouldn't listen. And now he's gone. Taken in front of my very eyes."

"I'm so—"

"Don't you fucking dare say sorry."

Pryderi launches at me but I fight back.

"STOP!" Kiera commands.

We freeze, including Elan who's mid-leap.

"Fighting one another isn't going to bring him or the others back."

"Others?" Arwyn asks.

"Look around you," she says, releasing her spell.

Elan lands awkwardly, having to turn away from Pryderi, his original target. We glance at the scene in front of us. I'd been so swept up in our own loss, I'd not noticed others yelling.

"EVERYONE. TO YOUR CLAN HOMES NOW!" I shout at the top of my lungs as the stench grows stronger again.

There is utter confusion as people run around, trying to converge. Teeth are bared and accusations are made. Fuck! Despite my anguish, I run into the fray to try to keep this from escalating.

"CLAN. NOW!" I yell at everyone I see. "FIGHTING LATER."

"RETREAT. GET TO SAFETY," Elan commands.

Most have scrabbled into their clan groups, their witches transporting them home, presumably. But other, more adamant ones are still snarling whilst others cower for cover.

Another flash of light flares. Rubbing my eyes, I try to focus, pushing people apart.

"FOR FUCK'S SAKE, GET TO YOUR ENCAMPMENT," I roar.

"EVERYONE. HOME CLANS NOW!" Kiera instructs.

Finally, everyone disappears. Our group is the last to leave. My heart is ripped out of me. Back home, emptiness fills my whole being as I collapse onto the ground.

"Kiera, I felt your fear. Are you alright?" a shrill voice asks.

There's a golden flutter at the edge of my vision.

Kiera's answer is a distant echo as I roll in agony. "Frydah, I'm so glad to see you. I'm fine. But these two need help."

"Oh no," the faery murmurs, flitting close, "Not again."

"Cerys, Chen, Frydah, I have to make some calls. Emergency! Help these two."

"I'm staying with you," Frydah chips in.

"Two? They're a triad, Kiera. Where's the third?" Cerys says.

"That's why they're in so much pain. Please. Help them. I need to find Hassan, and I have no idea where to start. It's not just him. Other clans had people taken too."

A roar almost deafens me. Then everything falls silent. I wonder if I've passed out. But then I wouldn't be able to think that, would I? I can't turn my head to look, it makes me dizzy.

"Yes, if you think you can find him, go look, Shui," Chen agrees, breaking the silence. "But please be careful."

Cerys is lifting my head onto her lap. "Here, sip this."

Wincing, I do as she says.

"Chen, you take this one to Elan."

Cerys strokes my hair. "Breathe, brave Arwyn. We will find him. I vow it."

Tears are falling down my cheeks. How long have I been crying? Clutching Cerys' arm, I plead, "Please. Find him. Heal me."

"Shh. I'm healing you. Both of you. We'll get you to my den in a moment once that elixir kicks in."

"No, I have to go now."

"And just where do you think you're going, hm? Besides, you're in no fit state to go anywhere, are you? Take a moment, Arwyn. I know every bone in your body is screaming for your mate. But let us find him. Get strong so you can fucking kill whoever took him."

I grunt and nod. The witch speaks sense. But fuck it all, I need to find Hassan.

"Focus, Arwyn. He needs you."

Well, doesn't that just make me grit my teeth and bare it?

"That's it. Can you get up and walk? There are supplies in my den. Let's get you to safety so I can get you properly back on your feet. Maybe if we get you better, he can feel it too, eh?"

"I'll call Threaris. Maybe he can help?" Frydah suggests.

"I should be able to do this," Kiera gripes.

Cerys consoles, "Kiera, dear. You can't be everywhere at once. The other clans need answers. And I'm sure they're all too ready to lay blame at your door. Call all the witches, let them know we're searching. Maybe they can help."

"My locator spell isn't working. Why would theirs?"

"We have to try everything."

"I know. I just feel so bloody useless."

"Kiera, get a grip. We'll find them. But we need help."

Frydah checks, "Tell me what happened. Where were you?"

Cerys and Chen help Elan and me to our feet and we creep towards her den as explanations are made. I will get healed. And I will find my mate. Then whoever did this will beg for mercy before they die.

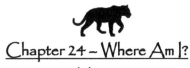

Chapter 24 – Where Am I?

– Hassan

"That's right, groan for me, elinefae," a gruff voice sneers near me.

It's dark. Someone is cradling me in their arms, but they smell of frankincense and roses, not the foulness flowing out from the speaker.

"Omar? Is that you? Where am I?" I ask through clenched teeth.

"Shh! I do not know the answers you seek."

"No talking!" our captor shrieks, slapping Omar across the face, jolting me in turn.

So, we're not in the Saudi Arabian clan. I thought maybe they'd dragged me back. But the face I just glimpsed…it's not even elinefae. I try to leap to Omar's defence but fall back down as pain ricochets through me.

"Pain is good. Fear is better. And you *should* be afraid, elinefae scum."

The stench is too much, like farts produced by blue cheese, cauliflower and Brussels sprouts with overtones of dead rat. I just about manage to roll over and throw up onto the floor, and not on Omar. He shuffles us away from the puddle.

"He needs water," Omar pleads.

I shrink as my former clan mate gets slapped again. "You're in no position to make demands. Shut it."

Where are Elan and Arwyn? Not wanting to give these villains what they want, I try to push down my panic. But the pain…it consumes me. I bite my lip so hard that the tang of blood hits my tongue.

"Deep breaths," Omar whispers.

I try, but any stale air comes in stutters. Omar quietly soothes, rocking me in his arms. How strange! But I am too thankful to question too deeply. I need to find out who these creatures are. But my mind is fogged.

My friend starts to hum a familiar tune we sing to younglings. The edge is taken off the pain. And I almost laugh when our captor squeals for him to stop. I manage to open my eyes and see them covering their ears.

"Stop! Stop that racket," they moan.

Brave Omar ignores their demands and carries on. At least, until another enemy comes over, hands still over their ears, and kicks him in the face. "You were told to stop."

Without another word, they skulk away.

Blood is seeping between Omar's fingers where he's clutching his nose. I reach my hand up and replace his hand with my own.

"*Confervo*," I whisper, to heal his broken nose.

"Thanks. But I'm supposed to be helping you," he whispers back.

"Works both ways," I say, flolloping back down.

He chuckles. Fortunately, our captors seem not to have noticed. They're huddled together along the opposite wall. Maybe our smell is as offensive to them as theirs is to us. Goddess, I hope so.

Slowly, I turn in Omar's arms and count…one, two…ten. Including myself, there are ten elinefae here. They're in various states of shock, some are crying. Looking back at the…goblins? There are only five of them. Why are we not attacking them? My foot tingles as I stretch my leg out. Argh! That outright stung me. Right, magickal barrier - that would do it.

Goblin isn't quite right, though. They're far too small for orcs. Right size and appearance for goblins; short, deceptively muscular, pale greyish green skin, huge nose, pointy teeth, protruding large ears which are pointier than ours or elves.

Then there are their eyes; although light blue, there is a total lack of the warmth found in Arwyn's loving gaze. There's something cold and soulless about them, more than goblin…argh, my head hurts. Everything hurts. I clutch my stomach again.

"Arwyn. Elan," I murmur, trying unsuccessfully to reach through our link.

"It's true, isn't it?" Omar whispers.

"Mates."

The effort of healing, moving and thinking has worn me out. Sweat breaks out across my brow.

"Shh, try to rest."

A wooziness creeps over me. My eyes close as Omar strokes my hair.

I must've fallen asleep. Sadly, this is real and not some terrible nightmare, I realise, opening my eyes.

"Here, I saved you some...of this," Omar says, nudging a bowl into my hands as I sit up.

My free hand rubs down my face. "How long was I asleep?"

Omar shrugs. "No idea. Do you feel any better?"

Frowning, I internally check. "Hm, groggy, but maybe a little better."

"Good. Eat if you can. It's not exactly your standard."

"Oh, this is not good."

"It's terrible."

"No. I mean, that they're feeding us. They want us alive."

"Well, that's not terrible."

"My friend..." I stop myself. What's the use in pointing out that we'll probably get tortured before they decide to end our lives? Instead, I spoon some gloop into my mouth.

"Shit," I exclaim, trying to swallow.

"Don't say I didn't warn you."

"Yeah. But why is nobody beating us up?"

"You, Hassan, are just looking for trouble. I think they ate their fill. They all fell asleep."

"Careless. Wait...ate?" I quickly count up our numbers. Phew, ten still.

"Riley, she's from an American clan, thinks they're eating our fear."

"From what that one said earlier, I think she's right. Goblin-like, fear-eaters, magick users…that would make them…graublin."

He nods. "That is my guess."

"But they've not been seen…"

"And because you cannot see something means it is not there, perhaps?"

Rubbing my forehead, I mutter, "Shit."

"Agreed."

"Has anyone got any ideas?"

"We've not had much time to talk. The graublins haven't been asleep that long."

I still can't feel my mates. But it doesn't hurt quite so much. I try again to reach out through our mind link but feel nothing. Goddess, are they alive? It shouldn't be so numb. Squinting, I push that thought aside. If I give into it, I'll crumble entirely. They're just far away, I tell myself.

Forcing down more slop, I look around at the terrified faces near us, and swipe an arm across my eyes.

"Firstly, we need to stop feeding these brutes."

"How do we do that?" one of the others asks, I think in an Australian accent.

I smirk. "Stop being scared."

"Riiight, just like that."

"What's your name?"

"El…Ella."

"Well, Ella. Have you seen these little bastards? We're twice their size and number."

Slow nods go around our group.

"And we are elinefae," I say, slapping my chest. My mates' behaviour has rubbed off on me already, it seems.

"Yeah," they all call out.

The graublins stir. Crap!

I focus on my mate link again, desperate to reach Elan and Arwyn. Ahh, there's a very faint echo. What can I send down it? I don't even know my location. So, I draw on love; feeling and giving. "*Find me,*" I think at my mates, also trying to send them an image of the graublins. Nothing comes back the other way.

I pray to the goddess it's enough. But I can't rely on that. If I don't know where I am, how will they?

A thought occurs to me, making me wish the brain fog would return. Even the graublins marked me out as weak. Looking at my fellow captives, I realise they picked out their prey with care. Fuck! I feel sick again. And I need to hit something. Roaring, I punch the wall.

I lick at the blood on my knuckles whilst relishing the sting. Anger boils in my veins. That's better than being sorry for myself. I'll show these arseholes who's weak.

As if responding to my inner threat, a graublin enters our area, lifts me off my feet and chucks me at the wall. "No damaging property!"

Are you fucking kidding me? I slide down on my behind, my head in my hands.

"Are you alright?" Omar asks.

"Just leave me alone," I whimper.

I will not cry. I will not cry. Fuck them! I will not cry.

The others are whispering in their corner. "How the hell did he pick him up like that?"

"Must be magick."

"NO TALKING! I won't tell you again," a graublin warns, striking one of us with his cudgel.

Great, now they're all awake. Come, witness my abject humiliation! I kick out but my foot doesn't contact anything, I just kick up a bit of dust off the floor. That'll show them!

There's a draught. Looking up, I realise I punched a dent in their dirt wall beneath the tiny, barred window. A sweet scent reaches my nose as I heave myself closer to the opening.

Realisation dawns - they're not even trying that hard to keep us contained. Wait. Does that mean there's more danger outside? They seem pretty confident we won't escape out of our flimsy cell. Although, kicking this wall in would probably bring the ceiling down on us all. Is it worth the risk?

The graublins are licking their lips. "That's better!"

Really? I get thrown like a ragdoll and now the elinefae are scared little kitties again? Wow! Yes, it was surprising that they could. But it didn't truly hurt. I've had worse playfights. Clearly, none of these elinefae are Watchers or Leaders. Presuming we were all taken at the same time, they must be cooks. Laughter bubbles up but I squish it back down. I don't even know what's so funny.

Oops! Too cheerful. A graublin is staring at me, its head cocked to one side. I offer it a sarcastic salute. It stalks closer.

"I wouldn't be so happy if I were you."

I shrug.

"Are you that stupid that you don't know what's going to happen?"

"Are you so stupid as to believe you will go unpunished?"

"Nobody will want to save snivelling specimens like you. You're not worth the effort. Besides, you're the ones who came into our home uninvited. We're defending ourselves."

"Oh, this is self-defence?"

"The grin will be on the other side of your face when we spit roast you alive."

There's surely something wrong with me. At hearing "spit-roast", my mind thinks of Arwyn. Oh, my gorgeous mate, taking me and Elan. I close my eyes and smile. My mates. They love me. They will want to save me.

"This one's broken," the graublin calls to its brethren.

"What do you mean broken? It seems intact."

"It just smiled when I told it we are going to roast them."

"Well, one or two of them. The rest we'll just swallow raw."

Perhaps the graublin's right; my mind has broken. But I laugh at the idea of being swallowed. Keeping my eyes closed, I imagine the glorious blowjobs I've been gifted. These graublins can kill me, but I'll die a happy male. I was united with the two best mates an elinefae could wish for.

"See! It's laughing. Why is it so happy? It's disgusting."

"We'll cook him first. The rest have enough fear in them."

"Hmmm…gobbling…" I murmur, still picturing fun times.

"Oh, my goddess, you're not…?" Omar begins, then laughs too.

"What? What's so funny?" the other elinefae ask.

"Blow jobs," Omar snorts out.

The graublins are seemingly lost for words.

"Yeeeeaaaah," I moan.

I've hit a horny nerve. My companions join in the groans of pleasure. I crack an eye open and see some are even touching themselves.

"Foul elinefae. I said it wasn't worth our trouble. Look at them. Revolting!" a graublin complains.

"Stop it. We're going to kill you," another graublin rages, coming up and hitting me.

"Oh, yes, harder! I like it rough," I moan, trying to stop bile from rising by picturing Arwyn.

The graublin hits me again, but I'm ready and kick out. It buckles over as my foot connects with its balls. So, magick strength but not protection. Idiots! The standing graublin drags the injured one out to their side.

"Fool! What did you let it do that for? Now, they're going to think they can attack us."

The other one's still wailing too much to say anything. Ha!

I yell over, "So, you want to eat us, right?"

One of the graublins turns and takes a couple of steps closer. "Yes, once you've worn out your use."

"Well, we're all cooks. Any one of us will tell you that what you feed your prey flavours its meat. Right?" I ask, looking at the others who nod.

"Your point?"

"Let me cook for us. We'll taste better."

It scrunches its face. "What's in it for you?"

"Edible food," I reply with a shrug.

It looks at the other graublins who shoot dubious glances our way.

"You speak true?"

"Yes."

"It could be nice to eat something tastier than plain elinefae flesh," it says towards its friends.

"And that one should be kept away from the others. It's interrupting our feast," another adds.

"Hmph. Well, alright. But no tricks."

"You can lead me to your kitchen in chains," I offer.

"Alright then."

"Keep back," it warns the others as it crouches to tie rope between my feet and then hands.

Tugging on the rope, it leads me out of the dank room and into the foulest kitchen I've ever seen. Bones and scraps litter every surface. Using my bound arms, I sweep detritus off a countertop to clear space.

"Let's see what you have, then," I say, pulling on my bonds and trying to gingerly walk to the cupboards.

My head reels back as the stench of mould hits me. I'm guessing food poisoning isn't a problem for these graublins. Goddess, their stomachs must be cast iron. In the corner, I notice some sacks of fresh vegetables. These bastards must've raided the market. Did they kill everyone else there? My stomach lurches, but then I remind myself that I felt *something* on my link. No, the graublins are too cowardly anyway. They must've raided what was left after everyone fled.

Fled? My mates ran away without me? Impossible. But where are they? Their presence is so faint. I mentally slap myself. I still don't know where I am. Don't give into melancholy. Believe in Elan and Arwyn. Believe in myself. Yes, right, my job.

I've automatically been picking through edible food, which I now take over to the vile counter, balanced in my arms. The graublin watches without helping, of course. The rope between my feet hangs loose, and I almost trip up.

"Right, I'll need some herbs. What have you got growing outside?"

313

"Growing?"

"Yes. There are green things in the ground, aren't there?"

"You'd eat the ground hair?"

Oh, good goddess, give me strength! "Of course. Where do you think these came from?"

"Market."

"Riiiight. But before that, these vegetables grew in the ground."

The graublin pulls a face.

"Will you just let me look?"

It grimaces, but the graublin leads me outside. I take in gulps of fresh air. Oh, sweet mercy! The wild herbs smell divine.

"I need a knife."

"No. You'll stab me. I'm not stupid. I said no tricks."

I roll my eyes. "I won't stab you. But if you're truly worried, stand back."

"It *is* a trick. You'll run away."

"Even if I tried, I wouldn't get far like this."

It snorts, backs away and tosses a penknife on the ground. I try not to wonder where it got that as I scout around. Ah! There, valerian, just as I smelled earlier. Praise be. I dig up as much as I can, including the roots. Some other herbs get picked too, so as not to arouse suspicion more than I already have.

"I need to pee," I announce, standing up, holding out the harvest in my hands, "Please hold these."

"Drop the knife and kick it over."

"Oh, for fuck's sake. Here," I grumble, doing as told.

Only then, does the graublin approach, pick up the knife and take the herbs. It stands and watches as I relieve my bladder. Oh oops, how did some land on the rope at my feet? Eww! But necessary. I'd apologise but the graublin doesn't seem to care or notice.

We go back inside, with me trailing my scent behind me.

"I'll need my hands free to chop," I say, holding them out.

"No. No more knives. You tell me, I do."

I grimace. The thought of those grubby hands near my food turns my stomach. "Fine. First, where's your water? Those need to be washed."

The graublin makes a face. Ha, don't like that, do you? But it complies.

The graublin is clumsy and lacks finesse, but eventually, a vegetable soup is prepared. It's licking its lips as steaming liquid gets ladled into bowls. We carry them through.

But horror surrounds me as we enter the room. There must be a sound barrier, otherwise, I would've heard something. The elinefae are huddled together, screaming and sobbing. The graublins are crunching bones. I count...no! Only eight remain in the cell. My stomach lurches.

Licking its fingers, a graublin snarls at me. "A delicious appetiser. Now for mains."

315

My blood freezes. I should've known this was going too well. Shit!

"*They ate Ella,*" I hear Omar wail in my head.

No. No, no, no. Not Ella. I swallow the bile back down as it tries to rise.

"You ate one without me?" my kitchen helper whines.

"Fuck off. There's plenty more."

Instead of grabbing me, it mercifully grabs the bowl from my hands.

It laughs. "You didn't think we'd let you eat such food, did you?"

My mouth hangs open; words won't surface.

Noisily, it slurps from the bowl.

"*Kol Khara,*" I think, wishing it would literally eat shit. But then it would probably enjoy that.

The others snatch bowls from the one who prepared the food. It goes back for the rest and returns whilst licking its lips. Clearly lower in the pecking order, it must've eaten its share in the kitchen. I'm still standing there, uselessly watching, unable to tear my gaze away.

<u>Chapter 25– Find Him</u>
~ Elan

"Hassan!" I murmur, waking up.

Goddess only knows what Cerys knocked me out with. I remember drinking another elixir, and the residual smell of burning herbs lingers in the air. I palm my eyes, trying to come fully into the waking world. I'm empty.

Arwyn crawls onto my bed and wraps himself around me. "Did you just wake too?"

"Yes. Eurgh, I'm so groggy. But we need to get out of here and find our mate."

"Agreed. Thank the goddess I have you. I think I'd be more crazed than Pryderi was without Kiera if you weren't with me. I know he's alive, I feel…love."

Rubbing my chest, I confirm, "Me too. But how can anyone do this? Why?"

"I have no answers. Only anguish."

My anger wakes me a little more. "He's our mate. We're Watchers. And yet some fucker took him. We were right there, Arwyn…" My anger turns to tears.

His mouth gapes and he clutches his head. "Oh, my goddess. It's my fault. Elan, I felt a disturbance. More than once. But I dismissed it as a squirrel, and then you another time. Fuck! I should've reported it. They were here. His captors. They've been spying on us. Shit! I've failed. I failed him, duty and clan…and you, us. We've got to find him. I can't live with myself if —"

I stop his ranting by rubbing his upper arm. "Shh! It's OK."

"But it's not though, is it?"

"It will be. We'll find him. Somehow. And then the thieves will wish they'd never been born."

"Damn fucking right!"

"Oh good, you're both awake," Cerys notes, coming back into her den.

"Oh, my goddess, I'm so sorry for what you're going through," Pryderi says, having followed the witch in and kneeling in front of us.

"I'm not sure you should be here right now," Arwyn growls.

"Let's get one thing clear. You are not to blame my mate. She's been working flat out to find Hassan. And if you dare accuse her of anything but good, I won't tell you where he is."

We both shoot up and pin him to the floor. "You've found him? Tell us. Where?"

Pryderi grins. "Actually, not far from where we were."

"At the marketplace?"

"Near but hidden. Shui can show the way. He's the one who picked up his scent."

We both stagger out of the den.

"Wait! You need to eat. And a plan," Cerys calls.

But we don't stop, breaking into a full run instead. We both skid to a stop as we get outside – a large dragon is in our way, drizzle dripping off his scales.

"Shui," I cheer, "Thank you, my friend. Can you take us to him?"

He does his 'yes' head bob.

A cackled roar has me peeking around the red body in front of me.

"Terrah. And you have backup." My eyes widen, trying to take in the scene.

Rhion and Ioan beat their hands to their hearts. Chen stands in front of Kiera, who is next to…her father - The Great Threaris, the sorcerer has come? And with his mate, Zondra. And a unicorn. It seems the whole clan surrounds them.

"Oh!" I exclaim on a breath.

"What?" Arwyn asks, catching up, having paused to stroke Shui. "Ah!"

Zondra steps forwards, bowing her head. "Kiera said Shui smelled goblins with your mate. I thought you may appreciate a little water power."

"Thank you, yes, I suppose, err…" I stammer.

"I requested Roger's assistance. Goblins are renowned for their fear of horses. So, a unicorn should have them pooping themselves," Frydah adds, flitting closer.

Dai steps out of the surrounding crowd. "For strength," he says, offering us each a cup of blood.

"Our gratitude," Arwyn replies, taking both cups.

"You get him back, you hear?"

There's a lump in my throat, so I just nod. Arwyn and I down our fortifying drinks.

"I'm so—" Kiera starts.

Arwyn holds up his hand. "Apologies later. Now, we must rescue Hassan. Tell us, what is your plan? It seems you have one."

Pryderi and Cerys have come outside and stand with their mates. Two Watchers approach with our weapons which we strap on.

As we prepare, Kiera explains, "There seems to be an isolated house, according to Shui. The area for the marketplace was a front, a trap of some sort."

"How many?" I ask Shui.

"He's not sure," Chen replies for him. "But no more than ten, probably fewer. It is a small dwelling."

"And you're sure there are no others in the vicinity?"

Shui snorts.

Chen continues, "Cerys, Rhion and some Watchers are remaining here, in case it's a diversion, and the clan come under attack."

We both nod. "Understood."

"Shui will fly above, showing the location. Roger will lead the way on foot. Surprise will be on our side as much as the fear he'll invoke. Ioan will be close behind him. Threaris will shield us and counterattack any magick. Presuming all the enemy are inside the house, we will sneak up to ascertain their positions. If they set off any incendiaries, Zondra will take care of them.

Kiera's bringing up the rear. Watchers and me at your side upfront."

"Reconnoitre, get in, strike, get our people out, got it," I confirm.

"How many elinefae were captured?" Arwyn asks.

"Ten. No other casualties."

I nod. With so many of us at that marketplace, I'm unsure whether that's good or not. It at least suggests a small number of elinefaenappers.

Looking at Rhion, I ask hopefully, "Sir, we take no prisoners?"

"There is no mercy, not for this." His ferocious look reminds me how this powerful male earned his place.

Taking a blade out of its casing on my back, I swipe the air in front of me. "This the best way to kill them?"

"With steel containing iron? I'd say so," Chen says with a wink, flourishing his own sword.

Arwyn's also testing the weight of his weapon. Placing it back in its sheath, he checks, "So, are we ready then?"

"*Deffro'r haearn!*" echoes around as swords are lifted. 'Wake the iron' being the Welsh battle cry of our clan.

Drummers thunder out a rhythm as we line up in attack formation. My heart beats all the harder as our feet march in time. On the spot, we stomp. Even Roger hooves the ground. The tempo picks up. Yelps, cries, growls then roars echo up to the skies as we truly prepare for battle. The strength of the clan fills our veins as we cry out together.

Arwyn and I may be focused on Hassan, but this is so much bigger than him. Other clan members were taken. We are all here for clan. We stand as one.

A deathly hush falls at the last drumbeat. As much as Ioan irks me, he is all ferocity now, coming to our aid as he takes the lead behind the unicorn. A communal breath gets drawn in and Kiera opens a portal.

With a shake of his mane, Roger steps through. My heart's in my mouth. This has to work. We will get Hassan back. It takes a lot of self-control not to let out another battle cry, but stealth is our aim. With a determined glance at one another, Arwyn and I march forwards.

Kiera and her father dissolve the glamour as we near, and the cottage is revealed. How had we not sensed this? My hand tightens its grip on my weapon as movement near a tree catches my eye. My fellow warriors have noticed too. I sense we're all coiled, on the cusp of charging.

What the actual..? Despite our training, without any other thought, Arwyn and I run towards our mate who meets us halfway.

"Hassan! You're safe. You're safe," I cry.

Arwyn pats him all over. "You are OK? You're not injured?"

"As well as I can be."

Our arms are all over each other, kissing and nuzzling. He's here. He's safe. Our mate. Tears pour out of us all.

"I knew you'd come," he whimpers.

"Our brave mate. Of course. Of course, we came. We had to find you first. But you didn't need us, it seems."

"Aher! As much as I hate to break up the reunion, might I ask where the enemy is?" Ioan interrupts.

"Inside. Second room," Hassan answers.

"What? All of them?" Arwyn asks.

That cheeky grin I've missed too much appears. "All five graublins. They ate something that didn't agree with them."

"They're all inside?" Ioan checks.

"Yes. No elinefae are left in there. But...I'm sorry. One of us didn't make it," He admits, looking over to the rest of the survivors who are huddling by a tree.

Ioan slaps Hassan's back. "Explanation later. Clan to me," he calls.

"Go! I'm safe," Hassan urges when we don't move.

Looking around, I see Kiera. "Guard him with your life."

"Of course."

Time for vengeance! Lifting my sword back up, I follow my clan Watchers. My breath is stolen by the stench as we enter the house. But instead of five graublins, there stands a small, green dragon.

"Terrah! What did you do?" I ask, my voice high-pitched.

She burps.

My arm shoots to my mouth. "Not nice, Terrah!"

"Bloody dragon stole our prey," Arwyn grizzles, "We're denied the satisfaction of slipping swords through their unworthy flesh."

"Come, Terrah," I call, turning to go outside into the fresh air.

"Kiera, you need to have a word with your dragon," I tell her, leading the guilty-looking familiar to her. "She ate all the graublins."

"What? Eww! Don't think you're sleeping in the den tonight, young lady. Your tummy will be all kinds of upset now. And I'm *not* cleaning up after you. Not to mention you might have been hurt..."

Her words fade as I embrace Hassan again, along with Arwyn. Goddess, I need in! "Get us home," I plead behind me.

We jump round as a shriek erupts. How did we miss that? A graublin must've somehow cloaked itself and escaped. With blood oozing from the dagger sticking out of its stomach, the graublin runs towards us, magick charging up in its hands. Kiera's hands circle, and I know she's created a barrier. The blast deflects off and lands uselessly on the ground before fizzling away.

"Permit me," Roger says in a sombre tone, already on his way.

Threaris holds onto the power already raised in his hands, clearly backup for the unicorn.

Head bent down, Roger gallops towards the now motionless graublin and stabs it with his horn and tosses it up into the air. It lands back down in a crumpled heap.

"Eurgh! Now there's graublin blood on me," Roger complains, raising a leg in an attempt to swipe it off his horn.

Picking up some moss, Hassan asks, "May I, Sir?"

Roger bows his head and lets our mate sponge off the residue. Whilst Kiera turns to Terrah.

"How many graublin did you eat?"

The dragon looks pointedly at her and chuffs.

"Five? Are you sure? Count with me, Terrah. One, two, three, four." She stops as Terrah nods.

"Four. That's one less than five. That was a dangerous mistake. We really do have to work on your numbers," she admonishes, shaking her head.

Terrah burps again and still looks pleased with herself.

"Thank you, Sir," Hassan gently tells Roger as he finishes cleaning.

"Well, at least it wasn't an entirely wasted journey." He looks around. "Frydah, I am not in the habit of running fool's errands. Although guarding the fae realm can grow dull, when one is called upon, it is expected that it's for a good reason. And that there will be something I am required to do. I had to leave Paul in charge of the doors."

"Well, excuse me. I didn't know the male was going to free himself and the others, did I?" Frydah bites back.

He rolls his eyes. "I suppose. Well, if that is all?"

Kiera calls, "Wait! Please. Roger, do you believe it will be safe here for our market now?"

He shakes his mane. "I don't see why not. Maybe use caution. It wasn't a graublin realm before. I sense no others. Hm, nice idea of yours. Shame about these ones. Pity about the guardian. Goddess only knows how they bested her."

"Guardian?"

"Did you not know? Really, if one goes realm-hopping, one should at least introduce themselves."

"I tried. Nobody answered my repeated greeting calls."

"Hmph! This was always intended as a gathering place. Not just for elinefae. I'm curious how graublins got in. The house was concealed, the guardian should have been safe. I shall launch an investigation and install a new guardian. She was here to ensure only those with peaceful intent entered. Perhaps you can strengthen the concealment spell when the next candidate is in situ? Very odd business this. Mostly, graublins sneak into the human realm where there is plenty of fear to feast upon without any need for coercion or killing. These ones got greedy. Not good. Not good at all."

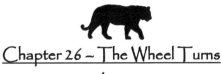

Chapter 26 ~ The Wheel Turns

~ Arwyn

Back at our encampment, Hassan explains, "Once the valerian took effect, and they were all asleep, I heaved a graublin over the threshold of the cell so the barrier would recede. Not wanting to risk being recaptured, I am ashamed to say, we killed them with their own blades in their sleep. Their strengthening spell made it too much of a risk any other way when we were unarmed. Then we made our escape outside. But we couldn't open a portal. I was just trying to make contact, free of the confines of our prison, when you all turned up."

Rhion tells him, "No, it was very wise under the circumstances. But were you not at risk of drugging yourselves? Or worse?"

Hassan shrugs. "I know the doses, Sir. Due to the size difference, we would probably have just been mildly sedated. But even if we'd been knocked out, it was better than being awake in that nightmare. Sir, I would never endanger clan."

With a few more explanations, Rhion completes the debriefing with an, "Alright, go."

No need to tell us twice. All three of us run towards our den, leaving Kiera to treat the other elinefae for shock and stress before returning them to their clans. Ordinarily, we would assist, but our mate comes first now. The urge to hold him overrides all else.

With a hand on his lower back, I guide Hassan towards the corridor, away from our den. He turns a scowl towards me.

Shrugging, I tell him, "The stench must first be removed."

He nods and faces back in the direction we're headed. Praise be for Kiera's shower. The smell of others on my mate is enough to drive me wild. But when it's also foul smelling, well, my teeth are grinding with the effort of not letting my frenzy burst out. Hassan needs my calm strength after what he endured. But inwardly I'm cursing yet again that I could not exact my vengeance upon the worthless…deep breaths.

Our brave mate strips, seemingly eager to distance himself from the remnants of graublins. Almost tearing our clothes, we hurry to do the same. Elan pulls the cord, and warm water cascades from the shower head. Tentatively, Hassan puts a hand underneath its stream.

"It's OK," I encourage, "We're here."

Taking another brave step, his whole body becomes encompassed by the flow.

Elan stands behind and squirts shampoo from a bottle into his hand. "Mmm…coconutty."

Hassan's eyes are scrunched closed but he sputters water from his mouth.

Chuckling, I take the bottle of body wash and sniff the coconut and vanilla scent. "Always said she was nutty."

"Ha, don't let Pryderi hear you say that. Can we just get on with the task in hand?" Elan admonishes.

I roll my eyes at him but lay my soapy hands on Hassan's beautiful, soft yet firm body. Elan's hands dive into Hassan's luxurious hair at the same time. We're both getting sprayed with water, but I barely notice once my hands start roaming.

I feel the tension ease as we work our mate into a lather. Tantalising moans come out of his mouth, making me wash him quicker so we can get back to our den all the sooner.

"*Good,*" I hear him say in my head.

His cock agrees as it raises a salute to me. My tongue traces across my lips, keen to taste that delight.

"Eager, handsome?" Elan teases.

"You haven't got the same view I do."

"Yeah, but I have got these perky orbs grinding against me."

Elan playfully smacks Hassan's arse as he grinds more. "No sexy time in here, remember?"

Water goes everywhere as Hassan vigorously shakes his head.

"Oh, you're learning to have fun in the water, kitty?" I ask.

His eyes still scrunched, Hassan nods with a wicked grin. I stroke suds up his shaft.

"Well, I know a place we can explore that more. But not here. And not today," I tell him, a purr in my voice.

He groans and juts his hips forward.

"Right. Sud free?" I check with Elan who nods in response, pulling the shower off.

Grabbing a towel, I waste no time wrapping it around Hassan before scooping him up. Elan jogs behind as I race down the corridor to our den. The door crashes closed behind us.

"Need you now," Hassan announces when his towel slips as I put him down.

"So, I see. Tell me, which do you need first, mate?"

"Both."

My mouth gapes.

Elan nestles up to Hassan's back, nibbling his neck. "Are you sure, honey? I don't think we can go very slowly right now. I don't want to hurt you."

"It's a risk I shall just have to take. I need you both."

"We could—" But Hassan holds up a hand, stopping my suggestion.

"Please." It's more of a 'shut the hell up' statement than a plea.

"OK, sweetheart, OK."

I wander to our bed and lie on my back. "Come here then."

It's a completely pointless instruction as Hassan is already covering me with his body by the time I finish saying it. Augh, his cock grinds against mine as he rubs into me.

Tears trickle down his cheeks as he kisses a trail up to my mouth.

"Missed you," he whimpers, nuzzling my neck.

My hands travel up from his shoulders to stroke his hair. "Missed you more."

"Me too," Elan murmurs into his shoulder.

Turning his head, Hassan cheek rubs then snogs Elan. Fuck, I'm going to come already if they carry on. A rather pained groan escapes me.

"Hold on, handsome," Elan soothes.

"Trying!"

"Ha, Hassan, how ready are you, honey?"

"So ready," he answers.

There's a pause.

"Auuugh, yeah you are. So wet for us, aren't you?"

In response, Hassan scoots up and aligns his hole to my cock. Looking directly into my eyes, he slowly lowers down. My head is thrown back in ecstasy. Fuck, that feels good!

"Make it quick," I plead.

As Hassan leans forwards and down, I nibble a nip. He squirms.

"Hold still," Elan commands with a smack.

"Mmmm…not if that's my reward."

"Fine. Squirm and no more smacks."

We all chuckle.

"OK, breathe for me, Hassan. Finger first, I promise. Just to be sure."

"No. *Zib* now!"

"Greedy. But if you get torn, remember it's your own fault."

I see Elan's hand grab the bottle of lube from the cabinet next to me. He must've put it there before he joined us. So careful and thoughtful. He squelches some into his palm. Peering around Hassan, I see Elan rubbing lube on himself and I almost lose it.

His weight shifts, and Elan, straddling my legs, gets closer to Hassan. Fuck, this is happening. He's going to do it. My hips want to buck so badly. My breath hisses out of me.

Elan gradually inches inside our mate. It's agonisingly slow. Both Hassan and I are grunting at the pace. Rising up, Hassan reaches behind him, and I know he's trying to push Elan along. He takes the hint.

"Aaaauuuuugh," I cry as his cock slides along mine. Inside Hassan. Fuck!

"Holy shit," Elan moans at the same time.

"Oh, my goddess, I'm so full," Hassan announces, his eyes glossed over and glowing.

"OK? I'm not hurting?" Elan checks.

"Trust me, he's fine," I answer for him, "But if you don't start moving, you won't be."

Without another word, Elan joggles back and forth in small movements, making us all groan loudly. Ahs echo between us. Hassan collapses back down into my neck.

"If you suck now, it's all over," I warn.

"Sit up for me, gorgeous," Elan requests.

Hassan stops to delve his tongue into my mouth, though. I can't stop myself from bucking now, my whimpers getting frantic. A smack resounds.

"Here. Now!" Elan demands.

Mercifully, our mate complies. But his blissed-out look as he does ricochets through me, sending my head back on a groan.

"Open your eyes, handsome," I hear Elan tell me.

Holy fuck, when I do, he's kissing Hassan's cheek who looks like he's in heaven. Elan and I both rock into him.

"Look at you, taking us both like a good, greedy boy, sweetheart," I murmur in awe.

"Ah! So good," he repeats over and over between whimpers.

His chest is upright, and I bathe in its furry glory. My fingers reach up and travel down through the hair on his chest and down his happy trail. Hassan's breathing hitches. My palm goes sideward so I can grip his hip.

"Like that, don't you?" I ask.

"Uh-huh." He's trying to keep his balance, hands on my chest.

"Can you sit back a little bit more?"

He does.

"Good boy."

I stroke his cock as Elan continues his rhythmic swaying. Our lover's close; his tone rises up a notch. My hand tugs him faster and firmer. So many delightful yelps. Then his arse clenches around our two cocks and he jets over my torso, collapsing backwards onto Elan's chest who holds him in place.

Elan thrusts against me, and I feel him throbbing. I grunt as my balls tighten, tighten, tight… "Aaaaauuugh!".

We fill our mate with our cum, who's still in his post-coital dreamland. He falls back down on me, boneless.

"Mmmmm…" is all he seems capable of saying.

Not that I'm much better. My eyes are closed as I draw in a breath, trying to find my way back to Earth. Elan slides out lies and next to me. I manage to wrap an arm around him and kiss his forehead. Pulling the covers with him, Hassan snuggles up to my other side, one hand interlacing with Elan's.

"Mine," we chorus.

Content in every sense of the word, I drift off.

Chapter 27 - Seeking
~ Hassan

Arms are wrapped around me from either side, covers enveloping us. My eyelids flutter open.

"Mmmm...home," I whisper, snuggling in all the more.

Relief floods through me as I fight off the memories of my ordeal. My mates came for me. We found our way back to one another. I'm lying on my side, facing Arwyn. Elan must have snuck around once I was asleep as he's now at my back.

Elan's arm squeezes tighter as he shnuffles into my neck. "You alright, my mate?"

I nod but don't say anything.

"I felt that. It's OK to not be OK, you know."

"I'm fine."

Arwyn's blue gaze is intent upon me now. "No false bravery, sweetheart. What happened was horrific. Elan and I were distraught at the sudden loss. So much so that Cerys had to sedate us. But where you—"

"Please, I don't want to talk about it."

Elan kisses my shoulder. "Alright, honey. But we're here when you need to. And know how sorry we both are we were unable to prevent it."

"It was not your fault. And we're together again now. It is done."

Arwyn's frown shows his doubt in my words. I'm lying, of course. I am not fine, and they know it. What happened was a shock for us all. I truly don't blame them, though. It makes me feel sick to think about it. For now, just feeling the presence of my males is all I need.

My hand runs down Arwyn's cheek as I jut out my chin, pouting. Taking the hint, he laps my lips before deepening the kiss. I grind my backside against Elan.

Arwyn taps my nose. "Insatiable male! But as tempting as you are, I need to make sure you're fed. You must be hungry."

My stomach growls at the mention of food. I smirk with a nervous laugh.

"Are you alright to go to the dining area? Or would you like me to bring back something here?"

Elan adds, "Our clan will probably rush to welcome you back. It might be a bit overwhelming."

A knock on our door interrupts any response I was going to make. All three of us tense up and are on full alert. The arms around me go from cuddlers to barriers. Snarls erupt from all of us.

"I can come back later if now's not a good time," Kiera calls out.

Arwyn's eyes close briefly as he breathes out deeply. Elan's exhale tickles my ear.

"Approach with caution," Arwyn replies, his voice hoarse and hissed around his elongated teeth, not moving.

Elan rises up, glaring at the door, ready to pounce. Kiera enters our den, but only one step in, her hands held up and out. "It's alright, fellas. I understand. Downright bloody sympathise, actually. I'm so sorry."

"What do you want, Kiera?" Arwyn asks, his teeth retracted, but his body still tense.

"Right. Straight to the point. Hassan, Omar is in Cerys' den. I won't lie, he's in a pretty bad way still. He's been asking for you. I wanted to give you guys time to reunite, but…"

"Of course. I'll go to him."

My mates growl.

"Bad kitties! Come on, let me up."

"You would go to another male this moment?" Arwyn sneers.

"He's in distress. My clan member. He was there for me…"

More growls.

Kiera raises her hands. "I don't want to start trouble. I'm sorry. It's fine. We'll sedate him again and try a different approach."

I bolt upright, shoving Elan out of my way. "NO! I said I will go. And I will."

"I'll wait outside."

Clambering over Arwyn, I jump onto the floor and spin to face the rumbling males who are on all fours on our bed.

"Challenge me all you want. But I have honour. I will not leave a clan member in distress when I can help," I seethe.

Both Elan and Arywn drop onto their forearms, their heads banging the mattress.

"You're right," a muffled Arwyn admits.

"Sorry, Hassan," Elan mumbles.

Crouching down, I stroke through their hair. "You're protective. I understand."

Elan looks up. "This is why we need to talk."

"Maybe. But not now."

Kissing their foreheads, I get up and go towards the wardrobe and yank out some clothing.

"We've upset him," Elan says to Arwyn.

"No shit," is the response.

"You don't get to control me," I clarify.

Elan stalks over and places his hands on my shoulders. "I know. I know that. But we only just got you back. We can't lose you again."

I roll my eyes. "To Omar? This will never happen."

Elan pouts as his hands travel down to my hips to joggle me. "Forgive us for being a little possessive?"

My hand runs down my face. "Of course, I do. But please try to be a little less snarly. Can you do that? For me?"

"We can try."

Arwyn joins us and we all nuzzle cheeks and plant pecked kisses on one another.

"If you come with me, do you think you can control yourselves? I don't want you to make the situation any worse," I ask.

Two heads slowly nod at me.

"Alright. But if you even start to get riled up you must leave Cerys's den. Understood?"

Two more nods are given before they pull on some clothes as quickly as possible. And we make our way to Omar, following Kiera. Only, I stop at the door. My stomach clenches upon hearing my once cocky friend's sobs.

Elan's eyes bore into mine. "You don't have to do this."

Biting my lip, I shake my head. "But I do."

Elan nods once.

Taking in a steadying breath, I open the door. It takes me a moment to take it all in. Omar is curled up on a bed whilst Chen holds his hand, smoothing his hair.

Kneeling down beside him within my next heartbeat, I ask, "Omar. Tell me what I can do."

His red, puffy eyes turn towards me. "You came."

"Of course. Of course," I soothe, replacing Chen and rubbing Omar's arm.

My mates remain silent at the door.

"Hold me." His plea breaks my heart with its quiet desperation.

I move around, looking at Arwyn and Elan. Their mouths are set in grim, thin lines, but they both jerk their heads in a sharp nod. Knowing they're trying their best to not be over-protective, I slowly lie down behind Omar who immediately curls into a ball in my embrace.

"Shh! It's OK. You are safe now. We are safe," I mutter repeatedly, my hands stroking his hair.

I begin humming the same tune he aided me with…before. Every so often, I glance towards my mates. I know this must be torture for them. But their feet are planted firmly where they stand, arms folded and all too quiet.

"I'm sorry," Omar whimpers.

"For what?"

"This."

"Tssaryar! You are not. There is nothing to be sorry for. Just breathe for me."

He tries, but it comes out stuttered.

Looking across, I try, "Elan. Do I ask too much of you—"

"Thank goddess! I thought you were never going to ask," he replies, rushing to Omar's side.

"Hey, me too," Arwyn chimes.

They both kneel in front of Omar and peel his arms away from his stomach so they can take a hand each.

"You are not injured?" Elan checks.

Omar shakes his head.

"*Twp*! Of course, he's not. Do you not think Cerys and Chen would have healed him by now?" Arwyn rebukes.

"I was only asking."

"Bothering the poor male with a stupid question is what you were doing."

With a snotty sniff, Omar chuckles.

"Oh, Arwyn's insults are amusing, are they?" Elan asks.

"And there you go again. Yes, obviously. But then I am quite funny. And charming. Don't forget charming."

"Oh, charming now, is it?"

"You love it."

"You know I do."

They kiss as Omar laughs. I hand him a handkerchief to wipe his eyes and nose.

"Are they always like this?" he asks me, sitting up.

"No. Usually, they are far worse."

Elan races around to tickle me. "Is that so, mate?"

Through my laughter, I manage to tell him, "Yes."

Omar shakes his head. "And these are your mates? You are certain of this?"

"I wouldn't question it if I were you."

Arwyn, still kneeling, curls his lip to reveal sharp teeth but then grins.

"See. He's fine. Omar, I think you were faking being upset," Elan says.

Quickly I add, "You get used to their teasing."

"If you say so."

Chen, who had planted himself against the wall, out of the way but still present in case needed, smiles.

"Did I see some soup?" I ask him.

He nods and brings over a bowl and spoon.

"Do you think you can eat some of this now?"

"I'll try."

"That is all I ask."

Gingerly, he scoops the soup to his mouth and sucks it in. "Hm, nice but not made by you."

"Pshh! Like you can tell."

"You think I cannot taste your cooking after all these years?"

"Fine, if you insist."

"I miss it," he admits, looking crestfallen.

"I am sorry for that. But my home is here now."

"This, I can see."

"That is not why you were so upset?"

He barks out a laugh. "You wish!"

I grin at him and wriggle my eyebrows. "I had to check."

He shakes his head. "I think these two are rubbing off on you."

"Only every chance we get," Elan says, pulling me to my feet and in for a hug.

Slapping his arm, I cry, "Eww! Not like that. Elan!"

"You see what you've started?" Arwyn cajoles.

Chen shakes his head. "Honestly. You do get used to them."

"Aww, Chen. You wouldn't have us any other way," Elan catcalls.

"I honestly don't think I would. You are all joyously you."

With Omar eating more of his soup, Arwyn joins Elan and me for a quick hug.

"So, which is which?" Omar asks.

"Oh, my apologies. Omar, these are my mates, Arwyn and Elan," I introduce, pointing at each in turn.

Omar bows his head. "My greetings and congratulations."

"Oh, he's as polite as you, Hassan. Can we keep him?" Elan chuckles.

Narrowing his eyes, Arwyn asks, "What? Two mates are no longer sufficient for you?"

"You're right. I have more than enough. I mustn't be greedy."

"That'll be the day."

"Hassan was always so quiet," Omar mutters.

"He still is," Arwyn replies.

"Only because I can't get a word in," I retaliate.

"Aww, poor little mate." He ruffles my hair.

Pushing his hand away, I blow him a raspberry.

Nestling in close to my back, Arwyn whispers, "You know I love it when you're petulant."

Turning in his arms, I look up into his eyes. "I know you love me always."

"Mmm...you got that right." Dipping his head, he kisses me.

Elan is immediately up against my back, his arms around us.

"Wow! You certainly are a special triad," Omar murmurs.

"Had you ever heard of such a thing?" I ask him whilst still gazing into a sea of blue.

"Never. But this should not surprise you."

I turn and look at him. "No. But I was curious if I was oblivious to common knowledge."

"And you would even suspect this why?"

"I'm not sure. Things here are so very different. I've begun to question everything I ever knew."

"Come here, please. If you can."

I crouch down in front of Omar. He takes my hands in his. "Never doubt who you are, my friend. You are the bravest, cleverest elinefae I've ever met."

Tears sting my eyes as I gawp at him.

Elan kneels next to me. "I'll second that."

"That makes me the third, then," Arwyn adds with a chuckle.

"No. Not you two. No. It cannot be. You are Watchers. Surely you know braver."

Elan's eyes are so kind as he smiles. "We do not lie, *ya shamsi*."

"*Ya shamsi*? You call him this?" Omar asks.

Elan has to answer as there's a lump in my throat. "Ha, yes. But I get *ya amar*."

"And I'm *njūmiyy*," Arwyn announces proudly.

"Oh, my goddess. Sun, moon and stars. So celestial. Magickal," Omar observes.

"Perfect," I confirm.

"Umm…Hassan…there is something I must say to you. But I confess your mates are a little intimidating."

They glower at him.

"Not helpful," I tell them.

"Can I speak with you alone, please? Just for a moment."

Arwyn grumbles, "You're not going to declare your undying love for him, are you?"

"No. I promise. I respect your mate, more now than I ever did. You three are obviously mates. But there is something…delicate I would say to Hassan. I fear it would be troublesome for you to hear."

"Hmph! Alright. But we will be just outside the door. No funny business."

"You have my word."

Chen follows Elan and Arwyn out.

"Hassan. Thank you. I wanted to apologise."

"I told you it is unnecessary."

"No, not about this. Although, yes, this too. But about before."

"That was not your fault either."

"No, before before. Hassan, I was selfish. I did not treat you with the respect owed to you. It was not until Kiera told me off that I even thought about what we did. It brought me untold shame that I never reciprocated your…deeds. That is why I volunteered to come to the market that day. I needed to seek you out and apologise. I was so very wrong."

"I accept. But I had not thought much about it either, in all honesty. Yes, I wanted it reciprocated. But it wasn't until I came here that I realised how equal all elinefae are supposed to be. We knew no better."

"It seems our clan have lost its way in some things."

"But we excel in others."

"You are generous. You always have been. I am not sure we deserve your or Kiera's kindness."

"I am sure you do."

"Did you know she has located a new settlement for us?"

I'm lost for words, so simply shake my head.

"Ah, clearly not. You know of the dragon, Shui?"

"Oh, yes, him I know."

"He flew over the deserts. There is another similar clan. Their Leader is elderly and wishes to establish a new home for them before his time ends. Our new home is further away but Shui sensed the water reservoir. It is so much bigger than ours. Your clan is helping build new homes so we can all live there. Two clans becoming one, returning to our roots."

"My clan?"

"Yes, *Habibi*. This is your clan now."

"But…"

"Please. You may not have changed your mark, and you are not yet hand-fasted. But these people are yours now. I see this."

My gaze is cast to the floor. "I cannot argue against you."

"I am happy for you. Truly. Even if your mates are a bit crazy."

"Oh, they are a lot crazy but in the best way."

"And they are very caring."

"Don't forget protective."

"Ha, yes, that too. They treat you right. None of us ever did. I am so sorry, Hassan."

"Please, stop apologising. It is past."

"How are you not falling apart after what happened? You're amazing."

I wince. "Maybe it will hit me later. I was just so relieved to be reunited with my mates that nothing else seems to matter. I'm trying not to think about what you and I went through."

"You were so brave. I would never have known the valerian was there, let alone to use it."

"Experienced cook."

"Genius."

I can feel my cheeks warming.

"You are the brains. And your mates are the brawn. You three will be unstoppable, I think."

I chortle. "I pray to the goddess that we are never tested like that again."

"As do I, my friend."

Slapping my thighs, I change the subject, "So, do you want some of my food before you go?"

"You're going to the kitchen now?"

"I'm not even sure what time it is. But yes, my hands are itching to feel my knives."

"Until your mates are in your grasp, at least."

"Dirty!"

"Truthful. I see you. And I am aware what newly mated couples are like."

"Elan says we are a throuple."

"I am sure it's even more intense for three. But nonetheless, if you manage to get as far as the kitchen, I will gladly accept your cooking."

"Do you feel like getting out of here?"

"I think I am capable now."

"Good. I'll see if someone can show you around whilst I cook. This place is amazing."

As we stand, Omar grabs me into an embrace. "My gratitude, my friend."

Chapter 28 – Just Desserts
~ Elan

I understand Hassan's need for distraction. For something familiar. But Arwyn and I are not prepared to let him out of our sight. So, we're perched on stools against the far wall of the kitchen, near the door.

We went to the other survivors before coming here. They are all cooks for their clans, hence them having been at the marketplace. It seems they were all eager to occupy their hands as they try to come to terms with their ordeal.

"None of us is overly hungry, are we?" Hassan had asked.

Everyone had shaken their heads, no.

"So, let us make our favourite comfort food and share? That way, we all experience different cuisine as originally intended. And we can just pick at bits."

His hands are now busy chopping as he issues orders to others. Riley is making a large pot of macaroni and cheese with the assistance of one of our clan cooks. There are chips in the fryer. Chen is showing some others how to make *jiānbǐng*.

"What were those cheese sausage things?" Hassan asks.

"Glamorgan sausages," I yell across.

"Yes. Them. Can someone make those, please?

Dai nods with a, "Yes, sir." And recruits others to help him.

Flatbreads soon start piling up high, and bowls of hummus and cut vegetables appear. Someone else is making pad thai. The smell of what I learn is called jerk chicken is making my mouth water. And there's some sort of curry bubbling away.

Being here, witnessing this hive of activity…it's like its own kind of magick. Everyone's focus is on the task at hand, and they all seem to, if not relax, at least appear less harried. And our mate is conducting them all, overseeing and supporting. He's amazing. Just as I think it's not possible, I fall in love a little bit more.

Arwyn nudges my arm with his own and whispers, "He's not only bossy in our den, then?"

"Ha, you love it."

"Yeah, I really really do."

I let my head fall onto his shoulder. "Me too."

All the food gets poured into trays. There's even French onion soup going into a large tureen. We help troop it all to the serving area, where a crowd is already gathered.

"You alright?" I check, quickly catching Hassan's attention.

His smile is weak and doesn't touch his eyes, but he nods before stepping in front of the dishes. "If I may, I'd like to say a few words?"

He's met with nods and murmurs of assent.

"Firstly, I would like to thank Leader Rhion and all of you for coming to our aid."

Cheers and applause erupt.

Hassan waits for it to die down before he continues, "I…errr…"

Arwyn and I dash to his side and hold a hand each as his voice cracks and his words disappear.

He takes a deep breath. "One of us didn't make it home. Ella, from another clan was…well, she is now in the afterlife. But her sacrifice shall not be forgotten. I wanted to honour her memory. To make it mean something. So, in a much smaller way, please enjoy some of the tastes of the world and let us know which you'd like again. Thank you."

"Hold it!" Rhion commands, raising his hand as the crowd surges forward. "I want to add my own words. Thank you, Hassan, for helping create this feast. Of course, we shall keep Ella in our thoughts and hearts. Now seems as good a time as any…"

He pauses and looks between the three of us. "I don't think I'm assuming too much, but, Hassan, I think it's about time we officially welcomed you into this clan, don't you?"

Our mate is motionless for a moment. "Um, yes. Yes, I would like that very much. Thank you, Sir."

He's still stood still, so I tug at the buttons of his cardigan and pull it off for him.

"Oh, right," he mutters, blushing.

The sounds of some of our clan admiring him do not escape my attention. I shoot them a fierce glance. Mine!

Rhion reaches his hand over Hassan's clan mark. Hassan flinches and hisses a little. But when our

Leader's hand is removed, our green, tri-headed dragon, Celtic knot, clan mark has replaced his red bird of prey.

"Welcome, Hassan, to our clan."

Whoops, hollers, cheers, applause, laughter and congratulations all burst into the air around us as our triad joins in a group hug.

"Welcome home," I chime in unison with Arwyn.

"Alright, don't let it get cold. You can eat now," Rhion yells above the din.

Hassan is grinning from ear to ear. "I truly am home," he says as people bump into us in their rush.

"Ours. Home," I affirm as Arwyn kisses the breath out of him.

Eventually, he breaks away, gasping for air, only to turn around to me. His dark peach, swollen lips launch at mine, and I'm all for it. My mouth opens wide, gathering our mate to me as Arwyn nuzzles him from behind.

"As much as you want to eat each other, here, have some actual sustenance," Pryderi interrupts, holding up some plates.

Kiera is grinning beside him, holding more.

"You didn't waste any time," Arwyn teases.

"Neither did you."

"Haha, very funny. Come on, then. Let's get this one seated and fed."

"I'm sure these two know how lucky they are to have you, Hassan. But you truly are remarkable," Kiera says as we find somewhere to sit.

He tries to bury his head in my neck.

"Nuh uh uh. You are. Own it, honey," I tell him, peeling him away.

He bites his lip but manages to look at Kiera. "My gratitude."

She smiles broadly. "It will get easier."

"Eurgh, I hope so."

"Of course, it will. You're one of us now."

He hums as he beams.

"Oh, for the love of the goddess, can we just eat?" Arwyn huffs.

"In a rush, mate?" I ask with a wink, one arm around Hassan.

"Aren't you?"

I shovel a fork load of food into my gob and chomp rapidly, making everyone else laugh.

Pryderi and Kiera wanted to try a bit of everything, so we share from the taster plates they loaded up.

"Hhhhhrrr!" I cry, fanning my mouth.

Hassan laughs. "Aww, did you find a chilli?"

My eyes are watering. "Uh-huh," I squeak. Then hiccup.

"Wait there, I'll be right back."

"Not without me," Arwyn warns, getting up with him.

I can't even protest. Maybe this is how I die? Please, goddess, not now. The water I sip does nothing to extinguish the fire. I push my tongue out, trying to get cool air onto it. What on Earth was that?

"Point to where that came from," Pryderi instructs.

Through my tears, I think I point to the right one. Pryderi turns the plate so that dish isn't near him, uttering, "I don't want to end up like that. Your face is all red and everything."

My mates return with a glass of milk.

"This will help," Hassan says as he holds it to my lips.

Milk trickles down my chin as I try to gulp it down.

"Mucky kitty," he admonishes, licking it away.

"Dirty boy!" Arwyn adds, his voice husky.

"Waste not, want not."

"Heeeeuurrrgh!" I breathe out.

"Better?" Hassan asks.

"A bit. My gratitude."

"We're avoiding this one," Pryderi says oh-so-helpfully, pointing at the offending item.

"Right you are," Arwyn remarks, biting into a Glamorgan sausage.

"Wuss puss," I jibe.

"I know where I am with these. I'm not risking looking like you, thank you very much."

It's then that I notice a few more clan members are in the same predicament.

"Well, we can build up to the hotter chillis. We have time," Hassan notes.

"Yeah, all the time in the world." I nuzzle my cheek to his.

"Bleurgh, I'm going to be sick," Kiera says but chuckles.

"Like you two are any better," Arwyn accuses.

Pryderi kisses his mate as if to prove the point. I noisily slurp some of the soup from the bowl.

"Thanks for that," Kiera moans.

"What?"

"Don't play innocent with me, Elan."

I flutter my eyelashes. "Who? Me?"

She chucks a piece of flatbread at me. "*Twp!*"

Raising my eyebrows, I slurp up another spoonful.

"Is it too late to change my mind?" Hassan asks.

"Yes. Sorry. No going back now," Arwyn replies, tickling him.

"Elan, save me!"

"Like you need it," I retort, adding my own hands to the tickle attack.

We both back off when he's really had enough. That is when he can't breathe properly.

Grabbing some hummus-dipped bread pieces, he stuffs them in my mouth and Arwyn's. "There, that should shut you up."

Arwyn laughs and talks around his mouthful. "Not likely."

Hassan sidles onto Arwyn's lap. "Well, I'll have to find another way."

I twirl some noodles onto my fork and offer it up to Hassan. "Food first. You've still not eaten enough."

"I don't want to get too full," he moans before sliding his mouth over the fork anyway.

"You little bugger!" He's deliberately sucking the food off my fork slowly.

"Not this again," Kiera mock moans.

Arwyn taps Hassan's nose. "Behave. Seriously. Eat."

"Oh, alright." Hassan sits back on the bench.

"And no pouting."

Of course, those lips protrude even more.

"Oh, you're in so much trouble later," I warn, sucking his lips into my mouth.

Breaking away, he grins and eats, the picture of innocence. We are so wrapped around his little finger. And I don't know anywhere I'd rather be. Well, maybe there's one place that springs to mind. With effort, I manage to carry on trying the food before me. And that's only because I've promised myself that Hassan will be my dessert.

Epilogue
~ Hassan

I couldn't hide from my trauma forever. I won't lie; it was brutal to face. But Arwyn and Elan helped me through. Maybe I helped them in return. They were not entirely unscathed by my elinefaenapping, after all. Kiera and Cerys lent assistance too. At such times, all clan come together in support. In a strange way, it helped me feel more at home as I adjusted to my new surroundings.

Of course, the Wheel keeps turning. I'd never seen a Lughnasadh like it. There is so much more harvested here. And a great many breads were made in celebration. Arwyn, Elan and I attended the sabbat festivities in the celebration realm. We danced and drank and sang as the fires burned. I would say all night, but, well, our own fires burned brightly too, so we snuck off to do our thing.

My clan keeps surprising me. I never knew I could be this happy.

And I even seem to be getting used to the weather. Although, Kiera did buy me some *trainers* to wear on my feet so they didn't get cold. Yes, as the summer ended, I discovered new lows in temperature. My first frost was a bit of an eye-opener. Literally.

Life has settled into a routine. Kiera kept assuring us we could take our time. It was a difficult process. My two mates would go off to fulfil their duties. Their routes had always been close, but they found ways of crossing paths so they could check in with one another. But they also pulled on my link, so I knew where they were. And I cooked up a storm in the kitchen. Two grinning faces always appear at the door to ensure I eat with them.

Kiera held another farmer's market. Hardly anyone attended, though, including me. There was no way I was going back there. Frydah and Roger had ensured the realm was graublin-free, and a new guardian was installed. Chen and some other witches created new wards. But I didn't want to risk it, even so.

However, after that first one went off with no repercussions, we all started going to more. And so, I found new recipes to try. Some great and some didn't go down so well. But the fun is in the trying.

At the Samhain festival, I was delighted to see *all* my old clan in attendance, along with their new members. Omar is doing well in their new home. Old habits die hard, but they seem to be relearning our old ways.

I kept my promise and made an apple, orange and cinnamon pie just for us three for Yule. It went down well. The abundance of greenery in the decorations around the encampment was mesmerising and smelled almost as delicious as the pie. Almost.

The weather got colder and colder as the Wheel turned from Yule to Imbolc. But my mates have their ways of keeping me warm. To be able to snuggle up under the covers in our den is one of the best luxuries in my life. To love and be loved is a gift. And by two of the finest elinefae who ever breathed.

My breath was taken away when it snowed. I'd never seen such a thing. Our home, covered in a blanket of white was even more beautiful. Stunning. And my mates took me outside to play in it. Not for long; we soon returned to the communal fire at home and drank hot chocolate in its glow. Snow is cold and wet.

I went out with my males as spring emerged. They took me around the encampment so I could see all the beautiful flowers emerging from the ground; a truly magickal sight. Especially the bluebell woods, which smell divine. I'm pretty sure I saw some sprites frolicking, but they flew away immediately. I didn't want to pry, so didn't call out to them. They don't pose a threat, so we let them be. It was there that Arwyn and Elan proposed to me. There was never going to be any answer but yes.

Terrah is still a mischief-maker. Maybe more so now she's grown even more. She's still very cute, so she gets away with it. And Shui is a great uncle figure to her. I've even started being able to 'hear' his voice. I visit him often between my mates leaving for work and before mine starts. He enjoys the company. Not to mention the treats I take him.

And so, Beltane arrived, and we were hand-fasted. The ceremony was a little awkward. A few other soul-matched mates were undergoing the ritual, but they were pairs. Everyone had to keep waiting for all three of us to tie the ribbons on one another. Not that anyone minded. In fact, they seemed to cheer all the louder for us. All our parents were there, even mine, wearing their best smiles.

I didn't think it would change me. That day, getting my new clan mark confirmed my place here, and my commitment to my mates. However, the bond we made on our hand-fasting day glows inside us all. I can sense my mates' feelings even more strongly now, and they mine. The distress as well as the joy. It's not always easy, but it is most definitely worth it.

I, Hassan, along with Elan and Arwyn might just have our happily ever after – a true HEA.

Thank you so much for reading Love Bites More.
Big squishy hugs to you!

If you enjoyed this book, please do consider leaving a review online – it helps other readers make an informed decision, as well as encouraging me to write more.

Honestly, writing can be a world of isolation and woe. Knowing there is someone somewhere who enjoys my book makes it all worth it.

Glossary

Some of the names, words and phrases in this book may seem new or strange to you, so here's a list of some of them, along with tips on pronunciation.

Name /Word	Pronunciation/Translation
Arwyn	*aar-wihn*
Babr	*BAE-b-r* – name of Saudi Arabian clan Leader.
Branwen	*braen-WehN* – Arwyn's mum
Cerys	*keh-rihs*
confervo	*CON-FERV-oh* - Latin – spell to heal/knit broken bones
Dai	*di*
deffro'r haearn	*DEFF-roe-r-HAY-arn* – Welsh; awaken the iron
dwt	*du:t* – Welsh; wee/small & cute (usually children)
Eirlys	*ayr-lihs* – Pryderi's mum (& Elan's adopted one)
Elan	*ee-lan*
elinefae	*ee-LINE-fay* – race of beings (cat people)
faery	*'fer-ee* – alternative spelling of faerie / fairy; a collective noun – a magickal being (usually small)
Frydah	*free-dah*
graublin	*GR'AU-blin* ('au as in ou of ouch)
gutrah	*goo-trar* – Arabic; head scarf
Habibi	*ha-be-bee* – Arabic; 'my love' (also; my darling/dear/beloved/honey)
Hassan	*HHaa-SAEN*
Ioan	*YO-an* (Welsh clan's second)

jiānbǐng	*jeeyan-bing* – Chinese; savoury pancake/crepe; street food
joie de vivre	*ZHWAH də VEEV(-rə)* – French; joy for life
kabsa	*KAB-sah* – A rice and chicken dish, served on a communal platter (origin; Yemen but popular in Saudi Arabia)
Kiera	key-air-uh
Kol Khara	*KOL KHA-RA* – Arabic; eat shit
njūmiyy	*noo-zhoo-mee* - نجومي – Arabic; my stars
Omar	*oh-MAAR*
Owen	*OH-en* – Pryderi's dad (& Elan's adopted one)
Perceval	*pur-Seh-Vuhl* – Arwyn's dad
Pryderi	*pruh-DAIR-ee*
roc	an enormous mythological, bird of prey from Middle Eastern legends; رخ
Rhion	*ree-on*
Shakira	*shu-KEER-uh*
Shui	*shw-aay*
Terrah	*tehr-rahr*
thobe	*THohb* – Arabic robe
Threaris	*three-AH-is* – Kiera's sorcerer father
tssaryar	Elinefae sound made when someone is talking bollocks/bullshit/nonsense
twp	*tʊp* – Welsh; fool/stupid
ya amar	*ya-ka-mar* - يا قمر – Arabic; my moon
ya shamsi	*yar-SHAM-see* - شمسي – Arabic; my sun
zib	Arabic; dick (penis)
Zondra	*zon-drah*

About the Author

TL Clark is an award-winning, best-selling, British author of love who stumbles through life as if it were a gauntlet of catastrophes.

Rather than playing the victim she uses these unfortunate events to fuel her passion for writing, for reaching out to help others.

Her dream is to buy a farmhouse, so she can run a retreat for those who are feeling frazzled by the stresses of the modern world.

She writes about different kinds of love in the hope that she'll uncover its mysteries.

Her loving husband (and mourned for cat) have proven to her that true love really does exist.

Writing has shown her that coffee may well be the source of life.

If you would like to follow TL or just drop in for a chat online, **@tlclarkauthor** will find her across most **social media**: Instagram, TikTok, Goodreads etc.

She also has a blog where she shares writing wisdom and book reviews. She's very kind and supportive, so often reviews other indie authors.

You can also sign up for her **newsletter** on her blog, to ensure you don't miss any exciting news (about new releases or special offers):

www.tlclarkauthor.blogspot.co.uk

Other Books by TL Clark

Fiction

The Darkness & Light Duology - (Love Bites and Love Bites Harder) – In case you've not read it yet; this is my award-winning paranormal romance (m/f)

Young's Love – a contemporary romance including gelato in Tuscany as Samantha strives for independence

True's Love – romantic suspense; Amanda finds more than cheap thrills in Ibiza

Dark Love – explore the love in a BDSM relationship and beyond with male submissive, Jonathan

Broken & Damaged Love – Tina comes to terms with her childhood abuse as she learns to love and trust again

Rekindled Love – Join Sophie on her rollercoaster ride through life, from first to last love

Self Love – Molly goes on a quest to change her perspective on life and even herself

Love Gaia – A cli-fi romance set mainly in an underground in New Zealand as nuclear war breaks out

Regency Love – Discover what Lady Anne really thinks as she enters the marriage mart in 1814

Love in the Roses – The fictitious tale of a knight's daughter, living life how it might have been in 1484.

Non-Fiction

How To Write A Historical Novel And Love It – A Beginner's Guide to Researching, Writing and Publishing a Historical Book

Ingram Content Group UK Ltd.
Milton Keynes UK
UKHW011829250523
422362UK00001B/18

9 780995 611788